A BODY
ON THE
BEACH

BOOKS BY DEE MACDONALD

KATE PALMER MYSTERY SERIES
A Body in the Village Hall
A Body in Seaview Grange
A Body at the Tea Rooms
A Body at the Altar

The Runaway Wife
The Getaway Girls
The Silver Ladies of Penny Lane
The Golden Oldies Guesthouse

A BODY
ON THE
BEACH

DEE MACDONALD

bookouture

Published by Bookouture in 2022

An imprint of Storyfire Ltd.
Carmelite House
50 Victoria Embankment
London EC4Y 0DZ

www.bookouture.com

ISBN: 978-1-80314-127-5
eBook ISBN: 978-1-80314-128-2

In memory of Michael John Brown

ONE

It was one of those swelteringly hot days without a breath of wind which was unusual, to say the least, in a Cornish field so close to the edge of the cliffs. It was even *more* unusual for someone to be pushed off these cliffs and end up on the sandy beach below, but that is what happened...

Kate Palmer had spent a very sticky afternoon at the village summer fair, in her nurse's uniform, tending to cuts, bruises, one bee sting, one nosebleed and a plethora of minor wounds requiring sticking plasters. She'd been a practice nurse in Tinworthy for the past three years, during which time she'd made a name for herself as something of an amateur super-sleuth due, in no small part, to being married to retired Detective Inspector Woody Forrest. Today Kate was in charge of the first-aid tent, assisted by a young volunteer called Carrie.

This was the Tinworthy Summer Fair, where everyone came along to peruse the stalls selling all manner of goods; to eat, drink and to take part in the various games and competitions, like welly-throwing, coconut shies and to try to win prizes on the hoopla stalls. All the proceeds were going to local charities. This was an event frequently rained off or that otherwise had everyone huddling under cover to dodge the Atlantic gales. But not this year. Although, in retrospect, Kate might well have wished that it *had* been rained off.

Things had started to take a downturn when Sienna Stone, a minor local TV celebrity, had wandered into the first-aid tent. Kate had just finished bandaging a boy's ankle when this red-haired vision appeared, clad in a flowing sea-green kaftan which coordinated with her cat-like sea-green eyes.

Without glancing at either Kate or Carrie, Sienna pushed her way into the tent and proclaimed to no one in particular, 'I'm feeling quite faint with this heat; I *must* have some shade and a cold drink.' She then plonked herself down on the seat behind the little screen that Kate had set up in case any visitor needed to display any intimate injuries.

There seemed to be very little wrong with Sienna Stone, but Kate felt she'd be failing in her professional responsibility if she didn't do some basic observations. She took the woman's blood pressure, pulse and temperature, all of which were completely normal, and tried to think of her purely as a patient and not as the person she'd had an altercation with on the Plymouth road some months back.

Carrie, her eyes out on stalks, was plainly in awe of the television personality. As she rushed to get a glass of water, Kate said firmly, 'Now, this area is for my patients and, as there appears to be nothing wrong with you at all, can you find somewhere else to sit please?'

Sienna Stone looked up, her green eyes glinting. 'Don't you know who I *am*? Do you realise that I am being hounded by those people out there for my autograph? I *have* to have some privacy.'

'Yes, I'm well aware of who you are,' Kate said, conscious of a throng gathering outside, 'and there's a refreshment tent a few yards along where you can sit in the shade and have something to drink.'

Sienna didn't move. 'We've met before, haven't we?' she asked after a moment.

'Yes, indeed we have. I'm the owner of the car you smashed into back in March. But I'm surprised you remember because you'd obviously been drinking.' Kate had vivid memories of that dark, rainy evening.

Sienna glared at her. 'No idea what you're talking about.'

'Oh yes you do,' Kate said, her voice rising, but she was unable to control the volume, 'and you've ignored all my letters and emails.' She could hear gasps from the small crowd that had gathered outside, plainly waiting for Sienna to exit the tent. Several people were now openly standing inside the entrance.

Sienna sighed. 'My secretary probably binned them. Such is the price of fame – everyone's always after me for *something*.'

Meanwhile, Carrie was hovering, her eyes still like saucers, holding a glass of water. 'Here we are, Miss Stone,' she said adoringly, 'and I just *love* your programme!'

'Now you have your water I'd like you out of my tent,' Kate said to Sienna. 'Find somewhere else to sit in the shade.'

Carrie gasped. 'Kate, that's S*ienna Stone!*'

Sienna still didn't move. 'You don't tell *me* what to do!' she snapped.

'I just did,' Kate snapped back, realising that the crowd had now ballooned outside the tent entrance, all craning to hear the altercation, 'so I'll say it again – please leave this tent.'

'Is there a problem, darling?' The deep male voice belonged to Irving Aldridge, who was pushing his way through the throng. The millionaire businessman had recently bought Tremorron, a large house in Higher Tinworthy after the unfortunate departure of the Hedgefield family. He was also Sienna's husband, although it was rumoured that he wasn't going to be for much longer and that Sienna was determined to relieve him of every penny he had.

Sienna gave an exaggerated sigh as she stood up, her hand carefully ruffling her mane of red hair. 'Unfortunately, Irving, I've been feeling quite faint and this wretched nurse refuses to treat me.'

'I have *not* refused to treat you!' Kate could feel her temper rising even more. 'I only asked you to find somewhere else to sit.'

Sienna walked across to lean against her husband. 'She doesn't *like* me, that's what it is,' she said, pouting.

'The reason I don't much like you,' Kate said, 'is because you smashed into my car a few months ago and refused to take responsibility.'

'I have no idea what she's talking about,' Sienna purred to her husband, while the crowd outside pressed against the entrance in the hope of hearing more.

'You were on the wrong side of the road,' Kate reminded her.

'Such rubbish!' snorted Sienna, tugging at her husband's arm. 'Where's your proof? Come along, darling, let's get out of here, away from this hateful woman. I'm *gasping* for some champers!'

Looking increasingly bewildered, poor Irving Aldridge did as he was told.

At four o'clock, when things began to quieten down, Kate said to Carrie, 'I think I'll have a stroll around to see the displays before everyone begins to pack up. Call me on my mobile if there's a problem.' More than anything she needed to cool down after her altercation with Sienna Stone.

She wondered if Woody, her husband of two months, might be free. He was manning the police charity tent, assisted by a young constable in uniform. After forty years on the force, Woody liked to help out whenever he could. He also had the dog with him – Kate's springer spaniel, Barney. She couldn't have him with her in the first-aid tent, so Woody had gallantly taken control.

As she neared, the dog began to bark excitedly. She found Woody surrounded by a group of youths, one of whom was asking admiringly, 'Is it true you caught all those *killers*?' The boy was referring to Woody's days as the local detective inspector when not only had he bagged a killer or two, he'd also saved Kate's skin on more than one occasion. Kate had admittedly got herself into some very tight corners with her new-found passion for detective work.

Woody winked at her over the top of the boy's head and she could tell he was enjoying reliving his moments of fame. Not for the first time she noted what a very attractive man he was, even at sixty-three years of age. She decided to take Barney with her for her walk and to leave Woody to it.

A few yards further along she came to Angie's 'Pimm's and Pasty' marquee. Angie, her older sister, ran The Old Locker Bistro (formerly known as The Locker Tea Rooms) in Lower Tinworthy, next to the beach and just below Kate's house, Lavender Cottage, on the hill above. Angie was serving some cheerful customers queueing up – plainly not for the first time, and more for the Pimm's than the pasties, it would seem – only pausing to take a swig of her gin and tonic. Angie was very fond of gin.

Kate, holding firmly onto Barney's lead, waited for the queue to be served before heading to the bar counter herself.

'*Pimm's*, madam?' Angie asked. Then, under her breath: 'I've been on my feet all bloody afternoon! Fancy taking over for a bit?'

Typical Angie.

'In case it's escaped your notice,' Kate said tersely, 'I've been on *my* feet all day too, tending to everyone's stings, aches and injuries, and I am now trying to cool off, particularly after my encounter with Sienna Stone.'

'What have you done to upset *her*?' Angie asked, handing Kate a Pimm's.

'Absolutely nothing. She swanned into my tent—' At this point Kate realised there was a queue forming behind her. 'I'll tell you about it later. *Damn* woman! Sufficient to say, I could cheerfully *kill* that Sienna Stone!'

Kate drank her Pimm's, then began the climb up the steep rough path, dotted with gorse bushes that led towards the highest stretch of the cliffs, Potter's Point, to gulp some sea air and to enjoy the breathtaking views of the rugged North Cornish coastline. There was a time she'd have sprinted up here in a few minutes, but her sixty-year-old body now dictated otherwise. She'd let Barney off the lead and he was running around manically, having been tied up for most of the day. She knew how he felt. She'd need to take a few deep breaths to calm down before heading back to pack up her medical supplies and assist in dismantling the tent. She could already see glimpses of the ocean ahead, turquoise and calm as the Caribbean today – unless you went for a dip in the icy water, when you'd rapidly discover the difference.

It was as she was almost at the top that she heard a woman's voice shout, 'Get *away* from me! What the *hell*...' followed by a heart-stopping scream which shattered the warm, humid air like an arrow from hell. Kate could see several other people behind her were now running towards the cliff-top as well, but she got there first. She glanced all around before finally daring to look down.

And there, on the beach far below, lay the spreadeagled body of a woman, her glorious red hair radiating out like a halo, clad in an unmistakeable sea-green kaftan.

It could only be Sienna Stone.

TWO

The first time Kate had encountered Sienna Stone was on the road from Plymouth to Tinworthy one dark stormy evening in March. Kate, on the way home, had been steering her red Fiat Punto carefully round a particularly sharp bend when a white Range Rover came hurtling round the corner towards her in the middle of the road. There followed the dreaded sound of brakes screaming and metal crunching as the front offside wing of the Fiat buckled.

Kate, badly shaken but miraculously unhurt, climbed out of her car to survey the damage and came face to face with a tall, glamorous, red-haired woman who'd emerged slowly and carefully from the Range Rover. Even before Kate got close to her she could smell the gin on the woman's breath. She knew it only too well because of Angie's predilection.

Trying to hold back tears, Kate shouted, 'You were in *the middle of the road!*'

'Of course I wasn't!' snapped the redhead, who seemed more interested in examining the front of her own vehicle which, as far as Kate could see, appeared to have little damage, if any.

'You can see for yourself,' Kate said, 'my car is on the correct side of the road and yours is not.'

The woman sighed. 'Sorry, but I really can't stop now because I must get to Plymouth. I'm *on air* in an hour's time!'

Kate recognised her then: the locally famous/infamous Sienna Stone, who presented an evening TV programme called *SeeVue* every week. Apart from covering local topics, Sienna gave a brutal lowdown and star-rating on businesses in the county, which frequently did not go down too well. She was not known to flatter.

'But look what you've done to my car!' Kate protested, trying hard not to cry. 'I don't even think I can drive it home.'

'Oh well,' said Sienna airily, heading back towards her vehicle, 'I expect you've got a breakdown service. And I'm getting wet.' With that, she smoothed down the front of her white trouser-suit.

Kate could feel the anger rising as she confronted this callous woman. 'You can't just leave me here! It's *your* fault!'

Sienna was already back in the driving seat. 'Honey,' she said, leaning out of the window, 'there's no one around so I'm afraid it's your word against mine. I'm sure you have a good insurance company.'

And then she started up the engine and drove off.

Now, nearly four months later, Kate stood aghast, staring at the horrifying vision beneath on the beach. Her husband would know what to do; she wished Woody was here now. Hopefully he'd be on his way up. Why hadn't she waited for him? Next she became aware of people around and then the young constable, who had been helping Woody in the police charity tent, was standing by her side.

'*That's* her!' someone in the crowd shouted. '*That's* the

woman who was having a slanging match with Sienna Stone an hour or so ago!'

'Yes!' someone else shouted. 'She was drinking in the Pimm's tent and I heard her saying she'd like to *kill* Sienna Stone!'

The policeman turned to Kate. 'Looks like you might have some explaining to do,' he said.

It was with great relief that Kate became aware of Woody's arrival at the scene.

'What the hell's going on, Alan?' he asked the constable.

Kate pointed mutely over the cliff.

'Holy moly!' exclaimed Woody, getting out his phone. Kate heard him talking to Charlotte Martin, the current detective inspector. 'We got a body! Get down to Corner Beach – that's just round the north side from Lower Tinworthy beach – like *pronto!* We need the whole team!' He put his hand on Kate's arm. 'I gotta get down there.'

'So do I,' Kate said firmly as she followed him and Alan, the policeman, down the steep path to the beach below, Barney trotting behind.

Woody looked round. 'Why are all these people following us, Alan?'

'This lady was there when the woman fell, or was pushed, off the cliff,' replied Alan. 'They seem to think she had something to do with it.'

'*What!*' Woody stopped in his tracks to glare at the policeman. 'This lady is my *wife!*' He looked back at Kate.

In the background a woman was yelling, '*She* wanted to kill Sienna – she said so!'

'I was in the wrong place at the wrong time,' Kate admitted ruefully. She was beginning to feel a little afraid. 'And I just happened to get up there first.'

'So what? Why do they think you've got anything to do with it?'

Kate swallowed. 'Because Sienna and I had an argument in the first-aid tent, which attracted quite an audience. And then I was seen having a Pimm's at Angie's tent and was overheard saying to Angie that I'd like to kill Sienna Stone.' She stopped for a moment and gazed at Woody. 'I didn't push the silly woman, Woody.'

Woody sighed. 'Nevertheless, if she *was* pushed, you're going to be a suspect, I guess. *Why* are you *always* in the wrong place at the wrong time, Kate?'

'Well, at least I've never been on the wrong side of the *law*,' Kate retorted.

As they neared the beach, Woody immediately reverted to being in control.

He pushed his way through the mob which had gathered round the body while Kate, holding firmly on to the dog's lead, took shelter from the hostile crowd in a narrow cleft in the rock at the entrance to Corner Beach.

'Please stand back,' Woody was shouting, 'and do not touch that body.'

Although not in uniform, Woody had that air of authority that no one questioned – due, of course, to his years in the police force. The crowd, most in bathing gear, unwillingly dispersed; children, goggle-eyed, clutching buckets and spades, and one very fat elderly woman, bulging out of a pink bikini, who was wailing, 'But that's *Sienna Stone!*'

Kate could already hear the wail of the approaching police cars, followed shortly afterwards by a group of police, some in uniform, and the forensic team, heading towards the body of Sienna. Alan had joined them and immediately began to tape off the area, moving away the last few spectators who still hung around, openly fascinated.

Woody came back to where Kate and the dog were half-hidden. 'Apparently, Charlotte was at a barbecue, so let's hope she managed to eat early. Any sign of the husband, Kate?'

Kate shook her head. 'He collected Sienna from my tent a couple of hours ago, but I haven't seen him since.'

'Strange,' Woody commented thoughtfully. 'We have to assume he's still at the fair. We'd better get a car over there.'

At that moment, Charlotte arrived round the corner from Lower Tinworthy Beach. She was clad in some very tight white jeans, a black T-shirt and a short black leather biker jacket. She looked stunning.

'We'd only just got the damn coals heated,' she said sadly to them both, 'but at least I had time for a glass of wine. Only one though!' She looked across at the cordoned-off area. 'Anyone we know?'

'Sienna Stone,' Woody replied.

'Oh my God!' Charlotte looked really shocked. 'What did she do, jump?'

'Most likely,' Woody said cautiously, glancing at Kate.

'Well, we'd better get moving before the tide comes in,' Charlotte said as she headed off to Corner Beach, 'or she'll be washed out to sea.'

'*That's* the woman who pushed her!' a tall, thin man shouted, pointing at Kate.

Charlotte stopped in her tracks and turned round. 'What's he talking about, Kate? Is this true?'

Kate shook her head, sighed and gave a brief résumé of what had happened.

'Oh no!' said Charlotte. 'That means I'm going to have to take a statement from you. Sorry about that, Kate. So where's this Sienna Stone's husband?'

'Not around here,' Kate said.

'Not been seen,' added Woody.

'Hmm,' said Charlotte. 'Ah, here's Paul. Wonder if he's found anything.'

'Paul's the police surgeon,' Woody informed Kate as they watched two paramedics running towards the scene, carrying a stretcher.

'Anything of interest?' Charlotte asked.

The police surgeon shook his head. 'No obvious injuries unrelated to the fall. We'll do a more detailed examination at Launceston but it's imperative we get her off the beach as soon as possible or else they'll all be swimming back.'

Charlotte nodded. 'I'm off to organise two of these guys to go in search of the husband, because I'm going to want to interview him as soon as possible. In the meantime, after I've had a look at the body, can I come up to your house, Kate, to take a statement? Either that or you come up to the police station?'

Kate nodded wearily. 'Yes, come up to Lavender Cottage when you're finished here.'

THREE

Detective Inspector Charlotte Martin sighed and sipped the glass of water Kate had just given her. 'I'm sorry, Kate, but you'll appreciate that I have to question you.'

Kate nodded miserably. She was in shock, tired and hot.

'I've asked Woody to wait in the other room,' Charlotte continued. She was a slim, stunning-looking blonde, and Kate had been in awe – and not a little jealous – when Charlotte had taken over the job of detective inspector in the region, particularly as it was Woody, recently retired from the force, who'd had to help her to settle in and to prime her on who was who in the area.

Woody had been as shocked by Sienna's death as Kate. 'I *do* believe you!' he must have said half a dozen times during the short walk up from the beach. 'I *do*! But Charlotte has to do her job, you *know* that. I'm betting there's a few folk around who'd like to see the back of Sienna Stone, so don't despair! I guess Charlotte will be spoiled for choice when it comes to suspects!'

Kate liked that he still had traces of his American accent, even after more than forty years in the UK. She also loved his dark brown eyes, inherited from his Italian mother, and his calmness in an emergency, inherited most likely from his English father.

It had been her lucky day when she'd met him, in similar tragic circumstances, shortly after her arrival in Tinworthy.

But that was another story.

'Tell me again about today, about her arriving in your tent,' Charlotte said, ten minutes later, pressing the button on her recorder.

Kate did so. 'I was firm, but I don't think I was rude, even though our voices were raised,' she said. 'Unfortunately, quite a crowd had gathered outside so they overheard most of it. Do you remember that I told you that she smashed into my car back in March and refused all responsibility?'

Charlotte nodded. 'It's fair to say that she wasn't a very nice woman, Kate, but nevertheless we can't have her being pushed off a cliff.'

'I suppose there's no possibility it could be suicide?' Kate asked tentatively.

'Very unlikely, if you're correct in what you think you heard. Hopefully we'll know more after forensics do some detailed tests.' She paused. 'The fact that you heard her shout "get away from me" and scream indicates that she must have been pushed, as opposed to an accidental fall. Tell me about your visit to the Pimm's and Pasty tent.'

'That tent – as you probably know – was organised by my sister, Angie.'

'I do know.' Charlotte grinned. 'And where was Fergal while all this was going on?'

Fergal, an Irishman with more than a touch of the blarney, was Angie's current paramour. He'd helped her set up The Old Locker to its current glory from the former wreck of a place it once was, and they now ran it together.

'Fergal was back at The Old Locker, holding the fort, so to speak,' Kate replied.

'Right,' said Charlotte. 'So, you ordered a Pimm's?'

'Well, I felt obliged to; but God, I *needed* it!'

'I have a statement here from someone who says they heard you say you'd like to kill Sienna Stone.' Charlotte laid down her sheet of paper and studied Kate for a moment.

'Well, yes, I did say that, if I remember correctly. But we say these things, don't we? I was *not* planning to push her off a cliff, for God's sake!'

'You weren't at all tempted to give her a little shove when you saw her standing up there?'

Kate was beginning to feel a little nauseous. 'I did *not* see her standing up there! There was no one at all there when I got to the top, and it was only when I looked down...' She shuddered.

'Nevertheless, you were the first on the scene, as far as we know.' Charlotte was studying her intently again.

'As far as we know,' Kate repeated. 'But someone *must* have been up there before me.'

'Tell me,' Charlotte said, 'when you heard the shouting and the scream, how far up were you at that point? Would you be able to retrace your steps and show me exactly where you were when you heard it?'

'I'll try to remember,' Kate said, 'but I can tell you this: whoever might have pushed her over must have had time to get away before I, or anyone else, got up there, and they obviously did.'

'Young Carrie Simpson, who I believe was assisting you in the first-aid tent, has confirmed that you and Miss Stone exchanged a few words and that you ordered her out of the tent. Carrie, who I admit seems to be a bit starstruck, was horrified.'

Kate took a deep breath. 'The wretched woman—'

'You're referring to Miss Stone?'

'Yes, I am. Miss Stone then. She swanned into the tent and sat down on my treatment chair behind the screen I use for examining people. For example, I'd had a teenager with a bee sting on his bottom just minutes before she arrived.'

Charlotte nodded. 'OK. Now we come back to Angie's tent. You were seen to be drinking a Pimm's.'

'Well, that was the purpose of Angie's tent, and yes, I had one.'

'So you can see why people might be confused if you were seen drinking and, at the same time, saying you'd like to kill Miss Stone,' Charlotte said.

'Not that there's a great deal of alcohol in Angie's Pimm's!' Kate protested. 'Furthermore, none of these people were there on that dark night when the wretched woman rounded the bend on the wrong side of the road and nearly wrote off my Fiat.'

Charlotte switched off her machine. 'You're unlikely to be the only suspect, Kate. But we do have to investigate thoroughly.'

'I'm not going to sleep a wink,' Kate informed Woody after Charlotte had departed, on the hunt for Irving Aldridge.

'Yes, you are,' Woody soothed. 'You're going to have a few nightcaps and then try to forget the whole thing.'

'How *can* I forget? Everything I said and did this afternoon has been taken completely out of context. I don't even know if Charlotte believes me or not.'

'It's Charlotte's job not to believe anyone. Privately, I'm sure she believes you, but she has to do it all by the book. You *definitely* didn't see anyone running away when you walked up there?'

'No,' Kate replied, 'and I didn't see Sienna either. Whatever took place happened *just* before I got to the top. You *know* how steep that slope is. I've been thinking, Woody, that perhaps it was suicide and it was just a seagull or something that she was shouting at.'

'I think you're grasping at straws, Kate. If she planned her own demise, it's unlikely she would scream,' Woody said with a shrug. 'A scream *generally* means that someone is taken unawares.'

'On reflection, I'd have thought she was far too fond of herself to take her own life,' Kate said. 'Anyway, there must be other people Sienna Stone has upset?'

'Quite a few, I believe,' Woody confirmed, 'beginning with her husband.'

'Well, he was there today, although they seemed friendly enough with each other when she finally left the tent,' Kate said.

'Well, she *was* an actress at one time, and known to be a prima donna. And I don't reckon that her husband, Aldridge, was any too thrilled to find out that she was having it off with the director of her programme and wanted a divorce.'

'In which case I don't suppose the director's wife will be all that fond of her either,' Kate said, 'if he has one, that is. I wonder if she was at the fair today?'

'We've no way of knowing who was at the fair, other than by seeing them there. And it doesn't necessarily follow that the killer was at the fair anyway. He or she could have been walking along the cliff-path or climbed up from one of the other fields.'

'We need to find out if that director has a wife,' Kate said thoughtfully. 'I wonder what they're saying about it on the news?' She glanced at her watch as she switched on the TV.

The local news presenter solemnly announced, 'We are sad to report the unexplained death of the famous television presenter, Sienna Stone, who fell from a cliff-top near the villages of Tinworthy this afternoon. Her husband, Irving Aldridge, was too upset to comment, but Roger Moran from *SeeVue* said that the whole TV crew was devastated, and he himself appeared tearful. Charlotte Martin, detective inspector for the North Cornwall area, has said, "We're keeping an open mind, but foul play cannot be ruled out.'"

Just then there was a knock at the door. Barney began to bark hysterically.

'Who the hell is that now?' Woody asked irritably as he got to his feet and went to find out.

Kate heard voices at the door, and then Woody saying, 'Well then, I guess you'd better come in.'

Kate groaned. Who on earth was calling at seven o'clock on a Saturday night? After the day she'd had...

'Someone for you,' Woody said, coming in with a huge grin on his face. He stood back to let the tall young man into the room.

'Hi, Mum!' said the tall young man. 'Thought I'd surprise you!'

'*Jack!*'

FOUR

'Any chance you can give me a bed for the night?' Jack asked as he enveloped his mother in a bear hug.

'Oh, Jack!' Kate was almost incapable of speech. 'What, er, why...?' She extricated herself from his embrace and shook her head to try to make sense of it all. 'But you're in *Australia*!'

'Not just at the moment,' Jack said cheerfully, bending down to stroke Barney, who was jumping around with excitement.

Kate hugged him again. 'But what are you doing *here*?'

'I've come to see *you*!'

'How did you get here?'

'Oh, buses all the way from Heathrow! God, it takes *hours*! You really are off the beaten track here!'

'But...' Kate hesitated. 'Where's Eva?'

Jack pulled a face. 'That's history. Things haven't been right for a while, and now she's met someone else.'

'I'm sorry.' Kate couldn't stop herself from staring at her tall, suntanned son. Then, suddenly remembering, she said, 'Oh, Jack, this is Woody...'

'Thought it might be,' Jack said, grinning, and shaking Woody's hand. 'Hey, am I supposed to call you Dad or something?'

Woody raised his eyes to the ceiling. 'Let's stick with Woody!'

'Sit down, Jack! Tell us why you're here,' Kate said, still coming to terms with the fact that her younger son, who she hadn't seen for three years, was *here*, in Lavender Cottage! Unbelievable!

Jack plonked himself on the sofa. 'Well, work sort of dried up, Eva had gone, I got fed up with the heat and I just suddenly thought, why not go *home*? See the folks, work out what I want to do next, and so here I am!'

'I am *so* pleased to see you,' Kate said. Which was the understatement of the year, she thought.

'You must be in dire need of a drink,' Woody said, 'and, if you aren't, I am and I'm sure your mother is because she's had one helluva day.' He looked at Kate. 'We need to eat and I guess you don't much feel like cooking right now, so why don't we all go along to The Gull?'

The Greedy Gull pub was just a short walk along the lane from Lavender Cottage, and therefore frequently visited.

'I'd do anything for a pint of decent draught beer,' Jack said, getting to his feet.

'OK,' said Kate, 'but first let me show you to your room. It used to be Angie's. I think I told you she's moved into The Old Locker now, but the bed's all made up.'

'How is Aunt Angie?' Jack asked as he followed her upstairs, lugging his backpack. 'Still on the gin?'

'Nothing changes,' Kate said ruefully as she opened the bedroom door.

. . .

Half an hour later, they were comfortably seated in The Greedy Gull and Des, the landlord, had taken their orders for fish and chips and served beer to Woody and Jack, and a large glass of wine to Kate.

'Your mother sure needs this,' Woody said to Jack.

Distracted, Jack looked round at the white walls, dark beams and polished brassware.

'What's with the artwork?' he asked, pointing to where, on each side of the inglenook fireplace, a large gull with a fish in his beak had been painted.

'Des has an artistic bent at times,' Woody explained. 'He likes to inform everyone how greedy these gulls really are because, if you're sitting outside, there's a damn good chance one of them will swoop right down and snatch your lunch away from under your nose.'

Most people were sitting outside tonight – seagulls or not – and the bar was half-empty. Des had wiped the bar top several times while looking pointedly at Jack. He liked to know who was who.

'You got a visitor then?' His curiosity had plainly got the better of him.

'Nosy bugger!' Woody said under his breath.

'My son,' Kate replied proudly, 'all the way from Australia!'

'Blimey!' said Des, his long, lugubrious face breaking into a glimmer of a smile. 'You'll be in need of a few pints then!'

'Too right, mate!' agreed Jack, raising his glass.

Kate had told Jack about Angie and Fergal, and was about to ask more about Eva, when Jack asked, 'Who are those girls over there?'

Kate followed his gaze to where two girls were sitting in the corner drinking wine and endeavouring, with much giggling, to wind Des's spaghetti bolognese round their forks. 'No idea,' she said.

'Don't you think the dark one's pretty?' Jack asked, taking another slug of his beer.

'Well, yes, I suppose she is,' Kate said.

'Don't reckon they're local,' Woody said, 'so I guess they're here on holiday.'

'Hmm,' said Jack, continuing to stare.

Kate noticed that the girl must have made eye contact, because Jack was grinning at her, and she was grinning back at him.

'He sure doesn't waste any time,' Woody murmured admiringly.

At that moment, the fish and chips arrived, as did a group of about a dozen people.

Kate had just brought a forkful to her mouth when she heard a man say, 'That's *her*!' All eyes swivelled to where the man was pointing.

'Yes, that's her,' a fat blonde woman agreed, 'that's the one who must have pushed Sienna Stone off the cliff!'

Des, his mouth open, had stopped halfway through pouring a pint. Beer flooded all over the counter. 'That's *Kate*,' he said to no one in particular.

Woody laid down his knife and fork, stood up and walked over to where the group were standing. 'My wife did *not* push Sienna Stone off any cliff,' he said slowly and distinctly. 'Right now, we're trying to eat a meal in peace after a very stressful day. If you persist in accusing people of things they didn't do, then the landlord will ask you to leave.' Woody turned hopefully towards Des.

Kate noticed Des gulp at this; he wasn't one to turn away any custom but, having seen Woody's furious expression, he nodded meekly.

As Woody returned to the table and the group began to order drinks, still stealing an occasional glance at Kate, Jack said, 'Hey, Mum, what have you been up to? Who is this Sienna person anyway?'

Kate, rapidly going off her food, gave him a brief account of what had transpired earlier. 'I don't want to talk about it any more today,' she said wearily.

Woody said, 'Let's get out of here when we're all done. We'll have a nightcap at home.'

Kate looked at him gratefully.

When they all stood up to go, Jack said, 'I'll catch up with you two in a moment, OK?'

'What's he up to?' Kate asked crossly as they left The Gull and began to walk home.

Woody took her hand. 'My guess is that he's chatting up that girl.'

'Dear God!' Kate sighed. 'He's only been here for a couple of hours! I just hope he doesn't turn into a womaniser like his father!'

Jack Palmer had been conceived in Singapore just before Kate and her then-husband, Alex, had returned to the UK after two years in the Far East. Tom, fifteen months old, had been born there and Kate, on the flight home, wondered how she'd ever cope with two young children and no *amah*! Everyone had an *amah* to look after their kids in Singapore, freeing them to continue as they always had, socialising and partying. However, the ex-pat socialising and partying had begun to wear a bit thin for Kate, if not for Alex.

When she discovered that Alex was having an affair, he explained it away by saying, 'Well, I was feeling a bit neglected, what with the baby and you being pregnant again...' to which Kate had spluttered, 'And *who* do you suppose *gets* me pregnant, for God's sake?' She'd wanted to return to the UK on the next fight, but Alex's engineering contract with the airline still had a month to run.

Swearing that the affair was over, and pledging undying love, a month later Alex accompanied Kate home. It took just six weeks to discover that the woman in question had also returned to the UK, and that the affair continued.

Their marriage did not.

FIVE

On Sunday morning, Kate studied her son as they ate breakfast, wondering how long he planned to stay. Already she was dreading the thought of him returning to Australia. It was so far away and she hated partings.

'I bet you're wondering how long I'm planning to stay,' Jack said, munching his fourth piece of toast.

'Of course not,' Kate lied.

'Well, if it's OK with you and Woody, could I bed down here for a few weeks? Would Woody mind?'

'Neither of us would mind one bit,' Kate replied with some relief. 'You can stay as long as you like.' Woody was in the shower, so unavailable to be consulted, but she was sure he wouldn't object.

Jack drained his mug of tea. 'I like your Woody,' he said. 'I'm giving him my seal of approval.' He grinned.

'Well, that's a relief!' Kate said, laughing.

'But he won't want me hanging around indefinitely so I thought I'd go up to Edinburgh to see Tom, Jane and family, and then I suppose I should go see Dad.'

'What's your father up to these days?' Kate asked.

Jack snorted. 'Last I heard he's bedded up with some woman or other in a remote Welsh valley or somewhere.'

'Surprise, surprise,' Kate said drily.

'Well, he's sixty-five so not much chance he'll change now. But I'm glad you've got married again, Mum. You were a long time on your own.' He looked longingly at the loaf on the work surface. 'Any more toast?'

'Help yourself. I wasn't on my own for *all* of the time,' Kate said.

'True, true.' Jack placed a couple of slices into the toaster. 'But I didn't fancy any of *them* as a stepfather!'

Woody, shaved and showered, arrived in the kitchen. 'Morning, Jack! Sleep OK?'

'Yeah, I went out like a light. Comfy bed.'

'I was thinking,' Woody said as he fed pods into the coffee maker, 'I might cook lunch for us today and give you a rest, Kate.'

Jack cleared his throat. 'Thing is, er, I hope you don't mind, but I've arranged to meet that girl in the pub at lunchtime. You know, the pretty dark-haired one who was there last night?'

'You sure as hell didn't waste any time,' Woody muttered as he poured himself a coffee.

'Who *is* she anyway?' Kate asked, a little annoyed. He'd only just *got* here!

'Her name's Beth, and she's working here for the summer,' Jack said, beaming. 'I'm meeting her at twelve, and she's going to show me around.' He looked at his mother. 'You don't mind, do you?'

'No, of course not,' Kate replied, minding very much indeed. *For goodness' sake*, she chided herself, *surely you're not jealous! After all, he's a young red-blooded male, so what did you expect?*

It's just that I didn't think I'd have to share him so soon! she answered herself.

'Have you got a spare key,' Jack asked, buttering a fifth slice of toast, 'so I don't have to bother you coming and going?'

Kate was still feeling emotional after the previous day's events and wondered what sort of hours he intended to keep. Still, it was worth it to have him back home. She opened a drawer and withdrew a key. 'Here you are.'

'Thanks, Mum, you're a star!' He looked at Woody. 'OK if I have that last piece of toast?'

Jack was gone for most of the afternoon so Woody decided to cook dinner in the evening. 'My guess is he's gonna be hungry,' he said.

Before he'd gone out, Kate had heard Jack tramping around upstairs, in the shower, in the bedroom. He finally emerged in a different pair of jeans and T-shirt. 'Wonder if you could put these in the wash?' he asked, handing Kate a bundle of clothing. 'No hurry. How do I look?'

'You look very nice,' Kate said truthfully. 'I'm sure she'll be impressed.' Then, as an afterthought: 'Will you want to bring her back here?'

'Oh God, no!' he said. Then, seeing Kate's face: 'I mean, not on a *first date*! Don't want to come on too heavy.'

'Oh, right,' said Kate with some relief.

Woody looked up from his *Sunday Times*. 'I'm doing roast beef tonight.'

'Jeez, that's great, I'll be there!' Jack said as he waved and headed out of the door.

He'd only been gone for a few minutes when the phone rang. It was Charlotte.

'Hi, Kate. We need to have a walk up to the cliff, you and I, so you can show me where you were when you heard the argument and then the scream. I was wondering if we could meet tomorrow? What time do you finish at the medical centre?'

'Half past four, five o'clock,' Kate replied, 'but I'm only working tomorrow and Wednesday morning this week. I've cut down my shifts since we got married.'

'OK then, let's make it Tuesday. How about we meet out at the field where the fair was at two o'clock and take it from there?'

'That's fine,' Kate said, 'I'll be there.'

She hung up and turned to Woody. 'What difference does it make where I was when I heard Sienna shouting and screaming?'

Woody laid down his newspaper. 'Well, however much time it took for you to get to the top from wherever you heard the shrieking is the time it would have taken for someone to get away from the scene. You did say you were the first there.'

'I was,' Kate confirmed, 'although someone must definitely have been there just before me if Sienna was pushed off the cliff.'

'They'll do an in-depth examination of her clothes to see if they can detect someone's DNA or some sign of who might have pushed her.'

Kate had never been a suspect before and she certainly didn't intend to take this lying down. No way! She'd become good at investigating, and that was what she was going to do, if only to clear her name.

Jack arrived back at half past five. 'I've had an amazing day,' he said, crashing onto the sofa, 'and seen a lot of Lower Tinworthy. What a great little place!'

'We think so,' Kate said. 'There's a Middle Tinworthy and a Higher Tinworthy as well.'

'So I believe. What happens there?'

'Well, Middle Tinworthy is further up the hill and is the biggest part of the village where the church, the school and the shops are – and, of course, the medical centre where I work. And there's quite a big housing estate up there as well. Then Higher Tinworthy is right up at the top with great views all around and a lot of expensive property.' She hesitated. 'Um, how did you get on with the girl?'

'Beth? Yeah, she's really sweet. Been here since the beginning of May, working for the summer.'

'Doing what?'

'Cleaning caravans. There's a big caravan park nearby, it seems.'

'That'll be Sunshine Park,' Woody said. 'It's just outside Higher Tinworthy on the road towards Boscastle. Great big place, rows and rows of caravans.'

'Yeah, she shares a caravan with two other girls and they spend all morning and afternoon cleaning, although Beth says they normally finish by half past three to four o'clock.'

'So, are you planning to see her again?' Kate asked tentatively.

'Oh yes. She's got a share in a little car and she's going to drive me around – tomorrow.'

'Where's she from?' Kate hoped she didn't sound too inquisitive, but really...

'Bristol. She's a hairdresser.'

'So what's she doing cleaning caravans?' Kate asked.

'She's between jobs at the moment and fancied spending the summer in Cornwall because she wants to learn to surf. I said I'd teach her. I'm going to have to get myself a wetsuit though, because, sure as eggs is eggs, this ain't Brisbane! Anyway, you said you were going to be working tomorrow so you won't miss me!'

SIX

The following morning when Kate arrived at the medical centre in Middle Tinworthy, she was greeted enthusiastically by Denise, the receptionist, who knew everything about everybody. 'Hey!' she called out merrily. 'Did you finally get your own back on that awful woman who wrecked your car?'

Kate knew – hoped – she was joking but realised there would be more remarks like this in the days ahead. She was beginning to wish she'd never told anyone about the damn accident.

Just as she was about to reply, Sue, the other practice nurse, appeared on the scene.

'Leave off, Denise!' she said. 'Kate's not the only one with a reason to dislike that woman.' She tapped her nose. 'I believe there's quite a list.'

'There *is*,' Denise agreed enthusiastically. She was the expert in local gossip. 'She was having it off with the director of her programme, you know, and apparently, his wife went ballistic when she found out.'

'How do you know that?' Kate asked, noting that the

director did indeed appear to have a wife. Had she been in the area? Where did she live?

Denise leaned forward. 'I've got this cousin in Plymouth whose daughter works at the studios and...' In fact, Denise appeared to have a great many relatives who lived in all manner of convenient places throughout Devon and Cornwall, and fed her exclusive titbits.

'I don't suppose Sienna's husband's any too pleased then,' Kate said.

The first of the patients had begun to filter in.

'Can't stand here gossiping all day,' Sue said briskly. 'Who's first on my list, Denise?'

During the course of her shift, Kate became aware that often, when she entered the waiting area, there seemed to be a sudden hush in the conversation, and all eyes swivelled in her direction. Surely no one seriously believed her to be a killer? Or was it all in her imagination?

'God, Kate, can't you go *anywhere* without getting involved in some crime or other?' Angie asked as she polished a wine glass before replacing it on the shelf behind the bar in The Old Locker. She and Fergal had done a good job on the place, transforming it from a rundown shack – in which fishermen and builders had stored their gear for centuries – into the smart bistro it now was. 'And I can't believe Jack's come back! You must bring him down to see his old auntie!'

'I will, I will, but he's otherwise occupied at the moment. And I don't go *looking* for crime,' Kate protested, sipping a lager at the bar after her shift. It was early evening and the place was beginning to fill up with people wandering in from the beach.

'I wonder if the stalker was at the fair?' Angie asked, smothering a yawn.

'Stalker?'

'Didn't you know? Some creepy guy who follows her every-where and writes her love letters – all that stuff. It was in the papers because she took out some kind of injunction against him. Boy, there are some weirdos in this world!' Angie patted her blonde coiffeur.

At this point, Fergal appeared. He'd recently taken to growing a beard, which was as black as his hair, in spite of his fifty-seven years. Angie had assured Kate that he didn't dye it; it was just his genes or something and he rather fancied himself as an Irish pirate. Kate wasn't at all sure that the Irish had had many pirates roaming the Cornish coast, but perhaps they had.

'Hi, Kate!' He poured himself a lager. 'Sure, that fecking woman upset a lot of people. Did you know about Marc, up at The Atlantic Hotel?'

'What about him?' Kate asked. Marc Le Grand had done a great deal to improve The Atlantic Hotel, and he was an excep-tionally good chef.

'Sienna Stone did a piece on his restaurant on that *SeeVue* programme of hers, and she *slated* him. Criticised the food and everything, called him a phoney and all that.'

'That's unbelievable,' Kate remarked.

'Well, 'tis a fact. And Marc was not well pleased.'

'No, I don't suppose he was,' Kate said, trying to remember if she'd seen Marc at the fair.

'And he did the catering for the hospitality tent,' Fergal added, answering her unspoken question. 'One of his waitresses was in here earlier. Nice girl – her father's the postman. I said to her that we're forever getting the wrong mail and she said he gets a bit confused.'

'He was confused again today,' Angie said. 'He still thinks Polly Lock lives here.'

Polly Lock had been the owner of the building when it was a tiny tea room, before Angie took it over. To add to the postman's confusion, Angie had originally lived with Kate at

Lavender Cottage until Woody had bought her out when he and Kate got married. Now he let out his own house across the valley. Popularly known as Postman Pat (his surname being Patterson), he was in his late sixties, and he liked everyone to stay put. Months later, he was still delivering Polly's letters to Angie, Angie's letters to Kate, and Woody's letters to whoever happened to be renting his house, On the Up.

'Where's Wonderboy then?' Angie asked.

Angie had referred to Woody as Wonderboy ever since they'd first arrived in Lower Tinworthy and Woody had been the detective in charge of a murder which had taken place almost under their noses. Angie had fancied him and said so, unlike Kate who'd fancied him but said nothing. Kate suspected the fact that Woody had fallen for her, Kate, had rankled not a little. However, since Fergal had come on the scene, Angie was definitely less bitchy about it all.

'Woody's cutting the grass over at On the Up,' Kate replied. 'The tenants are out for the day and it's part of the deal.'

The aptly named house was situated halfway up to the cliffs on the opposite side of the valley from Lavender Cottage. Two couples had rented it for a month.

Kate drained her glass. 'Well, I'd better be getting back as Woody will be home soon.'

Angie grinned. 'Another nice little murder mystery for you to solve, Kate!'

'I'd be much happier if I wasn't a suspect,' Kate said, standing up. 'But do let me know if you hear anything of interest, won't you?'

As Kate walked up the hill towards Lavender Cottage, she stopped for a moment to admire the view below; the sea a deep turquoise, the sand white and glistening in the summer sunshine, the swimmers venturing into the water. Seagulls were circling above the shops bordering the little river, including The

Old Locker, in the hope of snatching something to eat from an unaware tourist.

She thought about what Angie had said about the stalker, and about Marc, and she wondered if it might be time to make a list. Kate liked making lists of suspects. Should she write her *own* name at the top of the list? If only to have the satisfaction of eliminating it straight away?

She let the dog out, kicked off her shoes, made a cup of coffee and sat down with a blank piece of paper.

'I've made a list,' Kate informed Woody when they sat down with a glass of wine a little later.

Woody rolled his eyes. 'One of your famous lists?'

'It helps, if only in that you can eliminate people as necessary, and then see who you're left with,' Kate informed him.

'Surely it's a bit early to think of eliminating anyone?' Woody asked, feeding the dog a crisp. Barney was addicted to smoky bacon crisps, and Kate had put them on her shopping list for his sake.

'No, I've already eliminated someone,' Kate said.

'Like who?' Woody asked, looking genuinely puzzled.

'Like *me*!' Kate laughed. 'I am a suspect, so I have to be on it, but I *know*, of course, that I didn't do it!'

Woody snorted. 'However do they cope without you on the criminology courses at Oxford?'

'No need to be sarcastic.'

Woody, California born and bred, had won a scholarship to study criminology at Oxford University when he was just eighteen. His English father had been proud and delighted, his Italian mother less so. She didn't want her boy to be 'away back in Europe', although she was assured he'd come back home eventually. But Woody hadn't. He'd joined the Metropolitan Police in London, got married, had two daughters, been widowed, moved to Cornwall, and only went back to Los Angeles for holidays.

He fed the drooling dog another crisp. 'OK, OK, so tell me who's on this list?'

'Well, there's the husband, Irving Aldridge. Rumour has it she'd been planning to leave him and take him for every penny. And he was *there*, at the fair.'

Woody nodded. 'OK. Who else?'

'There's a *stalker*. I don't know his name, and I don't know what he looks like, so I've no way of knowing if he was at the fair or not.'

'I guess Charlotte will be on to that,' Woody said. 'Who else is on this list of yours?'

'The director of SeeVue of course – that one Sienna was having an affair with. I don't know his name yet, but I'm looking into that. What's interesting is that the director has a wife who, Denise tells me, is most unhappy about their liaison.'

'I daresay she is,' Woody said. 'It should be easy enough to find out the director's name. I'll google the programme.'

'Well, his wife might not have changed her name, of course. After all, I didn't change mine, did I?'

'Well, I shall always think of you as Mrs Forrest,' Woody said firmly, 'whatever you decide to call yourself.'

Kate ignored him. 'And then we have Marc, from The Atlantic Hotel!'

'*Marc?*'

'Apparently, she slated him on her programme, and Marc is none too pleased either.'

'I saw Marc at the fair,' Woody said thoughtfully. 'He did the catering for the hospitality tent, you know. But surely he could have slipped something into her drink rather than climb all the way up the cliff to push her off?'

Kate looked up from her list. 'Will you *stop* feeding that dog? He's put on a load of weight since you moved in here.

Now, we need to know if the director's wife or the stalker were at the fair.'

'What's the fair got to do with it?' Woody asked, giving Barney the last remaining crisp. 'Whoever pushed her didn't have to be at the fair at all. They could have got up there via any of the other surrounding fields, or they could even have been on the coastal path itself. Who knows? Someone might even have arranged to *meet* her up there for all we know.'

Kate sighed. She hadn't thought of that. No point in concentrating on the fair then. This one was not going to be easy.

SEVEN

Before Kate ventured out to the cliff-tops, she surveyed herself in the full-length mirror, as she frequently did. It wasn't conceit; it was to reassure herself that she was still presentable. And, if truth be told, to try to reassure herself that she was still reasonably attractive and worthy of a good-looking husband, because there was no denying that Woody was a handsome man.

Her main concern was, of course, Charlotte. Kate knew that it was purely police matters that had brought Woody and Charlotte together, and she also knew that Charlotte now had a man friend. It was just that Charlotte was *so* damn effortlessly attractive, and charming to boot. OK, so the woman was almost ten years younger than Kate, not to mention being slim, long-legged and beautiful. Most of the Tinworthy men fancied her, even the old codgers in the pub who rarely looked up from their dominoes. And Woody was only human after all.

Kate reminded herself on a regular basis to hold her tummy in and keep her weight down, but she was very fond of a glass or three of wine, unwanted calories which she could ill afford. Still, her hair was still thick and shiny, with very little grey permeating her natural auburn colour, although that was fading a little – she was very grateful to Guy, at Guys 'n' Dolls, for the highlights and lowlights. She did a little twirl in front of the mirror, gave herself one final look and decided she was as ready as she'd ever be to meet Charlotte.

'Show me exactly where you think you were when you heard the scream,' Charlotte ordered as she, Kate and a young policeman trudged upwards through the rough grazing land towards Potter's Point. A few bewildered sheep stopped chewing for a minute to stare at them.

'I think it was *somewhere* around here,' Kate said, rubbing her forehead and stopping at a gorse bush. She remembered a gorse bush but, then again, there were an awful lot of gorse bushes around.

'But you're not certain?'

How can I be certain? Kate wondered. *As if I'd known at the time that I was going to be asked all these damn questions!* 'Well, I can't be a hundred per cent sure,' she admitted.

Charlotte sighed. 'OK then, let's say it *was* here. So, what was your reaction when you heard the shouting going on?'

Kate shrugged. 'I was really shocked. I think I probably stopped in my tracks for a split second before I started moving on up as fast as I could.'

'How fast would you have been walking?' Charlotte asked.

The police officer who was accompanying them stifled a yawn.

'Not very fast,' Kate replied honestly, 'because of the rough, uneven ground, but I sort of walked and then ran a bit as fast as I could.'

'Let me see,' Charlotte asked, giving a nod to the policeman.

Feeling a little self-conscious, Kate demonstrated her erratic gait as she headed up the slope, while the policeman was checking the time and doing some sort of measuring.

As they all reached Potter's Point, Charlotte said, 'What did you do then?'

Kate, recovering her breath, said, 'Well, there was no one around, which seemed strange. And then I looked down.' She shuddered at the memory.

'And then what?'

'That's when I saw Sienna Stone's body on the beach below.' Kate looked down at the smooth white sand, unable to believe what had taken place only a few days previously.

'You're sure there was no one else around, Kate?'

Kate shook her head. 'Not when I first got up here. It was just after I'd spotted Sienna that people began to arrive.'

At this point, the policeman said, 'One minute, seven seconds.'

Both women turned to stare at him.

'That's how long it would have taken you to get here after you heard the scream,' he added.

'Assuming that's roughly correct, are you quite sure you saw no one around at *all* when you got here?' Charlotte asked, peering over the cliff edge.

Kate was rapidly becoming confused. 'Well, I suppose there were people in the distance, on the coast path and so forth, but no one in the immediate vicinity.'

'You *suppose*?'

'Honestly, Charlotte, from what I remember, there was no one *nearby*.'

'You're sure?'

Right now, Kate thought, *I can't be too sure of my own name*. 'Yes,' she said hesitantly.

'Just you then?'

'Just me. If I'd known I was going to be interrogated like this I'd have made notes!' Kate snapped.

'Thing is,' Charlotte persisted, ignoring Kate's remark, 'there must have been *someone*.' She gazed out to sea. 'Because if some anonymous person had just pushed Sienna Stone off the cliff-top, they had to have gone *somewhere*, didn't they? So *where*? Surely that person couldn't have got very far away in the minute or so it took you to get up here?' She looked at the policeman. 'Are we aware of any Olympic sprinters in this area?'

The policeman shrugged and said nothing.

'The coastal path dips down quite steeply that way,' Charlotte said, staring to the north, 'but if they were heading south, because the terrain is so flat, you'd have seen them. So the person must have run off in a northerly direction and wouldn't have been seen until he or she started climbing up the other side.' She turned to the policeman. 'Do me a favour and walk as quickly as you can down that path and up the other side, just to see how long that takes.'

He didn't look happy but he set off obediently. It was two minutes, according to Charlotte, before he could be seen climbing further up. She shouted at him to come back.

'Well,' she said, 'he could have gone that way and hidden down in the hollow for a while. Do you remember seeing anyone thereabouts when you began walking down to the beach?'

Kate shook her head. 'Not that I can remember, but I was so shocked that I really wasn't looking around.'

'In that case it would seem more likely that the person was heading down somewhere at the same time as you were heading up,' Charlotte said, looking at Kate. 'That would surely be the logical thing for him or her to do?'

Kate thought for a moment. 'I certainly didn't see anyone going down towards the fair when I was going up; I *was* looking straight ahead though.' *And trying to get my breath back and not fall into a rabbit hole*, she thought. 'But there are these clumps of gorse around so I suppose someone could hide behind one of them?'

'Possibly...' Charlotte demurred. 'Like I already said, this someone must have been either heading down, or hiding somewhere, while everyone else was going *up*. We have no way of knowing yet if this was a spur-of-the-moment or a pre-planned crime.' She sighed. 'There are times I wish I'd taken up gardening or catering.'

Later, Woody guffawed as he sipped his wine. '*Catering?* Charlotte? She doesn't look like she could boil an egg, does she? Still, I guess she must have boiled a few in her time with three kids. Talking of catering, though, I think it's about time we paid another visit to The Atlantic for a meal, don't you?' He grinned. 'It would be good to have a word with our friend, Marc.'

When Marc Le Grand had bought The Atlantic Hotel in Higher Tinworthy, he'd modestly advertised it as 'the best place to eat in Cornwall'. Naturally, several famous local chefs had taken issue with this claim. And then Sienna Stone had paid a visit and had been distinctly unimpressed, giving him an abysmal review on her television programme.

'Marc is a suspect too,' Kate said.

'Exactly. So this might be a good time to have a chat with him,' Woody said, 'and except for The Gull the other day, we haven't eaten out much lately.'

He and Kate were sitting outside, having demolished the steaks that Woody had cooked on the barbecue.

Kate laid down her knife and fork. 'That was delicious,' she pronounced. 'Better than anything Marc could do!'

'True,' Woody agreed, draining his glass of wine, 'although it kinda lacked the Gallic touch.'

Marc's Gallic ethnicity was questionable. Apparently, he had adopted his French mother's maiden name, and spelled his name with a 'C', which was presumably more fitting for his haute-cuisine aspirations than his father's name of Bloggs, or so rumour had it. Though since he hailed from somewhere in Essex, Kate wasn't sure how anyone could know that. However, his knowledge of the French language was scanty, in spite of his efforts to pepper his speech with the occasional French cliché. Even though his 'French' accent reverted to pure Essex now and again, nevertheless Marc was considered to be *un chef formidable*.

'Let's book for Friday night,' said Woody.

EIGHT

On Wednesday lunchtime, Kate finally had an opportunity to accompany Jack down to The Old Locker.

'Hi, Aunt Angie!' Jack said, hugging his aunt and handing her a bunch of supermarket lilies. 'I was going to bring you a bottle of gin but Mum said that would be like taking coals to Newcastle.' He pointed at the impressive array on the shelves behind the bar.

Angie shot Kate a hostile look. 'Your mother knows quite well that these bottles are for the *customers*.'

Kate decided it wasn't a good time to mention that Angie was her own best customer. At this point, Fergal appeared.

'Come and meet my gorgeous nephew,' Angie commanded, 'all the way from Australia! Jack, meet Fergal.'

As they shook hands, Fergal asked, 'And how long are you here for?'

'Well,' Jack said, 'I kinda planned on staying for two or three weeks maybe, but I've met this girl so, um, I might hang around longer if Mum and Woody don't mind.'

If that's what it takes to keep him here, Kate thought, *maybe I'm going to be grateful to this Beth or whatever her name is.*

'Sure, you don't waste any time!' Fergal said, echoing Woody's statement.

'So, who's the lucky lady?' Angie asked, handing him a pint of lager.

Jack explained that Beth was in Tinworthy for the summer, cleaning caravans so she could learn to surf.

Angie leaned across the bar. 'And what do you think of your American stepfather, Jack?'

'Woody's OK,' Jack replied and, putting his arm around Kate, added, 'I think they're well suited.'

'That's just what *I* thought when we all first met,' Angie said, avoiding Kate's eye. 'I could *see* the two of them together!'

Kate was amused. 'You have a short memory, Angie. You must have forgotten that you fancied him yourself!'

'Oh, only *very* briefly,' Angie said dismissively, 'because he wasn't my type.' She turned to Jack. 'You must bring your Bess in here for a drink.'

'Beth. Her name's Beth.'

'OK, Beth then. You bring her in for a drink.' She glanced at Kate. 'And what do you think about your mother being a murder suspect?'

'I don't think my mum would hurt a fly,' Jack said, looking surprised.

'Neither do I,' said Fergal, giving Angie a dark look.

'Of course she wouldn't,' Angie put in hurriedly. 'It's all quite ridiculous, particularly as there were loads of people around at the fair who had good reason to get rid of Madame Stone.'

'Loads?' Kate queried, anxious to add to The List. 'Like who?'

'Like the stalker, for one,' Angie replied. 'By the way, I've found out his name for you. He's a geek called Timmy Something-or-other.

'How did you find that out?' Kate asked eagerly.

'Polly Lock told me.'

'So where does he live?'

'Oh, he's local,' Angie replied. 'He lives alone in one of those assisted-living flats up on the Middle Tinworthy estate. Typical loner, if you ask me. Probably wears a belted raincoat and a beret. According to Polly Lock, he's been sitting on the beach for days, staring out to sea and not talking to anyone. Your friend Charlotte's been questioning him, I believe, but he refuses to say a word.'

Polly Lock, like Denise at the medical centre, was another local woman who seemed to know everything about everybody. If she didn't, she made it her business to find out.

'Does that make him guilty?' Jack asked. 'Perhaps he can't speak? Perhaps he's got a speech impairment?'

'No, he's not got a speech impairment,' Angie said, 'according to Polly.'

Fergal had reappeared from the other end of the bar. 'Perhaps the poor man was so besotted with Sienna that he lost the power of speech when she died,' he said sadly.

'You old romantic, you!' Angie said, prodding him gently in the ribs. 'Is that what *you'd* do?'

'Are you serious? *Me*, not talking? Jaysus, no! I'd have plenty to say. Now, who's for one of my Irish coffees?'

Two Irish coffees later, Jack was tottering slightly as he and Kate walked back up the lane. 'How much whiskey does Fergal put in those coffees?' he asked his mother.

'A lot,' Kate replied, 'which is why I only had one. Are you seeing Beth this evening?'

'No, not tonight, because she's arranged to go with one of the other girls to the cinema in Wadebridge. But we're going out tomorrow to get ourselves wetsuits. I noticed there's a shop selling stuff like that along the road from Angie's.'

'Yes, it's called Riding the Waves,' Kate said, 'and I believe they're quite reasonably priced. Talking of which, how are you for money?'

'Not too bad,' Jack replied as they reached the cottage. 'I've got some savings and I've made an arrangement so I can withdraw money over here.' He hesitated at the gate.

'So that means you might be able to stay for a while?'

'Maybe, Mum. Maybe.'

When Woody came in, he said, 'Why don't we take Jack up to The Edge of the Moor tonight? Just for a drink, to let him see the place. He might want to take his new girlfriend up there.'

'Good idea,' Kate said, 'although he's already had a couple of Fergal's famed Irish coffees. I'll suggest it to him.'

When Kate did so, Jack said, 'Great idea!' And so, after dinner, off they went, up the winding road towards Bodmin Moor. Jack sat in the front of the Mercedes with Woody, asking questions about the vehicle: how many miles to the gallon, how often did he get it serviced, and so on and so forth. Jack was equally smitten with his first sight of The Edge of the Moor, the old single-storey stone building, with its ancient wooden door, wonky stone floors and polished wood.

'Are they both lit in winter?' Jack asked, indicating the inglenook fireplaces at each end. When Kate confirmed that they were, he said, 'Wow! Maybe I'll need to stay for winter then!'

Kate felt a little glow of warmth, better than anything an inglenook could provide.

Woody got them both a drink and then went up to get a menu to show to Jack, so he'd have some idea how much it was likely to cost if he were to bring Beth up here. While he was chatting to the barman, Kate told her son all about coming here with Woody on their first date, and their regular visits since, including her sixtieth birthday treat when her other son Tom and his family, along with Woody's younger daughter, had all been waiting for her.

'I just wish you could have been there too,' she said, patting Jack's arm.

'You should have stayed fifty-nine until I got here!' Jack joked.

'You have to book well ahead to eat,' she said, indicating the full tables, 'because it's very popular.'

Jack opened up a little then and told Kate about his dwindling romance in Australia, and how Eva had met a New Zealander who was in Queensland on holiday.

'She's gone back there with him,' Jack said. 'He lives on the South Island, and it gets bloody cold there, so I think she's in for a bit of a shock. She's a gal who likes the warmth and the sea.'

'Do you think she'll stay with him?'

'No idea. I really don't care, Mum. She's made her bed, let her lie on it and all that. The relationship was dead before he came on the scene anyway.'

At least, Kate thought, *that's one less incentive for him to go all the way back there to live.*

Woody returned to the table. 'Ready for another drink?'

In the restaurant and in the surgery, Kate still had the feeling she was being scrutinised. She tried to think outside the box; OK, she'd been standing there on the cliff-top just minutes after Sienna had been pushed to her death. She could understand that that might certainly *look* suspicious, but surely everyone here knew her well enough to dismiss the idea? After all, she was a well-respected nurse, had a reputation as a sleuth and was married to a detective inspector! Nobody could possibly think... or could they?

'Woody,' Kate asked hesitantly when they got home, 'is it

my imagination or are the locals still pointing the finger at me regarding Sienna Stone?'

'Of course they're not,' Woody replied. 'They know you too well by now. Why do you ask?'

Kate shrugged. 'Well, I am a suspect, and they haven't found the killer yet, so I suppose I shouldn't be surprised.'

'There'll always be *someone*, I suppose, Kate. But of course the locals aren't all pointing fingers at you! I think it's your over-active imagination.'

On Thursday morning, after a sleepless night with the suspects going round and round in her head, Kate decided it might be a very good idea to take Barney for a walk along the beach.

Woody was busy emptying the shed in preparation for knocking it down and replacing it with a larger, more up-to-date one, which would accommodate the tools and equipment he'd brought with him from On the Up.

'Tide's in,' he remarked as Kate put Barney on the lead. 'You'd get more of a walk up on the cliffs.'

'I fancy the beach,' Kate said firmly, hoping he didn't remember that she'd told him about the grief-stricken stalker sitting there on his silent vigil. She hoped he'd be there today.

'Are you up to something?' Woody asked suspiciously.

'*Moi*? As if...' said Kate before she and Barney set off down the lane.

Woody was right; there wasn't a great deal of beach due to the high tide. But there was a man sitting on one of the rocks at the far end of the beach, where Kate herself liked to sit. As she approached, she noticed that he looked to be fifty-ish, round-faced, balding and probably not very tall. This man was wearing neither a belted raincoat nor a beret. He was sporting a grey-and-black-striped zip-up cardigan and beige combat trousers with a couple of bulging pockets down each leg.

'The tide should be on the turn soon,' Kate said conversationally, beaming at him.

He said nothing, just nodded and continued gazing at the sea.

'I find the sight and sound of the sea very soothing,' Kate went on as she sat down on an adjacent rock and threw a stick for Barney, 'particularly when I'm sad.'

He didn't meet her eye or react in any way.

Nothing for it then but to broach the subject straight away. 'Awful, isn't it, about that tragedy the other day, just round the corner from here? Sienna Stone?'

He looked at her for a brief moment but said nothing.

'Perhaps you didn't hear about it?' She studied him and suspected he'd been crying. 'It's been in all the papers, and on TV. She was the presenter of that programme, SeeVue. You must have heard of her?' Then she wondered if perhaps she might be laying it on a bit too thick.

He stared at her with narrowed eyes for a moment then got up, sniffed loudly and walked away.

Kate watched him walk along the beach.

'Well, Barney,' she said to the dog, 'I didn't make much progress there, did I? But at least I know now that he's the most likely candidate to be the stalker, given that he's not talking. And now I know what he looks like.'

She stood up and was about to walk a little further on when she noticed something red lying in the sand close to where he'd been sitting. She bent down and picked up what looked to be a small diary. Intrigued, she went back to her rock, sat down and began to flick through the pages.

It was a day-to-day account, from January, of the life of Sienna Stone, right up until her death, after which the pages were blank. The details included every programme, every hair appointment, every public appearance, every shopping trip. Even every dental appointment. And beneath each sighting were his comments: *She looked more beautiful than ever today*; *She didn't appear to be enjoying herself*; *I swear she caught my eye*, and entered on 30 April, *I'd like to kill the men in her life. I could make her so much happier. Sometimes I feel the need to kill her too. She haunts me.*

Kate, thoroughly shocked, slipped the diary into her pocket and began to head for home. She needed time to study this deluded man's ramblings. But the last remark bothered her; was it possible that he'd given in to his feelings and that *he* was the one who'd pushed Sienna off the cliff?

She stopped halfway up the lane and brought the diary out again. *Please let there be a name and address somewhere!*

There was. The name was Timothy Thomson, and he lived at 6 Parson's Court, Middle Tinworthy.

Feeling pleased with her progress, Kate popped the diary back in her bag.

NINE

After studying the diary, Kate decided she had two choices: she could hand it over to Charlotte or she could return it to its owner. If she decided to return it to the owner, *surely* he would have to speak to her?

Parson's Court was a dingy grey concrete block of flats on the eastern end of the Middle Tinworthy estate. There was no greenery, only parking spaces for half a dozen cars at the front. Unsure if these were allocated to the residents or not, Kate decided to leave her car on the road.

There were eight doorbells at the entrance, some with a name and number alongside, some where that had been scored out. Fortunately, the surname Thomson appeared alongside flat number 6. Kate had no intention of ringing any bell.

She made her way up the bleak concrete staircase. There appeared to be two flats on each floor, meaning number 6 would be on the third. The stench of urine assaulted her nostrils and, not for the first time, Kate wondered who were these people who felt the need to pee down the stairs in places such as this? It seemed it wasn't only cats that liked to mark their territory but drunks as well.

Number 6 had had a dark-green-painted door at some point, before most of it had peeled off. Kate hesitated for only a moment before she tapped on the door, took a deep breath with a tissue over her nose and waited. She was beginning to hope he wouldn't be in because she had little idea what she was going to say. She should really have given herself a day to dream up some dialogue, but tomorrow Woody would be at home and would wonder where she was going, whereas today he was off to order a shed.

She had almost decided to go away when the door opened.

Timmy Thomson was still in his striped cardigan and cargo pants but had removed his shoes, displaying his big toe protruding through the brown sock on his right foot. She reckoned he was probably in his mid-forties.

He stared at her but said nothing.

'I wonder if I might come in for a moment?' Kate asked. 'I have something for you.'

Finally, he spoke. 'You've got my diary?'

'Yes, I have,' Kate said, holding on to her bag firmly, 'but I'd like to give it to you inside.'

'Why?'

'Because I'd like to talk to you for a moment.' She saw panic in his watery blue eyes. 'Only for a moment – *please*.'

'About what? What do you want to talk about?'

'About Sienna. I was a great fan, and I know you are too. I just need to chat to someone who feels as bereft as I do.' Would he ever believe that in a million years?

'Are you from the police?'

'Of *course* not!' Kate rolled her eyes. 'Heaven forbid! *Not my favourite people!* Sorry, Woody; sorry, Charlotte – but this conversation really is in a good cause.

'The place is in a bit of a mess,' he said after a moment. 'I've been too upset to do much cleaning.'

'Oh, don't worry about *that*! You should see *my* place!' Kate hoped he wouldn't ask where she lived because she felt she might be making some headway.

'Give me my diary first,' he ordered.

'I promise you shall have it as soon as I come in,' Kate said, alarmed that her acting talents were not as good as she'd hoped. If she refused to hand him the diary now, what would he do? Chase her along the corridor? Down the stairs? She decided to take a chance. She turned, as if to walk away.

'All right,' he said, scowling at her, 'you'd better come in.'

'Thank you,' she replied as she entered a tiny dark hallway, 'and my name is Kate. I believe you are Timothy?'

'Timmy,' he corrected. 'I get called Timmy.'

'Well, nice to meet you, Timmy,' she said.

Later, Kate would tell Woody that the flat, or what little she saw of it, could only be described as a sacred shrine to Sienna Stone. The woman was *everywhere*! There were several life-sized cardboard cut-outs (where on earth had he got *those* from?) propped against the walls, photographs and newspaper cuttings glued to every wall, and – holy of holies – a signed photograph (*To Timmy, with love from Sienna*) in pride of place on a rickety old sideboard, surrounded on all sides by a clutter of empty cider cans. Timmy indicated one of the two scruffy armchairs which faced a giant television screen, on top of which was balanced, very precariously, a wreath of white lilies.

Kate gasped but sat down nevertheless, wondering for a brief moment if she was to be sacrificed to his Goddess of Goddesses, right there on the coffee table. She averted her eyes from the grey carpet, which was stained, and noted the faded unlined curtain pulled halfway across the window. Sienna glared at her from every other surface.

'I should have tidied up a bit,' he said lamely, picking up a few of the cider cans, one of which he dropped. It rolled towards Kate's foot and she resisted the temptation to give it a hefty kick towards one of the cardboard figures.

'I don't suppose you were expecting a visitor,' she said.

He didn't reply but picked up the can and disappeared into what she presumed was the kitchen. There followed much rattling as he disposed of the cans. The room felt stuffy and smelled of sweat and something else. What was it – pot? Could be. She wondered if she dared open the window.

He re-entered the room and stood directly in front of her. 'The diary,' he said.

'Yes, of course,' Kate said hastily, rummaging in her bag. She handed it to him. 'Would you mind if I opened the window a little? I've got a bit of a cold and wouldn't want to give it to you.' She gave a little cough as if to verify this.

Timmy looked at her doubtfully then crossed the room and opened the window all of an inch. 'What is it you want?' he asked.

'Just to talk to you about Sienna,' Kate replied, 'because I realise she was very important to you.'

He said nothing for a moment then sat down in the other chair and began to cry noisily. 'I can't talk about her,' he said after a minute, wiping away his tears with a grubby tissue, 'I *can't!*'

'I'm so sorry if I've upset you,' Kate said sincerely, 'but sometimes it's good to talk, you know. I can see that you were very fond of her.'

Timmy snivelled for a few minutes then got up and stood next to the nearest full-sized cardboard Sienna, this one clad in a voluminous white shirt and black leggings. 'See,' he said, 'she was taller than me. But I didn't mind, and neither would *she* have minded.'

'Of course not,' Kate agreed, wondering where this conversation was leading.

'I told her in my letters that I was a little shorter than she was but that it didn't matter to me.' He stood proudly beside the replica, a good three or four inches shorter.

'Did she reply?' Kate asked tentatively.

He shook his head. Then, suddenly animated: 'And do you want to know why?'

'I do,' she said. 'Why?'

'Because she had a jobsworth of a secretary who opened and censored all her mail,' Timmy said.

Remembering her own experience, Kate nodded. 'You may well be right.'

'I *know* I'm right!' he shouted. 'But the secretary wasn't at the Tinworthy Fair!' He looked at Kate triumphantly. 'She wasn't able to ruin my chances at the fair!'

Kate took a deep breath. 'But her husband was there, wasn't he?'

'There was always someone in the way, which is why we didn't stand a chance.' He disappeared into the kitchen again, re-emerging with two unopened cans of cider, one of which he offered to Kate.

'That's kind of you, but I won't, Timmy.' She waited a moment while he took a gulp and then sat down. 'So who do *you* think might have pushed her off the cliff?'

He put the can down and said, 'I *saw* who it was, but I'm not telling *you*. What I *am* telling you is that the husband probably found out about *us*! She planned to leave him, you know. I read that in one of the papers and I was delighted.'

That was true at least, Kate thought, feeling sorry for the poor delusional little man. 'You said you *saw* who it was, Timmy? The husband?'

He drank some more cider. 'Yes, I did see. It's my secret. The police suspect me,' he said, 'but why would I want to kill the woman I loved?'

'Of course you wouldn't,' Kate soothed. 'If it's any comfort to you, I'm a suspect as well.'

'*What?*' He turned to her, his eyes blazing. 'Why would you want to kill her?'

'I didn't want to kill her,' Kate replied. *At least not much.* 'Unfortunately, I was in the wrong place at the wrong time.'

He was staring at her intensely now, and she began to feel a little afraid. 'If *you* killed my beautiful Sienna,' he said, 'then I would kill *you*.'

'I did *not* kill her,' Kate said, feeling increasingly uncomfortable at his steady watery stare. 'You've just said you saw who it was, so you must know it couldn't have been me.'

He shrugged, and said, 'Maybe you paid someone to do it? Just like her husband might have paid someone to do it for him?'

Kate was now thoroughly confused. 'So you're not sure?'

'I didn't say I wasn't sure.' He stared at her for a moment. 'I'm just not about to tell *you!*'

This conversation was making little sense. 'Well, what *is* for sure is that *someone* did, and I intend to find out who, if only to clear my own name. And yours too,' she added hastily. She noticed his mood had changed again. 'But you said you *saw* who did it? Surely you've told the police?'

'I saw who did it, but the person was wearing a long coat and a hoodie, and that's what I told the police.' He sighed. 'I don't know how I can go on living,' he added sadly, gazing at the curtain, which was flapping feebly at the open window.

Kate stretched across and patted his shoulder. 'I think you might need some grief counselling, Timmy. Someone who can help you through all this. I'm a nurse, so perhaps I can find you a therapist.'

His mood had changed again, and suddenly he rounded on her. 'I don't need any bloody therapist! I need to find the person who killed the woman I planned to marry, and then I will kill him.'

'Or *her*. It might be a woman,' Kate said.

'It might be a woman, but I'm not about to tell *you*.' He tapped his nose. 'It's my secret.'

'But if you saw who it was, then you must know it wasn't me,' Kate said.

He thought for a moment. 'I know it wasn't you. I know who I'm looking for and I will find them and, when I do' – here he slid his finger across his throat – 'it will be the *end* for that person. Now, I want you to *go!*'

As Kate stood up, she unearthed a card from her bag. 'If you ever want to talk about this, or if you find any further clues, you call me either on my landline or on my mobile.' She jabbed her finger on the card as she handed it to him. 'Perhaps we can solve this tragedy together.'

He didn't reply but stared at the card as he led the way towards the door.

'Goodbye, Timmy,' she said as she went out into the dingy corridor.

He didn't reply but, after a moment, she heard the door slam behind her.

TEN

'How on earth did you know where he lived?' Woody asked as they sat out on the patio, with mugs of tea, enjoying the late-evening sunshine.

'Oh, I found it in the medical records.' Kate hated lying to him but had he known about the diary, he would have insisted she hand it in to the police. 'I just wanted to try to suss him out.'

'And did you?'

'Nope.' She laid down her mug. 'But he needs help.'

Woody sighed. 'You may be right, Kate, but, as the saying goes, you can lead a horse to water but you can't make it drink.'

'He's nowhere near any proverbial water yet! Doesn't think he needs any help. But what's really important is that he *saw* the person pushing Sienna off the cliff, or so he says.'

'You're kidding! So why hasn't he told the police?'

'He may have done, but he was very vague; said the person was wearing a long coat and a hoodie. One minute he seemed to know who it was, the next minute he was vague again.'

'A coat and hoodie in that heat?'

'Apparently, so perhaps they should be looking around for some sweaty garments.'

Woody gazed into space for a moment. 'Do you think he was telling the truth? About seeing the killer?'

'I've no idea. He's in a world of his own.'

'Why then wouldn't he tell the police?'

'He said he wanted to finish off this person himself.'

'*What?* Are you sure?'

'Yes, but I don't think he actually meant it. He's not very consistent. He's so grief-stricken for Sienna though; he even wept when he was talking about her, and he seemed to imagine that she was leaving her husband so she could marry *him*.'

Woody guffawed. 'That *proves* he's nuts!'

'Yes, maybe, but from some of the courses I've done, these obsessives live in an imaginary world of their own. The person often thinks the whole world is against them, which can lead to some bizarre actions – even murder occasionally.'

'From what you've said, I'd guess he's most definitely a loner with an overactive imagination.' Woody shook his head. 'He'll get over it and probably become obsessed with someone else – but in the meantime, make damn sure he doesn't think *you* killed her!' Woody drained his mug. 'Now, can we talk about something else? Like your son wanting to bring his new love to lunch on Sunday? How about *that*?'

'What, Beth?'

'So far as I know that's his only love at the moment. Now, shall we have lamb or pork? And don't forget, we're eating at Marc's tomorrow night.'

'*Bon soir!*' greeted Marc when he appeared in the dining room in his chef's gear at the end of the evening. 'I 'eard you were 'ere.'

Most of the other diners had left, having heaped Marc with praise as they went out, which he graciously accepted with much bowing. There was only one other table of four young people still occupied. Marc peered at them then plainly decided they were not worth his attention.

'You don't mind?' Without waiting for an answer, Marc pulled out a chair and signalled to the one remaining waiter who was standing by the door, smothering a yawn. 'Cognac, yes?' he asked them, before calling out, 'The Courvoisier, Frederick!' He drew the chair up to the table. 'We 'ave a little drink on me, no?'

They thanked him, agreed that the meal had been delicious, the wine superb and the service excellent.

'So,' he said with much sighing, 'what does our local sleuth think about Sienna Stone's death?'

'No idea,' Kate replied, 'but I'm keen to know who the murderer is as I'm a suspect myself.'

'Well,' said Marc, 'I, for one, am not sorry. You can perhaps understand how *incandescent* I still am at *that woman's* report!'

He broke off as Frederick reappeared with the bottle of Courvoisier and three brandy balloons. '*Merci*, Frederick!' He then shooed the waiter away and began to pour brandy into the glasses.

'She never told me she was coming,' Marc continued, 'and she came on my night off, *lundi*! Why would she come on a Monday when I am not cooking, hmm?' He gulped some brandy. 'Philip was cooking and he is very good but' – here he blew out noisily – 'he lacks the *je ne sais quoi*, you know?'

Both Kate and Woody nodded obediently.

'There was no foie gras that night, and then one of my new waiters dropped a glass on the floor. *Mon dieu!*'

'Very unfortunate,' Woody murmured, nudging Kate's leg under the table.

'Then she does this bloody *programme*! I tell everyone I want to kill her! *Of course* I want to kill her! Wouldn't you?'

Woody shrugged non-committally.

'For several weeks,' Marc went on, 'hardly *anyone* comes

here. Then a nice lady from the *Cornish Post* came and wrote us a great report.' He looked round. 'Now we are full again every night.'

'I should think so!' Kate said with enthusiasm. 'We've had a *lovely* meal here tonight.'

Marc leaned forward. '*Merci!* But now they think I had something to do with that woman falling off the cliff at Potter's Point – *moi!*' He shook his head in bewilderment. 'But you know what? If I'd been up there at the right time then, yes, I *would* have pushed her off! I'd have pushed her hard and listened with joy for the *splat* as she landed below! Ah, *oui!*' He waved the brandy bottle in the air. 'More? *Non?*' He then refilled his own glass.

'Well, join the club,' Kate said. 'I'm a suspect because I just happened to be in the wrong place at the wrong time.'

There followed some Gallic shrugging. '*C'est la vie!* It is not *you*, it is not *moi*. But let me tell you *this*, we have the sister of Sienna staying here!'

Woody stared at him in amazement. 'Sienna Stone's *sister?*'

'*Oui!* She is Sienna's older sister, and she does *not* seem to be in mourning!' He nodded sagely, looking satisfied at their amazement.

'Perhaps she's come because of Sienna's death? To make arrangements?' Kate suggested.

Marc moved closer across the table. 'Ah, *non!* This is what is *most* interesting and what I have told your lady detective. She arrived last Friday, the day *before* the fair!'

'Perhaps she wanted to go to the fair, to support her sister?' Kate said.

Marc shook his head. 'So then why doesn't she stay with her sister at Tremorron? Would this not be normal, eh? The Aldridges have seven bedrooms, I hear.'

'Perhaps she wanted to surprise Sienna?'

Marc shook his head. 'I got the impression there was no love lost between them. But indeed Sienna *would* get a big surprise when – for that split second – she must have realised that her sister had pushed her over the cliff! *Non?*'

Kate made a note to add Sienna's sister to her lengthening list, which featured Marc himself, plus Sienna's husband and the wife of the man she was having an affair with. She must find out more about this sister. 'Can you tell me the woman's name?' she asked hopefully.

Marc shrugged. 'No harm, I suppose. She is Mrs Sally Brand.' He patted Kate's arm. 'Are you going to be a super-sleuth again?'

Kate saw Woody roll his eyes. 'Let's just say that I need to clear my name,' she said.

'What do you think?' Kate asked as they drove home.

'About what?'

'About Marc. Do you think he *could* have killed Sienna?'

'Who knows? We already know he's a bit of an actor. Anything's possible.'

Kate shook her head. 'From the way he spoke, I doubt it. Surely if he'd done it he wouldn't have said how much he'd liked to have pushed her off the cliff?'

'Kate, sometimes you're far too trusting – have you never heard of a double bluff? I've told you before that some of the most fiendish criminals are brilliant actors; butter wouldn't melt in their mouths.'

'Yes, but Marc would have been busy in the hospitality tent, wouldn't he?'

'Interestingly enough, I saw him walking around during the afternoon, shortly before I saw you. Like you, he probably wanted to stretch his legs once it had all quietened down. He'd have had plenty of time to get up to the cliff and back again.'

'Have you told Charlotte about this?'

'Yes, of course. Furthermore, I think you should tell her about your visit to Timmy and his life-size cardboard Siennas. She'll be fascinated, although I expect she's seen them herself. It could be useful though. She's been interviewing the Morans today.'

'The Morans?'

'Roger Moran is the director of Sienna's programme. And his wife Delia Moran has left him and is renting a cottage up on Bodmin Moor.'

'The wronged wife,' Kate said thoughtfully. 'I wonder if *she* was wandering around the cliffs last Saturday? How very interesting!'

'She may well have fancied some sea air. I believe she's got a couple of Labradors or something. Now, to change the subject, what do you think we should cook for your prospective daughter-in-law on Sunday?'

ELEVEN

They settled for roast pork for Sunday lunch, which was planned for around half past one.

'There's no bus service on a Sunday, Mum,' Jack said as he emerged from his bedroom at nearly 11 a.m., 'and one of the other girls is using the car so' – here he put his arms round his mother – 'I wondered if I could possibly borrow your car to go up to collect Beth? *Please?*'

'Have you still got a UK driving licence?' Kate asked anxiously, imagining her Fiat about to get another bashing.

'Yes, of course I have, and I'll be very, *very* careful!' He grinned as he released her. 'I thought it best not to ask Woody.'

'You're right,' Kate agreed, imagining Woody's face if anyone asked to borrow his precious Mercedes.

'Which is a pity,' Jack added, 'because I'd love to see Beth's face if I rolled up in that big beauty!'

'There's nothing wrong with my Fiat,' Kate said defensively.

'Of course not – it's a great little car! Thanks, Mum!'

. . .

At quarter to two, just as Kate was beginning to worry about her son and her Fiat, they arrived.

'Sorry we're a bit late, Mum,' Jack said cheerfully. 'Beth, this is my mum.'

'Hi,' she said, following him into the kitchen and handing Kate a bottle of red wine. Beth was small, slim, with long dark-brown hair and large brown eyes. She was undeniably pretty.

'Well, nice to meet you, Beth,' Kate said, wondering if she should shake hands or not but as Beth showed no inclination to do so, Kate concentrated on placing the wine on the worktop. 'And this is Woody.'

Woody, who'd been in the sitting room surrounded by countless pages of the *Sunday Times*, came into the kitchen smiling. 'Hi, Beth,' he said.

'OK,' Kate said, 'would you like red or white wine, Beth?'

'White, please,' the girl replied, looking at Barney, who'd come up to sniff her and was wagging his tail frantically.

'That's Barney,' Kate said as she handed Beth a glass of wine. 'Do you like dogs?'

'I prefer cats,' Beth said, sidestepping Barney's attentions.

'In your basket, Barney!' Kate ordered.

The dog looked at them all reproachfully before slinking away.

'Shall we all sit down?' Woody suggested, clutching a glass of red as he led the way into the sitting room. He folded up the newspaper and asked, 'And how are all your caravanners, Beth?'

Jack and Beth had positioned themselves on the sofa, close together.

The girl pulled a face. 'There's an awful lot of them. Still, it's a job.'

'Just for the summer, I believe?' Kate prompted.

Beth laughed. 'Yes, and that'll be enough,' she said, sipping her wine.

'Beth's really a hairdresser,' Jack reminded them.

There followed some general conversation about hairdressing, Kate enthusing about Guy at Guys 'n' Dolls. She waited hopefully for a comment, such as 'Great cut!' or 'It really suits you!' but none was forthcoming.

Lunch was a success although Beth turned out to be vegetarian and so filled up on vegetables and roast potatoes.

'I believe you live in Bristol?' Kate said as she produced the trifle she'd made.

'Yes, I do.'

'Nice city, Bristol,' Woody commented. 'Your folks live there?'

There was a short silence before Beth said, 'I don't have any folks. My mother died when I was only three, so I was brought up in foster care.'

'Oh, I'm *so* sorry,' Kate said, 'that must have been dreadful. You poor thing.'

'I survived.' Beth gave a ghost of a smile before taking another mouthful of trifle.

Kate's heart went out to the girl. *Some people have such unfortunate lives*, she thought. *I must be particularly nice to this lass*. 'Oh, Beth,' she said, 'I hope they were kind to you.'

Beth shrugged. 'Sometimes, not always, but never mind – it's in the past now. This trifle's lovely.'

'Do have some more,' Kate said, getting up to retrieve the bowl. She was now rapidly warming to Beth. *What a life she's had! We just don't know how lucky we are!*

As she went back to her seat, she noticed that Beth's left hand was busily stroking Jack's right thigh. Jack, looking very happy indeed, was also tucking in to his second helping of trifle.

Am I being an old fuddy-duddy? Kate wondered. *But surely it's a little bit naughty – not to mention embarrassing – to be so bold on the very first visit to her new boyfriend's family? Then again, she's probably been starved of affection for years. But she*

*must have known that I could see. Why didn't she remove her
hand when she knew I was right behind her?*

With very mixed feelings, Kate sat down and listened to
Jack and Woody discussing the merits of various German cars.

'I'm guessing you're called Woody because of your surname
– Forrest – right?' Beth asked Woody casually when the conversation lulled.

Kate smiled to herself; she could see what was coming.

'Correct,' Woody said, feigning sudden interest in studying
his wine glass.

'Hey,' said Jack, with a grin, 'I can understand why you
prefer to be called Woody because I remember your real name
from the wedding video! I keep meaning to ask you about how
you got that moniker.'

Woody cleared his throat. 'It was down to my dad. He
emigrated from here to the States as a young man and did very
well for himself. So, in some form of crazy gratitude, I guess, he
decided to name his offspring after US presidents.'

Beth leaned forward. 'And so you're...?'

He took a deep breath. 'Abraham Lincoln. Abraham
Lincoln Forrest.'

'You should be proud of that,' Jack said as Beth giggled.

'It has been known to cause great amusement,' Woody said
drily. Then, looking at Kate: 'And your mother has been known
to call me Abe when she's particularly annoyed with me.'

At this, Beth dissolved into further giggles, the only display
of mirth Kate had yet witnessed from the girl.

'More trifle?' Woody asked, passing the dish along.

A little later, shortly after they'd had coffee, Jack asked, 'Is it OK
if I borrow the Fiat again, Mum? Beth fancies a trip to Boscastle,
don't you, Beth?'

Beth nodded.

'I'll be ever so careful so you needn't worry,' he added.

Kate nodded mutely, now more concerned about the relationship than the car. 'Yes, of course,' she said distractedly.

'Thanks so much,' Beth said.

'That poor girl,' Kate said, as she watched the Fiat going down the lane, 'She's had such an unfortunate life.'

'She seems to have come out of it OK,' Woody commented.

'But you don't know how it affects her *really*, do you?'

'I'd say it makes her fairly tough. Self-sufficient.'

Kate looked at him for a minute. 'Did you not like her?'

'I didn't *dislike* her,' Woody replied, looking up from the newspaper.

Kate wondered if she should mention the hand on the thigh. Damn it, she would; she'd like his reaction. 'Did you know she was caressing Jack's thigh under the table?'

'Some guys have all the luck!' Woody replied with a grin.

'Don't you think that's a bit, er... *forward*, on a first visit?'

'Well, much as I might have been tempted to, I don't think I'd have risked it on a first visit to your mother, if I'd ever known her, which I wish I had.'

'Exactly, Woody. But, you see, she plainly craves affection after the sad upbringing she's had, so we mustn't be too judgemental.'

'I wasn't being judgemental. I'm just stating a fact; I wouldn't have done it until I was *well* away from your mother's house!'

'Be serious!'

'What else do you want me to say? I didn't warm to Beth all that much but Jack's old enough to know what he's doing, and it'll probably fizzle out when she goes back to Bristol and he goes back to Australia. *If* he goes back to Australia.'

Kate felt a glimmer of hope. 'Do you think he might stay here then?'

Woody shrugged. 'I don't know, although I wouldn't be altogether surprised. But don't raise your hopes, just in case.'

Kate decided that putting up with a bit of thigh-stroking might well be worth it if it kept her son in the UK. *Yes,* she decided, *I am being silly and old-fashioned.*

TWELVE

On Monday, when Kate got home from work, she found a silver Renault parked alongside Woody's car and a strange woman standing in the garden.

Woody, who was dismantling the shed, raised an eyebrow and said, 'This lady insists on talking to you, and you alone, Kate.'

The woman was tall, not unattractive and probably in her early fifties. She had noticeably green eyes, and brown hair with a multitude of highlights and lowlights. There was something vaguely familiar about her. 'My name's Sally Brand,' she said simply.

So *this* was Sienna's sister. No wonder she looked familiar, although she didn't have Sienna's fine bone structure or the stunning red hair.

'I'd really, really like a word with you,' she said, looking hesitant.

'Of course,' Kate replied, unable to believe her luck. She'd planned to go in search of this woman and now here she was, on her very doorstep. She obviously hadn't given Woody her name, which was just as well.

The woman followed Kate into the kitchen.

'Tea?' Kate asked as she filled up the kettle.

'That's kind of you.'

'So, what can I do for you, Mrs Brand?'

'Please call me Sally. I understand you're a dab hand at catching criminals,' the woman said with a glimmer of a smile, 'and that your husband's a detective.'

'My husband *was* a detective,' Kate said, 'but he's retired now. And I certainly wouldn't agree that I was good at catching criminals. It's more of a coincidence because I seem to get involved with them without *knowing* they're criminals. Woody says it's because I'm nosy, and I guess he's right.'

'Well, I want to find out who killed Sienna Stone.'

Kate's hand wobbled slightly as she poured the boiling water onto the teabags. 'We *all* want to find out who killed Sienna Stone. Milk? Sugar?'

'Just milk please.' She accepted the mug and sat down on a kitchen chair.

'Why are you so interested?' Kate asked disingenuously, not wanting Sally to know that she, Kate, was already aware of who she was.

'I'm her sister.'

Kate feigned surprise, sat down opposite and sipped her tea. 'You're Sienna Stone's *sister*?'

Sally Brand laughed. 'I can understand you find that hard to believe; everyone does.'

'Well, no, I, er...' Kate could understand why people found it hard to believe, because even though she saw the slight resemblance – particularly the eyes – Sally had none of Sienna's flamboyance.

'Yes, you do. I'm older, of course, and I never had her looks. Mind you, she spent a lot of money improving hers.' She sniffed.

'Really?'

'Yes, really.'

'Well, Sally, I'm so sorry for your loss. It must be awful for you.'

Sally sipped her tea. 'No, it's not awful,' she said, 'because I hated her guts.'

Kate's tea went down the wrong way, causing a coughing fit. '*What?*' she asked as she recovered.

'I hated her. I realise that's not a popular thing to say about your sister, but I don't care. She wasn't a nice person. She wasn't Sienna Stone either. She was Sheila Potts.'

'She was a good TV presenter,' Kate said diplomatically, trying to think of something positive to say about the woman.

'I suppose she was, because that was an act, just like everything was an act. She was a cow in real life. She was a cow from the time she was tiny. From when she was a *calf*!' She sniggered at her own wit.

'Well, that's as may be,' Kate said, 'but I've no idea who killed her, if that's what you want to know.'

'*I'm* a suspect of course,' Sally went on, 'and now I have to stay in Tinworthy until they find the killer.' She looked Kate straight in the face. 'I *could* be the killer. I hated her. I told the police that.'

Kate was none too sure how to react to this. 'I, too, have a sister,' she said after a moment, 'who frequently drives me mad. We're very different in lots of ways, but I've never wanted to kill her. Perhaps you're overreacting, Sally?'

Sally was staring out of the window. 'I was five when Sheila was born. She was a beautiful baby and my parents doted on her. Both of them. She could do no wrong. As she got older, she had them both wrapped round her little finger, and she knew it. She was always the centre of attention – always.'

'And you felt left out?'

'Yes, I did. I'd had five years of their undivided attention and then, suddenly, it was as if I hardly existed. I wasn't as pretty or as clever. I struggled at school, while she sailed through her exams. She was bridesmaid at my wedding, and *she* stole the show. I'm divorced now, by the way, so I'm fighting my own corner. Not that *he* was much good. Then, after that, she goes off modelling, acting, getting on television and marries a millionaire.'

'Some people have all the luck,' Kate admitted.

Sally narrowed her eyes. 'It wasn't just luck. She was ruthless. She'd stop at nothing to get where and what and *who* she wanted.'

Kate was fascinated. 'Would you like a glass of wine?' she asked, opening the fridge. *Because I sure as hell would.* 'Pinot Grigio?'

'Thank you; you're very kind. I hope you don't mind me calling on you like this but Marc, at The Atlantic Hotel where I'm staying, told me that you liked solving mysteries.'

Kate handed Sally a glass. 'Oh, *did* he now? Marc, as you may know, is also a suspect. And so am I. And so is Sienna's husband.' For a moment, Kate wondered what on earth Charlotte would think if she knew all her suspects were discussing the murder with each other.

'Oh, *Irving!*' Sally snorted. 'Irving has far more money than sense. Everyone, except him of course, could see straight away why she married him. It was common knowledge even then that she was having it off with Roger Moran, which is most likely why she got the presenting job in the first place.'

'Do you think, then, that Irving might have finished her off out of jealousy?'

Sally shrugged. 'I doubt it but who knows? She was a trophy wife, I suppose, because he liked showing her off. They probably used each other. Then again, he's a hard-nosed businessman and he would not have relished her affair becoming public knowledge – it might make him look weak or something. You haven't told me why *you're* a suspect?'

Kate gave her a brief account of her dealings with Sienna on the day of her death, before asking, 'So why are *you* here in Tinworthy, Sally, and staying at The Atlantic Hotel?'

Sally sighed loudly. 'I'm a freelance journalist and I live in Bath. A well-known women's magazine has commissioned me to do an article on sisters, particularly when one is famous and one isn't; they likely knew I was an expert on the subject! So I thought I'd make a start close to home. I came down to study Sheila – sorry, Sienna – because, just for a start, we don't get the *SeeVue* programme in Bath. So I wanted to see that and also to observe her everyday life – without her knowing of course.'

'Were you at the fair?'

'Yes, but I kept well back from wherever she was wandering, so I missed her argument with you.'

Kate took a deep breath. 'Did you follow her when, for whatever reason, she decided to go up to Potter's Point?'

'No, there was somewhere else I had to be.' She gazed out of the window. Kate decided not to pursue the point.

'I went back to where my car was parked and then drove back to the hotel.'

'If Charlotte Martin – the detective in charge of the case – tracked you down, how did she know you were Sienna's sister?' Kate asked.

'I got in touch with the police as soon as I heard about Sienna's death,' Sally replied. 'I didn't want them to think I had any reason to hide.'

Kate suddenly remembered what Woody had said about a double bluff. 'And did she question you?'

Sally drained her wine. 'She certainly did. In depth. I was completely honest with her, just like I've been honest with you, which is why I'm a suspect and still stuck in The Atlantic Hotel. Still, at least I've made a start on the magazine article.'

She stood up and placed her glass on the table. 'Thanks so much for the tea and the wine, and for listening to me. I wanted you to be aware that I'm as keen as you are to solve this crime, so perhaps we can work on it together?'

Kate followed her to the door. 'I think it's probably best left to the police, Sally. Charlotte is very efficient, and my husband, Woody, is very much against my getting involved in any more crime-solving.'

Sally smiled as she unlocked the door of her car. 'But this time you're actually a *suspect*, are you not? You must be as keen as I am to solve this crime. Think about it.' She waved cheerfully as she drove away.

Kate walked over to where Woody was working on the shed. He laid down his hammer for a moment. 'Who the hell was *she*, and what did she want?'

'You wouldn't believe it,' Kate replied with a grin.

THIRTEEN

'I don't believe it,' Woody said when she told him. 'She's after something, and she's using you. Don't get involved with her.'

'I don't believe it,' Angie echoed when Kate popped into The Old Locker for coffee and a chat on Tuesday. 'Why would she want to involve you?'

'Because she reckons I'm some sort of super-sleuth,' Kate said, 'although modesty forbade me from agreeing with her.'

Angie snorted. 'Only because you're so *nosy*. If you ask me, she's obviously trying to draw attention away from herself and onto everyone else.'

'I'm not sure. She freely admitted that she hated her sister, that she'd had her nose put out of joint when Sienna was born and, from then on, Sienna seemingly stole the limelight at every opportunity. Furthermore, she wasn't Sienna Stone, she was Sheila Potts.'

'Doesn't have quite the same ring to it,' Angie agreed. 'So, sibling jealousy?'

'Yes. Sienna was prettier, cleverer and, by the sound of it, more ruthless. I did try to tell her that most sisters irritated each other from time to time, and that there was many a time I'd have liked to murder you but managed to resist.'

Angie scoffed. 'What have I ever done to upset you, other than being more beautiful and delightful? And adventurous.'

'Adventurous? Whose idea was it to come down here?'

'Well, OK, it was your idea, but you've just carried on with your boring old nursing while I've tried different things.'

'Like painting pictures that didn't sell?' *And I won't bother to mention the so-called acting.*

'One did sell,' Angie protested, 'and look at the success I've made out of The Old Locker.' She waved her arms around the bar.

'Yes, you have done well here,' Kate conceded, 'and just to prove my sisterly devotion, let me buy you a gin!'

Angie stared at her sister. 'You *never* encourage me to have a gin!'

'That's true, so you'd better pour it quickly before I change my mind. And, while you're at it, I'll have one as well.'

Angie poured the drinks. Then, turning back to Kate: 'Cheers! How's that lovely son of yours?'

Kate hesitated for a moment. 'I hardly see him. He's with Beth most of the time, surfing every evening. You know I want him to stay here and not go back to Australia?'

'That's understandable,' Angie agreed, taking a hefty gulp of her drink. 'I often wish my Jeremy would come back from Sweden – with the boys, of course, but not that wife of his.' Angie referred to Ingrid, her Swedish daughter-in-law with whom she'd never got on. 'You're so lucky with Jane.'

Kate realised that was true; daughters-in-law could be tricky, although her elder son Tom's Scottish wife, Jane, was extremely easy to get on with.

'Yes, I know. And now Jack has found himself a girlfriend...'

'That's good, isn't it? You could be lucky with this Beth too. Might keep him in Cornwall?'

'Ye-es,' Kate said hesitantly.

Angie took another gulp and narrowed her eyes. 'So, what's wrong with her?'

'Nothing, nothing!' Kate replied hastily.

'I don't believe you.'

'No, really. She's only here for the summer anyway. I *told* you, she's learning to surf.'

'So what's wrong with that?'

'*Nothing* wrong with that!' Kate sipped her gin. 'She's an orphan; lost her mother when she was just two or three years old and was brought up in care.'

'The poor girl!'

'Yes, I know, but there's just *something* about her...'

'For goodness' sake, Kate!'

'I know I'm probably being silly, old-fashioned even, but she came to lunch with Jack last Sunday and all went quite well until...' Kate hesitated.

'Spit it out!'

Kate related the hand-on-thigh incident.

Angie roared with laughter. 'For God's sake, Kate, it's the twenty-first century!'

'I know, I know. I just thought it was a little bit naughty, at our dining table, on her first visit, when she knew that I could see.'

'I know we weren't brought up to do that sort of thing, but don't forget it was *such* a different age, and we had a very conventional mother who wore a hat to go shopping, baked cakes every afternoon and insisted we were home by ten o'clock every bloody night!'

Kate smiled. 'I guess you're right. Dear old Mum!'

'And this whatshername didn't have a mum at all, did she?'

'That's true,' Kate said, 'and I must remember that.'

She glanced at her watch. 'I'd best be getting home, but it's been good chatting to you, Angie.'

'Kate, for the price of a gin, you can come in here any time you like for a bit of counselling.'

When she got home, and while Woody was loading up his trailer with the remains of the old shed, Kate got out The List.

Marc le Grand; Sally Brand; Timmy Thomson; Irving Aldridge. Who else? Ah yes, Delia Moran; she had a name for the woman now. She now knew, thanks to Woody, that Mrs Moran had left her errant husband and was residing in a rented cottage somewhere on Bodmin Moor. The woman also had dogs. Dogs meant walks. No doubt Barney would be delighted with a change of scenery from the coast, but Bodmin Moor was a big area. She'd have to try to discover exactly where Delia Moran might be renting.

An hour later, as they sat down with a glass of wine, Kate said casually to Woody, 'I wonder where this Delia Moran is renting?'

'I can tell you exactly where Delia Moran is renting,' Woody said.

Kate cleared her throat. 'So where's that then?'

'Where's what then?'

'Where Delia is living.'

Woody leaned forward. 'I'm not telling you because you'll go knocking on her door if I do. I *know* you!'

'Why on earth didn't you tell me you knew where she was living?' Kate asked.

'I've just told you why.'

'As if I would,' Kate said, aware that knocking on Delia Moran's door was precisely what she'd intended to do.

'If she's on that damn list of yours, you'll be there, banging on the door.'

'I promise I won't,' Kate said earnestly. 'Honestly!'

Woody studied her through narrowed lids. 'You promise?'

'Promise!'

'OK then. I've been tempted to tell you because she's renting that pretty little cottage just up the lane from The Edge of the Moor.' This was where they'd recently taken Jack on one of the rare nights when Beth had been otherwise engaged.

'Ah,' said Kate, 'we often wondered who lived in that dear little cottage.'

'I don't know who originally lived there but it's rented out now. Delia Moran chose it because it's off the beaten track and can only really be seen from the restaurant itself. Apparently, a la Garbo, she "wanted to be alone".'

'How very interesting,' Kate said truthfully. 'How come you found out all this?'

'When we took Jack up to see The Edge, I got chatting to the barman and he told me all about her. And,' added Woody, 'by no knocking on the door I mean no *ringing of a doorbell* either.'

'Quite so,' Kate replied.

'The poor woman's entitled to her privacy. Now, what are we having for dinner?'

As Kate prepared the food, her thoughts wandered to Delia Moran. Had she really come to this area to get away from it all – or for a more sinister reason?

FOURTEEN

The following day, while Woody was awaiting delivery of the new garden shed, Kate decided Barney needed a good, long walk. As she ushered the dog into the back of the Fiat, Woody called out, 'Where are you off to?'

'I thought we'd go up to the woods or somewhere,' Kate replied vaguely. She often did walk Barney up in the woods above St Piran's Church in Middle Tinworthy, or even on the rough moorland above Higher Tinworthy.

'Hmm,' he said, looking suspicious.

Kate got quickly into the driving seat before he quizzed her further. 'See you later!' she called out as she headed down the lane and sped up towards Bodmin Moor. She parked in a lay-by about a hundred yards from the cottage where Delia was supposedly in residence. Then she and Barney tramped over the moorland for around forty minutes, with no sign of Delia, or anyone else for that matter. She came home via the church woods where she dutifully walked the dog for a few minutes, so she would not be lying to Woody.

There was a repeat performance the following day and she

wasn't able to find enough time on Friday, so it wasn't until Saturday afternoon that she finally succeeded in finding her prey.

Woody, absorbed in erecting the new shed, did ask, 'What? You're going up to the woods *again*? Have you got a lover up there, hidden in the trees?'

On this occasion when Kate parked her car in the lay-by, a large black Labrador came bounding across from the direction of the cottage. He sniffed everything very thoroughly before loping off obediently when she heard, 'Come *here*, Larry!'

Kate let Barney out of the car, and before she had an opportunity to attach the lead to his collar, he'd raced off in pursuit of this prospective new friend at the cottage gate. A cream Labrador had also joined in the general frivolity and now all three dogs were chasing each other excitedly around while a tall, slim woman in a red T-shirt and jeans was shouting at them in vain.

Kate dashed towards the gate. 'I'm so sorry,' she yelled above the cacophony of barking. 'Barney, come *here*!'

After a minute, the barking subsided and, as Kate grabbed Barney by the collar, she said apologetically, 'He just *loves* other dogs!'

'Oh, so do these two,' said the woman, closing the gate behind her. 'Since we've come here, they've been a bit short of company.' She smiled and Kate noticed how her face was transformed, and what beautiful teeth she had.

Kate wondered what to say next: introduce herself? Talk about dogs generally? Say how nice it would be to have some adult company on a moorland walk?

After some consideration she said, 'I'm Kate, and the dog's Barney. We often come up here as it makes a change from the coast.'

Fortunately, the woman took the bait. 'I'm Delia, and these

two mad creatures are Larry and Loony. We were just heading out for a walk too.'

They took a few steps alongside each other a little uncertainly before Kate, desperate to break the ice, said, 'This is such an idyllic spot! Have you lived here long?'

'No, not long,' the woman replied, 'just about three months.'

'So you haven't had a winter here yet?'

'No.' Then, a little hesitantly, she added, 'I may not stay for the winter; it might be very bleak up here.'

'Yes, it can be,' Kate said, wondering what to say next.

Before she could summon up something else to say, Delia spoke. 'I've only taken the lease until the end of September. After that, I may move back to the city.'

Kate was pleased to see that she seemed interested in keeping the conversation going. It could make Kate's task a lot easier. 'Did you fancy some country air for the summer?' she asked.

'Something like that. Incidentally, I *love* your hair!'

'You do?' Kate patted her windblown coiffeur.

'Yes – where do you get it done? Round here?'

'I go to Guy, at Guys 'n' Dolls in Middle Tinworthy. He's a great cutter.'

'Guy? I'll remember that.'

They walked in silence for a few minutes before Delia spoke again. 'Did you say you lived on the coast?'

'Yes, in Lower Tinworthy. Do you know it?'

'I've walked the dogs along the coast path there a couple of times,' Delia said. 'Pretty place.'

So she *could* have been there that day. Kate took a deep breath. 'We had an unfortunate incident there recently.'

'So I believe.'

'Yes, a TV presenter fell to her death. Horrid business.'

'Hmm.'

'Still, I don't think she could have been all that popular because there are several likely suspects apparently.'

Delia stopped dead in her tracks. 'Like who?'

'Well, *me* for a start! I'm a nurse and I was taking a break from the first-aid tent at the Tinworthy Fair. I was walking up towards the cliffs to cool off when I heard the shouting and the scream.'

'So?'

'So I was first on the scene. Well, obviously, I wasn't really the first. Whoever pushed her was first, but it *looked* as if I was. And because I'd had an argument with Sienna Stone earlier, everyone pointed the finger at me. I can assure you it was *not* me, although I wasn't fond of the woman.'

They walked on, the dogs running around examining interesting bushes and rabbit holes.

'Why weren't you fond of her?' Delia asked at last.

Kate gave a brief résumé of the car accident and follow-up again. Then she decided to go for the kill. 'Have you ever watched her on TV?'

Delia gave a loud snort. 'Oh yes.'

'Well, I gather she upset a lot of people, including our local hotelier.'

They continued in silence for a few minutes before the cream Labrador found a muddy puddle and began happily luxuriating in it. The other two dogs were trying to get in on the act, but the puddle wasn't big enough.

'Loony!' Delia bellowed.

The dog ignored her and rolled around in ecstasy.

'Labs love water unfortunately,' she said, 'and if there's a pool or puddle anywhere around, they'll damn well find it.'

Kate laughed. 'That beautiful cream coat...!'

'Fortunately, I have a hose connected outside the cottage purely for occasions like this, so I can wash her when we get back.'

'I hope you don't mind having company on your walk,' Kate said several minutes later. 'We kind of foisted ourselves on you, didn't we?'

'No, I don't mind at all. To be honest, it gets a bit lonely at times up here, but I needed some time on my own.'

'Have you got family in the area?' Kate asked casually.

'In Plymouth,' Delia replied briefly.

'Oh well, not far to go then.'

'No.'

The conversation then moved on to traffic, weather and good eating places. It transpired that Delia had eaten several times at The Edge of the Moor and rated it very highly.

Kate realised that she'd made some headway with Delia but that the woman was not about to bare her soul to a complete stranger. It was also time to be going back.

'Well, Barney and I should be heading for home,' she said, 'but it's been great having some company. Perhaps I'll run into you up here again?'

'Yes, I'd like that,' Delia said.

'And should you be walking the coast path any time, why not pop in for a cup of tea? I live in Lavender Cottage, which you'll pass as you come down from the cliffs to the beach. I work a couple of days a week at the medical centre, but I'm usually home by five, and I rarely work Thursdays or Fridays.'

Kate delved into her bag, hoping she didn't sound too eager. 'This is my card.' For the umpteenth time, she blessed the day she'd had these cards printed.

'I'll bear it in mind,' Delia Moran said, studying the card. 'Kate Palmer – that name has a familiar ring to it. Where have I heard it before?'

'No idea,' Kate said cheerfully. She called out for Barney then turned around and said, 'Hope to see you again!'

'Yes, nice to have met you,' said Delia.

. . .

'You *promised* not to go to her door,' Woody said as he poured himself a coffee while Kate was stacking the dishwasher after lunch.

'I didn't go anywhere near her door,' Kate protested as she banged the front of the machine shut.

'You just *happened* to join her for a walk?'

Kate sighed. 'Woody, I am not lying. Her dog discovered us, then Barney went off to play with her two Labs, we got chatting and ended up walking together. I assure you it was pure coincidence.'

'Pure coincidence that you just *happened* to be up there, miles from home?'

'I fancied a change of scenery.'

'I bet you did. So, have you interrogated the poor woman?'

'No, I have *not*. We chatted about all sorts of things.'

'And you made no mention of Sienna Stone at all?'

Kate sighed. 'Well, I casually mentioned that we'd had a tragedy in the village and asked if she'd heard about it, which she had, of course. And that's as far as it went.'

'You didn't give her the third degree?' Woody looked at her suspiciously.

'Woody! Honestly!'

'What are you two shouting about?' Jack hollered from the sofa in the sitting room where he and Beth were sprawled together watching an afternoon movie. Beth had come to lunch again but, on this occasion, Kate was not aware of any thigh-stroking.

'We're not shouting!' Kate shouted back.

'Your mother is unable to keep her nose out of things that don't concern her,' Woody said with a loud sigh.

'But it *does* concern me,' Kate protested, 'because I'm still a suspect!'

'Surely the police are dealing with all this?' Beth piped up.

'Of course they are,' Woody confirmed, 'but Kate here thinks she can do a better job.'

'No, I don't, I just want to clear my name.' Kate poured herself a coffee and sat down on a kitchen chair. She was feeling weary and had no wish to watch the movie. She was also becoming increasingly concerned that she hadn't heard anything further from Charlotte – the silence was making her uneasy.

'You mark my words,' Woody said, 'she'll find a way to speak to every single suspect.'

'Good on you, Mum!' said Jack. 'You made any progress yet?'

'Not with Delia Moran. Not yet anyway. I'm not too sure about Sally Brand, and I haven't had a chance to chat with the husband, Irving Aldridge. I've got a feeling about Timmy Thomson though.'

'Who's Timmy Thomson?' Jack asked, turning down the volume on the TV.

'He's a funny little guy who used to stalk Sienna,' Kate replied. 'He comes across as a bit confused at times, but I'm pretty sure that not only does he know who the killer is, he wants to finish off that person himself. Which would explain why he hasn't told Charlotte anything.'

'Sounds scary. Don't go getting involved, Mum.'

'Thank you, Jack,' Woody said, 'because perhaps she'll listen to you. She sure as hell pays no heed to me.'

'I won't get involved,' Kate said, 'but I just feel sorry for the poor, lonely obsessive guy.'

'Nutty as a fruitcake,' added Woody.

'No, just obsessive,' Kate said, 'but I'm afraid he's out for the kill.'

So I think it may be time to pay him another visit, she thought.

. . .

Before Kate could organise a visit to Timmy, she had a visit herself from Charlotte Martin.

'Sorry to come unannounced, but there are a few further questions I need to ask you.'

'You'd better come in then,' Kate said. 'Coffee?'

Charlotte shook her head. 'No thanks, just had one.' She sat down on a kitchen chair and studied Kate. 'I need to go over one or two points again.'

Kate sat down opposite. 'OK, fire away.'

'How long would you say it was from the time Sienna was in your tent until the time of her demise?'

'In other words, what time was she in the tent? At a guess I'd say around three o'clock.'

Charlotte nodded. 'And how long after that did you visit Angie's refreshment tent?'

'I'm not sure, but probably forty-five minutes to an hour later,' Kate replied.

'And how long were you in there?'

'Half an hour maybe? I really wasn't noting the times, Charlotte.'

'Hmm. And it was immediately after that when you headed up towards the cliff-top?'

'We've already been through all this!' Kate was becoming more and more agitated.

'That's as may be, but I still need you to answer all my questions,' Charlotte said firmly.

Kate stared at her. 'Are you saying that I'm still a prime suspect?'

Charlotte stared back, unflinching. 'Of course you are, and so is everyone else. Everyone has a reason to dislike the woman and I must treat you all equally. One more question, Kate.'

Kate braced herself. 'Yes?'

'Why were your fingerprints on the back of her kaftan?'

'Probably because I encouraged her – no, I *ordered* her – out of the tent and so, yes, I would have pressed her back. I've told you all this already!'

'Just routine, Kate.'

FIFTEEN

Dr Andrew Ross called a meeting in his office after the surgery closed on Monday evening, ostensibly to discuss general administration and to announce that, as Kate was now working only two days a week, they planned to recruit another nurse on a part-time basis.

Dr Charlie Barratt, nearing seventy, now only worked part-time and had gone home early. Dr Graham Smith, red-haired and liberally freckled, and not long qualified, was there, along with Denise, Sue, Kate, an agency nurse and the physiotherapist, who usually worked at Tinworthy on Tuesdays.

Young Graham had a bad allergy problem, greatly exacerbated by the high pollen count, and spent most of his time sneezing, blowing his nose or sniffing.

At the end of the meeting, Andrew Ross said, 'Prompted by all the tragedies in this village, I was wondering if we should perhaps become more involved in grief counselling?' He turned to Kate. 'I know you've had some counselling experience, Kate, so I wondered what you might think?'

'I think it's a great idea,' Kate replied, thinking of Timmy Thomson and Irving Aldridge.

Graham sniffed loudly then blew his nose.

'Well,' Andrew continued, 'with severe cases, we do have access to the professionals but – as with everything at the moment – there are long waiting lists.'

Kate cleared her throat. 'Well, I'd be prepared to call on anyone who might need help, to have a chat and, if it looks as if they need more help than I can provide, at least refer them to a professional.'

Graham sneezed twice then blew his nose lustily again.

'Who did you have in mind, Kate?'

'In the case of Sienna Stone, then obviously the husband. And possibly the stalker. He's an odd little guy and seems convinced that he knows who the killer is.'

'So you've met him then?' Denise asked.

'Only briefly at the police station. We had a chat.' Kate had no intention of mentioning her visit to Parson's Court.

'The stalker's obviously a nutcase,' Denise said witheringly, 'so why waste time on someone like that?'

'Because he may need help too,' Kate replied. *And doesn't he just!*

'Rumour has it there's a sister around somewhere too,' Andrew said as Graham sneezed again.

'Yes, there is,' Kate said, 'and I've met her briefly too. I'd say she was not in the least grief-stricken and I very much doubt she'd need any counselling.'

'Some strange folk around,' Andrew said, shaking his head sadly. 'So, I'll leave it to you, Kate. Personally, I think I'd concentrate on the husband. I understand he generally uses the private sector for his medical care, so hopefully he's going to be able to pay for any counselling he might need. But it would be nice if you had a chat with him so he knows we're here to support him, and you can perhaps steer him in the right direction if he needs it.'

'I'll go up to see him when I finish here tomorrow,' Kate said.

Andrew shuffled his papers together. 'Well, if that's everything...?' He glanced at his watch. 'Time to go home.' He turned to Graham. 'Aren't those antihistamines working then?'

'No,' said Graham, wiping an eye, 'they bloody well aren't.'

Kate was familiar with Tremorron from when the Hedgefields had lived there. She'd narrowly escaped her demise during an encounter at Tremorron, so it was with mixed feelings that she drove up to the place at half past four on Tuesday. She hadn't phoned to make an appointment, having decided that a casual visit might be more appropriate. Apart from anything else, Irving could well have declined a meeting, and this was an opportunity not to be missed.

The view from up here was magnificent. The farm fields, mostly inhabited by sheep, rolled down towards Middle Tinworthy, Lower Tinworthy and the turquoise sea in the distance. It was a bright day but windy, and even from this viewpoint, Kate could decipher the turbulent Atlantic rollers and the tiny silhouettes of surfers. She wondered if Jack and Beth were amongst them.

She was relieved to see a couple of Jaguars parked outside, which presumably belonged to Irving, so hopefully he was in. There was also a silver Renault, which she'd seen somewhere before.

A rather dishevelled Irving opened the door, buttoning up his shirt and smoothing down his hair as he did so. He was a tall, thin man, with dark eyes and hair, and a small, tidy beard. 'Yes, what can I do for you, Nurse?'

'I'm sorry if I've disturbed you, Mr Aldridge,' Kate said, aware that he must have been having a siesta. 'I wonder if we could have a brief chat?'

'About what?' He studied her for a moment. 'Have we met before?'

'Yes, very briefly.' There was no reason to elaborate. 'I'm a local nurse and the doctors at the surgery wondered how you were coping with your bereavement and if we could help in any way?'

'I'm coping reasonably well, thank you,' he said. 'I shouldn't think I have need of any help.'

'Sometimes there's a delayed reaction, you know,' Kate said, 'and I'd really like to chat to you, so I wondered if I could come in just for a moment?'

He frowned. 'Just for a minute then,' he said very loudly as he led the way through the hallway towards the snug, which was alongside the kitchen. Kate remembered that snug very well from her experiences with the previous owners. Was he trying to warn someone that a visitor was approaching? 'We, er... I wasn't expecting any guests,' he said, still speaking very loudly.

As they entered the room, Kate was astonished to see Sally Brand sitting on the sofa, also looking dishevelled. She and Kate stared at each other in amazement while Irving said, 'This is my sister-in-law Sally.'

'Yes, we've met,' Kate said.

'Um, yes – yes, we have,' Sally confirmed, doing up the top button of her blouse then smoothing her hair.

Irving looked from one to the other.

'I popped in to see Kate,' Sally said after a brief moment, 'because of this article I'm doing on sisters. Kate has a sister so I thought I could start there. She's quite famous, you know, for her detection skills, so I'd also hoped she might have some ideas as to who had killed poor Sienna.'

Poor Sienna? Kate remembered Sally informing her that she'd hated Sienna's guts. And this *sisters* business! She only mentioned sisters when Kate had asked why she was here shadowing Sienna. Interesting. And what was Sally doing *here* anyway? Kate wondered if her imagination was running riot.

As if reading her mind, Sally said, 'I just popped in to see Irving to discuss funeral arrangements.'

'That's right,' said Irving, looking relieved.

'Have they released her body then?' Kate asked.

'No, but...'

'Soon...' They both spoke at once.

'Well, I've obviously chosen a bad time to call,' Kate went on, 'but I'm here to offer counselling because I realise it's hard to lose someone, someone so *close* to you both.'

Sally was giving her an odd look. *She certainly won't need any counselling*, Kate thought. *And I'm not sure Irving does either.*

'It's a kind thought, Nurse,' Irving said, 'but I think it's highly unlikely I shall have need of counselling. Now, I'd offer you a drink, but I imagine you'll want to be on your way.' He stood up: interview over.

Kate knew she was being dismissed, and she was also aware that Sally was studiously avoiding any eye contact.

'Yes, well, if you change your mind...' Kate dug into her bag for one of her cards and laid it on the coffee table. Then she turned to look Irving straight in the eye. 'Since we are *all* suspects,' she said, 'you may want to stay in touch.'

As she headed towards the door, she turned to Sally. 'Nice to see you again.'

When Kate popped back to the surgery to file her report, she wrote that neither Sienna Stone's husband, Irving Aldridge, nor her sister, Sally Brand – who, by coincidence, was there as well – had any wish for counselling. She'd left her card and suggested they get in touch if either of them changed their minds.

Before she left, Kate decided to have a look through the files to see if there was anything relevant about Irving Aldridge. There was – under 'New Patient Check' – a brief note to say that he was known to have alcohol and anger issues but that he paid for private treatment. This, Kate thought, was surely worth googling to see if any of his past antics had made their way into the newspapers.

When she got home, she sat down with a coffee, opened up her laptop and scanned his details: Irving Aldridge, born 1958 in Torquay, Devon. There followed details of his education and his meteoric rise to fame in the business world. He was known to have a violent temper and, in 2000, his then-wife accused him of physical abuse but later dropped the charges. He was now married to TV presenter, Sienna Stone. No children.

Violent temper. Physical abuse. She certainly would *not* be removing Irving Aldridge from The List.

'There was definitely something funny going on there,' Kate said to Woody later as they ate dinner. 'Just for a start, what was Sally Brand doing at Tremorron?'

'Visiting her brother-in-law? Seems reasonable enough.'

'Mmm. Not sure why though.'

'Making funeral arrangements probably?' Woody suggested.

'Do you know what, Woody – I don't think so. That's what they said, of course. I think there might have been some hanky-panky going on there because they both looked a bit rumpled and crumpled to me, and they appeared very guilty.'

'Oh, Kate, come on! Your imagination is running wild again! Why on earth would Sienna Stone's sister and husband be having some sort of relationship?'

'I don't know,' Kate replied as she cleared away their dinner plates. 'I do know that Sally had a funny look about her and wouldn't meet my eye.'

Woody grinned. 'She's probably heard you're a bit of a Rottweiler. Have we any cheese?'

'Yes,' Kate said, digging in the fridge. 'Not only that, she told Irving that she'd come to see me because of the article she's supposed to be writing about sisters, but when she arrived here that day, she didn't have the foggiest idea if I had a sister or not. That only came out when I asked her why she wasn't staying at Tremorron with Sienna.'

'In that case, it'll be interesting to see if she follows it up with doing an article on you and Angie,' Woody said, cutting himself a hefty wedge of cheddar.

'I bet she doesn't. That was probably just a front and I bet she's not writing any article. I seem to remember that the article about sisters was supposed to be when one is famous and one isn't.'

As she spoke, Kate decided she would seek out Sally Brand at The Atlantic Hotel and tell her how delighted she and Angie would be to be interviewed for the article – though she'd better clear it with Angie first.

Angie was wiping vacant tables when Kate arrived at The Old Locker on Wednesday morning. She and Fergal had made a good job of extending and renovating the place, emphasising its history – or the better bits of it anyway. For years after any pirates had come near it, it had been a dumping ground for fishermen's nets and builders' tools. Nevertheless, Angie had concentrated on the pirates/smuggling/treasure-chest aspects of the old building and had decorated accordingly, covering the old stone walls with photographs of shipwrecks, old lanterns and – the *pièce de résistance* – a glass door in the floor looking down into a cellar full of so-called treasure chests. Only Angie and Fergal knew that they all contained clothes and general supplies, for which there was no room upstairs.

'To what do I owe this honour?' she asked Kate as she replaced a candle in its glass holder.

'Thought I'd pop in for my morning coffee,' Kate said. 'Woody's over at his house replacing a couple of roof slates before the next family move in at the weekend.'

'Fergal's off to the cash 'n' carry,' Angie said, 'so I'll do us both a coffee. It's been fairly quiet this morning so far because everyone's on the beach.'

A few minutes later, when Kate was sitting up at the bar with a cappuccino, Angie asked, 'So, have you solved the crime yet, super-sleuth?'

Kate shook her head. 'I wish I could, but it's proving tricky. Did I tell you I paid a visit to her stalker?'

'What?'

'I thought he might need some sort of therapy, and he does. However, he seems to think he knows who the killer might be, but he isn't telling.'

'He's hardly likely to tell *you*; he'd tell the police, wouldn't he?'

'I'm not at all sure that he has. Anyway, that's not why I came here. Do you remember I told you about Sally Brand?'

Angie screwed up her face. 'Remind me who she is.'

'Sienna Stone's sister,' Kate replied and went on to describe her visit to Tremorron. 'They both had that guilty look, like they'd been caught being naughty!'

'Maybe they *had* been naughty,' Angie suggested with a giggle.

'Now,' Kate went on, 'I don't know if she was telling the truth when she said she was writing this article about sisters, or whether it was just a front to explain why she was staying at The Atlantic Hotel and not at Tremorron.'

'Well, if Sienna was still alive, and she was having it off with Irving, she couldn't very well stay there, could she?'

'*If* she's having it off with Irving.'

Angie stared at her. 'You just said—'

'Yes, I know what I just said, but I couldn't swear to it. I mean, I'd have to find them in flagrante or something.'

'Surely even *you* wouldn't be creeping round the house, staring in windows?'

Kate ignored Angie's remark. 'Anyway, I thought I'd call her bluff. I thought we'd invite her to interview *us* for her article.'

'Us?'

'Yes, us – we're sisters, aren't we?'

'Believe it or not!' Angie guffawed. 'But what would be the *point*?'

'The point is that either she's bluffing, and we should be able to see through her, or she's genuine and you and I might feature in an article for a women's magazine. Goodness, we might even get *paid*!'

Angie refilled their coffee cups. 'So how are you going to find this woman, other than snooping around Tremorron and getting done for trespassing?'

'I *told* you. She's staying at The Atlantic, and that's where I shall be heading.'

SIXTEEN

The receptionist at The Atlantic Hotel was Danish, blonde and beautifully groomed with not a hair out of place. She didn't fit in with Marc's Gallic image but, then again, if he'd found someone French, his own limited knowledge of the language might have been put to the test.

'May I help you?'

'Oh yes please,' Kate said. 'I wondered if I could have a word with Mrs Sally Brand, who I understand is staying here?'

The receptionist fiddled with her computer screen and then looked round at the key deposit boxes. 'Her key is here, so it would appear that she's not in the hotel.'

'Oh,' said Kate. Well, it had been a bit of a gamble, and perhaps she'd try again tomorrow.

'*Kate!*'

At the sound of her name, Kate swivelled round to find Marc Le Grand right behind her. 'Oh, hi, Marc!'

'So nice to see you! How can we help?'

'Well, you can't really because I wanted to talk to Sally Brand, and apparently she's out.'

'Ah, *chérie*, she is always out!' Marc said with a sigh.

'Really?' Kate didn't want to appear too eager but she was desperate to know where Sally had gone. 'Perhaps evening would be a better time to catch her?'

'Mmm, *non*. She is out most evenings, I think.' Marc took her elbow and steered her away from the desk. 'She comes in very late or' – he looked both ways and lowered his voice – 'she does not come in *at all!*'

'How very interesting,' Kate said.

'We know when the key is there, you see. *Un café, peut-être?*'

'No thank you, Marc. I wonder where she goes?'

'*Je ne sais pas!* So why is she staying here if she has a lover? She *must* have a lover, *non?*'

'Very possibly,' Kate said.

'How does she find one so soon?'

'Good question.'

'Sometimes she comes back for siesta. Too much love-making perhaps?'

'Who knows? I'll try to contact her later.'

At two o'clock, Kate rang the hotel and was put through straight away to Sally Brand.

'Hi, Sally,' she said, 'it's Kate Palmer. I just wondered when you planned to interview my sister and me?'

'Interview?' Sally sounded vague.

'Yes, you know, for this article you're doing? You mentioned it the other day?'

'Oh yes, yes of course.' There was a pause. 'Maybe tomorrow, Thursday?'

'Well, I'm around tomorrow but my sister's permanently on duty at The Old Locker down by the beach. So why don't we meet there?' She thought for a moment. 'Probably around four o'clock before the bar begins to get busy?'

'Four o'clock,' Sally confirmed before swiftly putting down the phone.

On Thursday morning, Kate, feeling very apprehensive, had her fingerprints taken yet again, as did all the suspects, according to the constable selected for the job. 'Just routine,' was all he'd say. Kate remembered Charlotte asking her why her fingerprints were on the back of Sienna's kaftan, so they *must* already have them. She couldn't remember whether or not she'd touched Sienna Stone when she'd ushered her out of the first-aid tent. Possibly, she thought, and what about the possibility of DNA traces? Kate had taken her blood pressure after all...

Then the thought struck her that if, according to Timmy Thomson, the killer had taken the trouble to wear a coat and hoodie, then surely he or she would have thought to wear gloves as well? The more she thought about this, the more determined she was to see Timmy again. She'd go tomorrow. For now, she had to concentrate on Sally Brand and try to dream up some sisterly reminiscences.

'You don't look much like Sienna,' Angie said bluntly after they'd shaken hands and she'd made coffees.

'You don't look much like Kate either,' Sally retorted.

'Touché,' said Kate. Then, turning to Sally: 'I seem to remember you said something about you writing about sisters when one is famous and one isn't, so perhaps we don't really fit the bill?'

'Ah, but Kate, you are famous, or is it *infamous*, around here!' Angie cut in with a giggle.

'Exactly! You are famous around here, Kate! I've been doing my research in the local press,' Sally said.

'So you'll know then that she gets herself into no end of

trouble,' said Angie, 'and often nearly gets herself killed, just so she can try to solve a murder. Or two. Or... well, we won't go into that. Have you noticed that Palmer is an anagram of Marple? Need I say more?'

'No, you needn't!' Kate snapped. She turned to Sally. 'It's all pure coincidence, but I have to admit I do like trying to solve these things – beats crosswords any day!'

'And that's how she managed to snare the local detective inspector,' Angie added for good measure.

'Thank you, Angie,' Sally said drily, 'but we can come to that in a minute. Tell me about your childhood, Kate.'

'Angie's two years older than me,' Kate explained, 'but, like yourself, her nose was pulled out of joint when I arrived on the scene. She was never *nasty*,' she added hurriedly, observing Angie's scowl, 'but, like Sienna, was always looking for attention.'

'No, I *wasn't*!' Angie shouted.

'Yes, you were, which is probably one of the reasons why you wanted to become an actress.'

'You were an actress?' Sally asked, studying Angie with interest.

'Oh yes,' Angie replied airily, 'for several years.' She looked from one to the other. 'Either of you fancy a proper drink? No? Oh well, I might just have a tiny wee gin.' With that, she served herself a double from the optic.

'So when did you give up acting?' Sally asked.

'Oh, you know, marriage, children, one thing and another...'

Not to forget the gin, when you forgot to go to rehearsals, when you were too damn hungover to remember your lines, Kate thought.

'I've always been artistic of course,' Angie continued, 'and I've done some rather interesting work. Canvases, mainly. In fact, I do believe they still have one in The Gallery, just along the road here.' She indicated the venue with a dramatic sweep of her arm and almost knocked over her gin. 'Whoops!' She straightened her glass with the speed of light.

Kate had memories of Angie, shortly after they arrived at Lavender Cottage, ensconced in the summerhouse, in a smock with her hair tied artfully back, dabbing paint randomly on the canvases – and the floor. She still hadn't managed to get all the marks off the floor.

'And then you came *here*?' Sally prompted, scribbling in her notebook.

'Ah yes. This place was *asking* for a makeover, you know. It didn't look anything like this when I took it over, did it, Kate?' Without waiting for affirmation, she continued, 'It needed my artistic touch, and sheer hard work of course.'

'Aided by Fergal,' Kate said.

'Who's Fergal?'

'He's my partner,' Angie replied. 'He's having a lie-down at the moment because it gets *very* busy in here in the evenings.'

'Yes, I'm sure it does,' Sally agreed. Then, turning to Kate: 'Tell me something more about yourself, Kate.'

'As you know, I'm a nurse, always have been. I've never acted, but I did win prizes for my drawings and paintings in school. Nothing like Angie's abstracts of course.'

'You can say that again,' said Angie.

Kate ignored her. 'I still fancy having a go at some water-colours, now I have more time.'

'Like when she's not sticking her nose into other people's business,' said Angie.

'I'm sure that's all in a good cause,' Sally said diplomatically. 'So, what brought you both down here?'

Kate explained about herself being divorced, Angie being widowed, children flown the nest, memories of childhood holidays, escaping the rat-race and crime in the South-East – this punctuated by loud snorts from both women – for the sea, village life...

'And you still enjoy nursing?' Sally asked Kate, who then explained about being a practice nurse based at the local medical centre.

'I used to do three or four days a week,' she told Sally, 'but since I got married, I only do a couple of days now.'

'So you met your second husband here in Cornwall?'

'Like I said, she snared the local detective inspector,' Angie said, 'before someone else grabbed him.'

'Did you see my lips move?' Kate asked Sally.

'No, I didn't,' Sally said grinning. 'Shall we try again? So, you met someone here in Cornwall?'

'Yes, and as I told you, Woody *was* the detective inspector at that time. We had a very good relationship for a couple of years and then decided to get married back in the spring.'

'Congratulations!' Sally said, feverishly making notes.

'She finally took my advice,' Angie said with a sigh. 'I'd been telling her for months that she should grab him before someone else did!'

'I did *not* grab him!' Kate snapped. 'I wish you'd shut up, Angie, because Sally's talking to *me* at the moment.'

'My lips are sealed,' said Angie. She then opened them just enough to finish off her gin.

'I hardly dare ask this,' Sally said, her pen poised, 'but what are your criticisms of each other, if any? You first, Kate: what would you say were Angie's good and bad points?'

There was a moment of silence before Kate said, 'Angie is generous, she's always willing to try something new and she's good fun. Unfortunately, she drinks far too much.' She paused for a moment before adding, 'But none of us is perfect!'

'Angie?'

'Am I allowed to *speak* now? Well, OK, Kate is a very caring person, and she's always been there for me. Unfortunately, she has this stupid idea that she's become some sort of super-sleuth, probably because she's so bloody nosy.'

'Right. So now, can you briefly sum up your feelings about each other? Kate?'

'OK,' said Kate, 'I love her really, although she drives me nuts at times.'

'Angie?'

'Yeah, I love her too, the silly cow.' She put her arm round Kate to illustrate this fact.

Sally wrote for a moment before snapping shut her notebook. 'You both seem very honest and very normal in your relationship with each other. I only wish that I'd had that kind of relationship with Sheila – sorry, Sienna – but it's too late now unfortunately. Thank you both so much for cooperating. I'll send you copies when it's published.' She smiled, gave a brief wave and headed towards the door.

After she'd disappeared, Kate said, 'Well, what did you make of *that*? I wasn't sure about her at first. But she seems genuine enough, doesn't she? I daresay we'll find out if and when the article is published.'

'I feel the need for another gin,' said Angie.

SEVENTEEN

On Friday morning, Kate finally caught up with the dusting, the vacuuming and the washing. Feeling very worthy, she sat down with a cup of coffee just after eleven o'clock, as Woody came in to announce that his electric drill had given up the ghost and he was going up to Bude to buy a new one.

'I'll be back about half past two, I should think,' he said. 'I'll just go get my wallet.'

Faced with a few hours to herself, Kate wondered what more she should do: mow the grass, clear out the fridge, tidy up Jack's chaotic bedroom? Ugh. None of that appealed in the slightest. What did appeal was paying another visit to Timmy Thomson. She hadn't wanted Woody to know that she was planning to see Timmy again, so this was an opportune moment.

When Woody reappeared, she asked, 'Could you give me and Barney a lift up to the church on your way?' It was a steep climb up the road to Middle Tinworthy.

'Yeah, of course. You planning on walking Barney in the woods up there?'

'Yes, I am.' Well, that was only a little white lie because she would be *passing* the woods on her way to the housing estate.

'So will you walk back home?' Woody asked.

'Yes, no problem – it's downhill all the way.'

Ten minutes later, he'd dropped her and the dog at St Piran's Church, and the two of them set off along the road. Barney looked less than delighted to be walking on a lead and on a road, as opposed to running around freely. To compensate for this thoughtlessness, he sniffed everything thoroughly on the narrow grass verge, which slowed down their progress considerably. At this rate, Timmy might be having his lunch, but that was a chance she'd have to take.

As she wound her way through the estate, even the grass verges disappeared, and Barney consoled himself with examining every lamp post. She could hear sirens going off somewhere ahead and wondered idly if it was a fire or an ambulance call-out.

The nearer she got to Parson's Court, the louder the sirens and then – as she turned the corner – Kate saw a cluster of police cars and an ambulance outside Timmy's block of flats. What on earth was going on? It was doubtful she'd be allowed into the flats, but there was little point in turning back now, and anyway, she wanted to see what was happening.

One policeman was busy taping off the whole area round the flats and another was standing by the main door.

'You can't go in there,' he said firmly.

'Why not?' Kate asked. 'What's happened?'

'There's been an incident.'

'What sort of incident?'

The policeman shook his head. He was saying nothing.

At that very moment, Charlotte Martin appeared. She

looked at Kate with undisguised amazement. 'What on earth are *you* doing here?'

'I've come to see Timmy Thomson, to offer him counselling,' Kate replied. She noticed Charlotte and the policeman exchanging glances.

'You've left it a little late,' Charlotte said tersely. 'But since you're here, perhaps you could make yourself useful and have a look at that old gentleman sitting in the hallway. He's suffering from shock so tread carefully.' She turned to the policeman. 'Could you tether up the dog for a moment please?'

Barney was not having a good day. He looked at Kate reproachfully.

Kate followed Charlotte into the hallway where an old man with a thatch of white hair sat, grey-faced and red-eyed, on a chair which had plainly been positioned there for his benefit. He was holding a glass of water in his shaking hand and was staring into space.

'This is Sidney,' Charlotte said briefly. 'Kate's a nurse, Sidney, and she'll have a chat with you.' Then she turned and quickly headed back up the stairs, leaving Kate to work out the situation for herself.

'Hello, Sidney,' Kate said gently, 'I gather you're not feeling too good?'

For a moment, Sidney didn't react at all, and Kate could see he was in a complete state of shock. She patted his arm. 'You can tell me – I'm a nurse.'

Finally, Sidney began to focus on her.

'What's wrong, Sidney?'

'Wot's wrong?' Sidney sniffed. 'Wot's wrong is that I found 'im, that's wot's wrong.'

'Who did you find?' Kate asked with that sinking sensation in her stomach again.

'Timmy, wot lives next door to me.'

'Timmy Thomson?'

'I just told you that.'

'Why are you so upset, Sidney?'

The old man looked at her as if she was a complete lunatic. ''E were *dead*!'

Kate's worst fears were now being confirmed. 'I'm so sorry – that must have been an awful shock. Do you know how he died? Had he been ill?'

Sidney continued staring at her. 'Haven't you seen 'im?'

'No, not today. I came here to see him, but they wouldn't let me in...'

Sidney was now coming into his own. ''E'd got a plastic bag over 'is 'ead, all taped round his neck, like.' Now warming to the subject, he added, 'And there was all this blood in the bag too...' He shuddered. 'Made me throw up, it did.'

'Oh my God.' Kate wished there was another chair available so that she could sit down herself as she was beginning to feel decidedly wobbly. *Poor, poor Timmy! So he did know who the killer was, and the killer knew it.*

The white-clad forensic team were now coming slowly down the stairs, carrying a small figure in a body bag, followed closely by Charlotte.

'I'll follow you shortly,' she said to the team as they went out of the door. She turned to Kate. 'Why are you *really* here, Kate?'

'I told you. Timmy Thomson needed help.'

'Is that so?'

'Yes. Not only that, he said he *knew* who Sienna Stone's killer was.'

'You were hoping for some sort of confession?'

'Well, I hoped so,' Kate admitted.

'I wonder why he would tell *you* if he wouldn't tell *me*?' Charlotte said.

Kate decided to come clean. 'It seemed like he wanted to finish off the killer himself.'

Charlotte appeared shaken for a brief moment. 'He told you that?'

'Yes, but I thought it was just his grief talking. I didn't think he was serious.'

'When did he say this?'

'When I came to see him a couple of weeks ago.'

'And why, exactly, did you come to see him a couple of weeks ago?'

'Because he was obviously obsessed with Sienna and I wanted to help.'

'I'd like to know exactly what was said on that occasion,' Charlotte said, 'so I need to take a detailed statement from you at the police station.'

'What, now?' Kate began to feel a little panicky. 'I've got the dog outside.'

'Well, the dog will have to come too, along with poor Sidney here. I'm sorry, Kate, but it would appear you've been interfering in police business, and this doesn't look good – particularly as you're a suspect.'

'I wasn't interfering,' Kate protested. 'You can check with Andrew Ross at the medical centre. He asked me to offer bereavement counselling to anyone close to Sienna who might need it.'

'Nevertheless, I need a statement from you, and one from Sidney too.'

They both helped Sidney to his feet, and slowly made their way outside, Kate picking up Barney en route. She then got into the back seat of the car, next to a silent, trembling Sidney, the dog on her knee, with Charlotte in the driver's seat, a policeman alongside her in the passenger seat.

At the police station, after filling in a mountain of paperwork, Kate waited while Sidney was ushered into the office and presumably gave his statement. The poor old fellow would take some time to recover from finding Timmy in such a horrific state. He was also taking some time giving his statement.

After nearly an hour, Kate was finally directed into the office, by which time she was beginning to worry whether Woody had got home and would be wondering where she was. He was not going to be at all happy about this turn of events – at the fact she'd been using her professional obligations as a cover for a bit of sleuthing – and he would be appalled that there had been a second horrific murder.

Charlotte interrogated her on every detail of her visit to Timmy. He had apparently *not* told the police that he had any idea who the killer was, only that the person was dressed in a long coat and was wearing a hoodie. He had certainly not told them that he might have been planning to finish off the killer himself.

'Did you not think it was important to tell us all this?' Charlotte asked after nearly forty minutes. To add to the general misery, Barney – who had been tethered up again in the waiting area – had barked and whined to such an extent that Charlotte had, with much sighing, permitted the dog to come into the office where he sat staring at Kate with big sad eyes.

'OK,' Charlotte said at last, 'you can go.'

'I'll phone Woody to come to collect me,' Kate said as she stood up, beginning to feel a little weepy. In the waiting area, she located her phone.

'I was beginning to get worried about you,' Woody said. 'What's happened? Where are you?'

'At the police station in Launceston.'

'*What?* What the hell are you doing there?'

Woody came marching into the police station some twenty minutes later. After he'd hugged Kate, he stood back and asked, 'What's going on?'

At that very moment, Charlotte emerged from the office.

'Woody, would you get Kate out of here before I throw the book at her! Obstructing the course of justice, just for a start... and don't forget she's still a suspect herself!' She turned to the sergeant on the desk. 'Can you please organise a car to take Sidney home?' With that, she went back into her office and shut the door.

Woody took Kate by the arm. 'You have some explaining to do, my love,' he said as he steered her outside.

Kate struggled to keep her composure as she followed Woody to his car. As they drove away, he said, 'Explain!'

Kate had to confess then about her proposed visit to Timmy. 'You knew about my first visit, because I told you.'

'Yes, but you didn't convince me then that you thought Timmy Thomson knew who the killer was. You said he went back and forth on it. Mind you, I thought he would have told Charlotte exactly what he had told you.'

'I thought the same,' said Kate. 'Damn it, I wasn't doing anything *wrong*!'

'Nonetheless, Kate, this investigating of yours has to *stop*! I'll talk to Charlotte later and we'll smooth this out.'

'I'm sorry, Woody, but it's not fair! I had nothing to do with Sienna's murder but I'm a suspect. And all I was doing was trying to help Timmy, and now I'm in even more trouble...' Kate could control her tears no longer.

Woody patted her knee. 'Don't go upsetting yourself. Let's go home and have a drink and relax. I imagine Barney's had enough for today too.'

Kate blew her nose. 'The thing is, it's probably all my fault.'

'What is?'

'That Timmy's been killed. I might have alerted the killer one way or another, mightn't I? Did *you* tell anyone what I said about Timmy possibly knowing who the killer was?'

'Of course I didn't,' Woody said as he parked the car. 'Who the hell would I tell? It wasn't even a definite fact.'

A few minutes later, Kate was sitting on her sofa sipping a coffee which Woody had laced with brandy. Her mind was going round in circles.

'I'm trying to think who I might have mentioned it to? I think I may have said something at the meeting at work. Denise would have picked up on it. And I think I mentioned it to Angie. Would any of them have repeated it to anyone else...?' Kate shook her head in consternation and bit her lip.

'Will you stop torturing yourself?' Woody sounded exasperated. 'I know you want to clear your name, but this is becoming ridiculous. I really can't let you out of my sight for one moment, can I?'

EIGHTEEN

The following morning, Saturday, Kate decided she needed some eggs, which would necessitate a visit to Bobby's Best Buys down in the village, and she might pop into Angie's for coffee on the way back.

'I promise,' she said to Woody, 'not to interfere and not to ask questions. Just eggs from Bobby and coffee with Angie – OK?'

Woody looked at her doubtfully. 'Promise?'

'Promise!' Then she grabbed her bag and strolled down to Bobby's.

Bobby sold the basics and not a great deal of anything else. He refused to retire although he was well into his seventies, and had also refused several offers to purchase his shop. He had no desire whatsoever to modernise the dark, dated interior, and he was proud to tell everyone concerned that he wouldn't stock anything he couldn't pronounce. It turned out that there was a fair amount that Bobby couldn't pronounce. He filled his window – the only source of daylight – with buckets, spades and windbreaks all summer, Halloween stuff through October and half of November, which left December free for his annual array of dusty tinsel Christmas trees, a mountain of shortbread boxes and, inexplicably, two garden gnomes.

As she entered the shop, Kate reckoned he would doubtless have heard about the previous day's tragedy.

'Mornin', Nurse,' he said, wiping some biscuit crumbs from his mouth.

'Good morning, Bobby. I wondered if I could have half a dozen eggs please?'

'Lovely, new-laid they are,' Bobby said, burrowing under the counter. Then, as if remembering something, he stood up straight. 'You heard about that Timmy Thomson?'

'Oh, indeed I have,' Kate said with feeling.

'Terrible business that,' said Bobby. 'Mind you, he wasn't the full shilling, was Timmy.' He tapped his forehead to illustrate the point. 'And neither was that mother of his! Mary, she was called, but no virgin *that* one though.' He snorted. 'Don't know where she got that Timmy from, or *who* she got him from more like! Likely she didn't know who it was either. There was never no sign of no father.'

Kate had lost count of the double negatives but got the gist of it all.

Bobby wasn't finished yet. 'She never had no husband, and a boy should have a father, shouldn't he? That Timmy never did no work, just hung around and chased after some bleedin' actress or whatever she was. She was probably no better than she should be neither – I'm telling you!' He paused. 'What was it you were wantin' again?'

'Six eggs please, Bobby.'

'Right-o.' He bent down under the counter again and his eye caught some packs of yellow apples. 'Have you seen them lovely apples I got, all wrapped up nice in little packets, see? Golden Delicious they are; fallin' off the trees round here, and in my shop the very next day!' He slid the pack across the counter to Kate, who picked it up obediently.

'Very nice, Bobby. But in the small print here it says "Produce of France".'

Bobby picked it up and peered at it for a moment under the strip light. 'That wholesaler said they was *local*! Oh well, they probably came across on the ferry this mornin'. Now, what was it you wanted?'

With the eggs finally stowed in her bag, Kate made her way along the fifty yards or so to The Old Locker, where she found Fergal dusting the array of bottles on the shelf.

'Morning, Kate. Have you heard about that hellish murder up on the estate?'

'Yes, I'm well aware of it, Fergal. Where's Angie?'

'She'll be down in a minute after she's made herself beautiful. Would you be wanting a coffee now?'

'Thank you, I would.'

'Would it be too early for an Irish one? On the house?'

'Yes, far too early, thanks all the same. I'll have a cappuccino please.'

As Fergal pulled the levers on the coffee machine, which sighed and gurgled a little in protest, he said, 'I hear he was cut up in little bits and put in plastic bags.'

'I'm not sure that's exactly correct, but I think it was all a bit nasty anyway.'

'Probably some woman he'd upset,' Fergal went on blithely, 'a woman scorned and all that – although chopping him up would be a bit extreme, wouldn't it?'

'He was a suspect for Sienna Stone's murder,' Kate said, 'like me.'

'Oh, holy mother of God! Does that mean you're in danger yourself?'

'I hope not,' Kate said truthfully, that exact thought having crossed her mind in the early hours of the morning.

At that moment, Angie appeared, fully made up and with newly blow-dried hair. 'Have you heard about—'

'I was there,' Kate interrupted.

'You were *there*?' They spoke in unison and both turned to stare at her.

'I'm afraid so. I went to see if I could offer Timmy some counselling and hoping that he might tell me who he thought had killed Sienna. I told you that I was pretty sure he knew, didn't I?'

Angie nodded mutely.

'Go on, Kate,' Fergal pleaded.

'You didn't *find* him, did you?' Angie's eyes had widened in horror.

'Fortunately not. But one of his neighbours did, and I think the poor man's going to take some time to recover.'

'He was all chopped up, wasn't he?' Angie asked.

'In Sainsbury's carrier bags?' added Fergal.

Kate sighed. 'I don't know who told you all that. I haven't got all the gory details yet, but, according to the old man who found him, Timmy was probably suffocated with a plastic bag which was taped round his neck.'

'Jaysus!' said Fergal.

'Doesn't bear thinking about,' said Angie, 'but why would he let someone tie a plastic bag over his head?'

'I suspect he was whacked on the head first. Sidney said there was blood inside the bag.'

'Ugh!' Angie pulled a face.

'You wouldn't be seeing through a Sainsbury's carrier bag now, would you?' Fergal was scratching his head. 'I'm trying to remember who it was that told me it was Sainsbury's.'

'The thing is,' Kate said, 'I'm afraid I might have told someone that he thought he knew who the killer was. I think I mentioned it at the medical centre, I told Woody and I told you.'

'Well, I didn't say a word to anyone,' Angie said then paused for a moment. 'Oh, wait a minute – I might just have mentioned it to Sally Brand when she came in that night.'

'What night?'

'Thursday night, after the interview she did with us.'

'Sally Brand came in *here* that same evening?' Kate could scarcely believe her ears. 'Why would she do that?'

'Well, for a drink, what else? She said she'd heard about Fergal's wonderful Irish coffees and so she decided to pop in and try one for herself.'

Fergal beamed. 'And didn't she just *love* it! She stayed for another one, didn't she, Angela?'

Kate studied her sister. 'So you got chatting?'

'Oh, you know, just about this and that.' Angie was looking a little guilty. 'You know how it is.'

'No, I don't know how it is,' Kate said, 'so tell me. Did she talk about Sienna?'

'Well, she kind of *referred* to Sienna, and who might have pushed her off the cliff. She didn't think it was you, and she assured me it wasn't her.'

'Very generous of her. So you might just have let it slip that I'd visited Timmy Thomson and that I reckoned he knew who did it?'

'I suppose I might've done,' Angie said. 'Good heavens, Kate, you don't think *she*...?'

'I don't know what to think,' Kate replied as she drained her coffee cup. 'Anyway, I'd better be heading home because Woody's keeping a tight rein on me at the moment.'

'Well now, there's a surprise,' said Angie.

As she walked up the lane, Kate looked back at the ocean which today, for once, was calm as a millpond, unlike the chopping and churning going on in her tummy. Would she herself ever be able to feel really calm again?

NINETEEN

While she'd been out, Woody had been on the phone to Charlotte.

'Your friend, Timmy, did indeed come to a rather nasty end,' he said casually to Kate as she and the dog came into the kitchen.

'Did you manage to find out all the gory details?' Kate asked as she placed the eggs in the fridge.

'As many as she was prepared to give me,' Woody replied. 'Apparently, he'd been hammered repeatedly on the head – hence the blood – and, while he was out for the count, a strong, transparent plastic bag was placed over his head and taped very securely in place. I doubt he ever woke up.'

'That's exactly as Sidney described it,' Kate said. 'Did she say where he was actually found?'

'Sprawled on the floor with a large cardboard Sienna lying on top of him – so perhaps the poor guy died happy!'

'Oh, Woody, for goodness' sake!'

'I know, I know! And he hadn't been dead long apparently. Probably just an hour or so before he was found. It's horrible and Charlotte's really got her hands full now. No fingerprints again, so presumably gloves were worn. What was a little worrying was that she thought it was quite a coincidence that you appeared a short time after he was found – as if you'd been in the area for a reason. I told her that you'd been at home until I dropped you and the dog off at the church around midday – that I had no idea you were planning to visit Timmy, only that you were going to walk the dog in the woods. We reckoned that the walk from the church to Parson's Court couldn't have taken more than about twenty minutes, so I think she's satisfied with that.'

'Damn it, so she should be! Surely Charlotte didn't think I had anything to do with it?' She yanked open the cupboard door and pulled out a bottle of wine. 'Now perhaps you understand why I feel it's so important for me to clear my name when I always seem to be in the wrong place at the wrong time.'

'Yes, but you're on dangerous territory here, yet again. This case is becoming real nasty, Kate, and – for the umpteenth time – I beg you to leave it to the police.' He moved across and put his arms round her. 'I do not want to lose you.'

'I know, I know, but—'

'No buts!' he said firmly.

'No buts,' she echoed.

'Good!' he said.

Woody now insisted on accompanying Kate almost everywhere she went, even when she walked Barney on Saturday and Sunday afternoons. She was working Tuesday and Wednesday of the week ahead and somehow or other she really wanted to see Delia Moran again, although it was highly unlikely that Delia was the killer. There was no way she could have known about Timmy and what he might have known or not known. Deep down, she wondered if she was asking for trouble – being in the wrong place at the wrong time yet again.

She'd almost given up on the idea when Woody remembered he had a routine dental appointment in Exeter the following afternoon, at the practice he'd been attending ever since he came to Cornwall.

Woody eyed her suspiciously. 'You're sure you don't want to come to Exeter with me?'

'Not really, if you don't mind. It's not as if I want to buy anything, and I've got a few chores to do round here.'

'So you promise not to go snooping around again?'

'Of course I won't go snooping around! Good luck with the dentist!'

'Purely routine,' Woody said.

She waited until he'd driven down the lane, and she could no longer hear the sound of his engine, when she said to the dog, 'Come on, Barney, you and I are going for a nice walk on the moor!'

As Kate parked in the lay-by a short distance from Delia's cottage, she kept her fingers crossed that Delia was a creature of habit and walked her dogs every afternoon. She knew she couldn't hang around indefinitely and – quite apart from the fact that she'd promised Woody not to knock on the door – she had no real reason to do so anyway.

However, when she let Barney out of the car, the first thing he did was run, barking with excitement, straight across to the cottage where the two Labradors were chasing each other around in the garden. The Labradors then joined in the barking and, as Kate got to the gate to try to retrieve Barney, Delia appeared at the door to see what all the noise was about.

'Apologies!' Kate shouted above the barking. 'I let Barney off the lead and he headed straight here!'

'Don't worry,' Delia shouted back, 'we were just about to set off for a walk anyway. Mind if I join you?'

Kate could not believe her luck.

A few minutes later, they were tramping along, side by side, saying how often you met interesting people who you'd never meet otherwise, thanks to walking your dog.

Furthermore, it was Delia who said, 'Are the police any nearer knowing what happened to Sienna Stone?'

'Not that I'm aware of,' Kate replied.

'Incidentally, I was in Tinworthy at lunchtime on Friday. I went to your Guy at Guys 'n' Dolls to get my hair done,' Delia went on, 'and he's done a great job. Thanks for the recommendation.'

'Yes, I was just thinking how lovely it looked,' Kate said truthfully.

'Oh, thanks. Anyway, while I was having my hair done, I heard sirens and alarms blasting all over the place. Any idea what that might all have been about?'

Kate was dumbfounded for a moment. *Delia was in Tinworthy around the time of Timmy's murder!* 'Unfortunately,' she said, 'there's been another killing – the stalker. Did you know Sienna had a stalker?'

Delia stopped in her tracks. 'What? You mean Tiny Tim?'

'Timmy Thomson – did you know him?'

'I didn't exactly *know* him, but I knew *of* him. Sienna told me about him in the days when we were quite friendly, before she took a liking to my husband.'

Kate was unsure how to react to this. Finally, she said, 'I'm sorry about that.'

'Not as sorry as I am. She turned out to be a real bitch. In fact, I wouldn't insult any female dogs by calling her that. She was actually quite evil.'

'So she called Timmy Thomson Tiny Tim?'

'She mocked him,' Delia said. 'He'd sent her his photograph

and asked her to marry him so she knew what he looked like. Once, at an award ceremony, she saw him standing in the crowd and blew kisses at him. The poor little man went quite pink. It was cruel because she didn't give a damn about him, just laughed at him.'

Kate decided not to mention the cardboard Siennas. 'I went to offer him counselling a few weeks ago,' she said, 'and the poor guy was convinced that Sienna was leaving her husband for *him*.'

Delia laughed. 'Sienna was quite fit to let him think that. She liked taunting people; she even taunted me after she'd slept with Roger. But I'll tell you this, she'd never have left Irving Aldridge because she was far too fond of his money. Anyway, why would she when she could have her cake and eat it too?'

'Why indeed?' Kate was tempted to tell Delia about Sally Brand and her suspicions but decided not to. She didn't know her well enough. And now that Delia had admitted to being in Tinworthy that fateful day, Kate had to keep her on The List.

'I don't envy your lady detective because I reckon she's got a real job on her hands. There were lots of folk who didn't like Sienna Stone,' Delia said. 'Finding her standing on the edge of a cliff would have been a huge temptation to an awful lot of the people she'd elbowed out of the way over the years.'

Kate was beginning to feel that her crushed Fiat was of very little significance in the scheme of things.

They ambled on for half an hour or so but didn't mention either Sienna or Tim again. Kate hoped that Delia wasn't the killer because she rather liked the woman.

Normally, Kate discussed everything with Woody when they sat down together in the evenings. She wasn't ready yet though to tell him about her moorland walk, and the fact that Delia had been in the neighbourhood when Timmy had been murdered.

She'd have to choose her moment carefully. In the meantime, she'd have to listen to everyone's expert analysis of the situation when she went to work tomorrow.

'You won't catch *me* out on my own in the evening,' Denise assured them all the next morning as they convened in the tiny staff room. 'Not with a serial killer running around.'

'You never go out on your own in the evenings anyway,' Sue put in as she plugged in the kettle. 'I'm desperate for a coffee.' She turned to Kate. 'What do you make of all this, super-sleuth?'

'I haven't a clue,' Kate replied. That much was true anyway.

At that moment, Andrew Ross came in. 'Nasty business all this,' he said, looking at the three of them. 'You girls keep safe now and don't go out and about on your own.'

'Just what I was telling them,' Denise said. 'It can't be that he has a fixation for women though, because otherwise why would he kill that little weirdo in Parson's Court?'

'It's got to be the husband,' Sue said.

'Why?' Denise asked.

'It's *always* the husband,' Sue replied, 'or at least it is on TV. Perhaps he got fed up with Sienna being unfaithful with that director bloke? Maybe the director's next on his list? Still can't quite work out why he'd want to kill poor Timmy Thomson though – he was hardly competition, was he?'

Andrew shook his head and went into his office.

'Ssshh!' Denise pointed towards the door. 'Here come the customers!'

The 'customers', regardless of their aches and pains, all had theories on who was doing the killing.

Kate listened patiently to everyone's theory on the matter. Her head spinning, she couldn't wait to get home.

TWENTY

When Kate eventually arrived back at Lavender Cottage, she was pleasantly surprised to find Jack cutting the grass.

'Woody's gone to get some beers,' Jack said. 'There's an offer on at Tesco or somewhere.'

'OK, well I'm just going to put the kettle on,' Kate said as she opened the door, the dog jumping up in welcome, 'so, if you fancy some tea...?'

'Be right there in five minutes,' Jack replied, switching on the mower again, 'I've only got a teeny bit more to do.'

Kate was glad to see him on his own. Sometimes he came back overnight and sometimes he didn't. She had no idea what the sleeping arrangements might be up at the caravan site, and she didn't ask. He hadn't yet brought Beth back to Lavender Cottage overnight, which was a relief. So far as she was aware, his relationship with Beth was still going strong. She hadn't asked about his plans either, afraid that he would say he was about to go back to the other side of the world.

He ambled in after about ten minutes, pulling off his sweaty T-shirt to reveal his tanned, toned torso. 'Bloody hot work,' he said, 'so I'll stick this in the machine.' He then popped round the corner to what Kate liked to refer to as the laundry room but was in fact a tiny porch with only room to squeeze in a washing machine and dryer.

When he sat down and Kate handed him a mug of tea, he said, 'Good to see you on your own, Mum. I think we need a chat.'

Kate felt her insides plummet. Did this mean he really was going back to the other side of the world?

'I don't want to outstay my welcome,' he said.

'Jack, you'll never outstay your welcome; I'm just so pleased you're *here!*'

'Thanks, Mum, but I've been scrounging off you for long enough. I thought I might look for a job with a construction company.'

'What *here?* In the UK?'

'Yeah, here. Now I'm home, you know, and with one thing and another...' He sounded vague.

She felt a little explosion of happiness. He was staying! 'Jack, that's great! There's a lot of building work going on in Cornwall and Devon so I'm sure you'll find something with your qualifications.'

Jack cleared his throat. 'Thing is, Mum, I was thinking of Bristol. We could get a little flat up there.'

'*We?*' Kate echoed, feeling her spirits slowly sinking again.

'Yeah, Beth and me. She'll be going back up home at the end of the tourist season, and she's arranged to go back to her old salon, as they need a stylist. Thing is, we plan to get hitched when we've saved enough money.'

'*Married?*' Kate wondered if she was beginning to sound like a parrot. This had come as a considerable shock.

'Yes, eventually.'

For a moment, Kate could think of nothing to say. She sipped her tea. 'Are you *sure* you want to be married?'

'Yeah, of course I'm sure! Why do you ask? I thought you'd be thrilled!'

'Yes, yes, I am!' Kate lied. 'But you haven't known each other very long, have you?'

'Mum,' he said patiently, draining his mug, 'when it's love you *know*. *You* should know that!'

'But perhaps you should go up there to meet her friends first? Perhaps she's got some distant relations somewhere?' Kate knew she was clutching at straws.

'She has no family, Mum. You know that. And I'll meet her friends when we move up there. Why are you acting like this?'

'Acting like what?'

'Acting like you're doubtful about the whole idea. You like Beth, don't you?'

'Yes, but I hardly know her.'

Jack sighed. 'I know she can be a bit reserved at times. She's had a tough life – had to become very self-contained, but I'm sure you'll come to love her.'

Kate was at a loss for words again. She was definitely feeling the need for something stronger than tea.

'What worries me,' she said eventually, 'is that you may be on the rebound. I mean, it's not that long since you broke up with Eva, and you'd been together for quite some time.'

'Eva is history! I never felt for Eva like I feel for Beth. In fact, if Beth hadn't agreed to marry me, I'd probably be on the first plane back to Oz!'

Well, full marks to Beth for that *at least*. 'You're a grown man, Jack, and you must do what you feel is right for you. I must admit I'm over the moon that you've decided to stay in this country...' She hesitated.

'I can feel a "but" coming on?'

'But don't go rushing into marriage, like I did. Like me, you could live to regret it. Take your time. Surely you can live together for a year or two to see how you get on? Couldn't Beth get a hairdressing job down here? It would be so nice to have you nearby.'

'Bristol's near – only a couple of hours up the motorway. Anyway, Beth wants to go back.'

'When will you look for a job?'

'I've already applied to a couple of construction companies to say I could start in October. Beth will finish here towards the end of September, and then we'll take ourselves off for a couple of weeks. Go see Tom and family and stuff like that.'

'Well, I do hope something comes up,' Kate said.

'I'm pretty optimistic. Anyway, I'm off to have a shower now.'

When he'd left, Kate thought longingly for a few minutes of a glass of wine. Woody was due home any time now and they'd normally have a glass or two before dinner, but she wasn't sure she could wait that long.

After a further moment's deliberation, she stood up, got the bottle of Merlot out of the cupboard and poured herself a generous glassful. Then she sat down and mulled over what Jack had told her.

Why was she not feeling elated that Jack had found someone he wanted to marry? After all, she'd been delighted when Tom had introduced Jane into the family. Of course she'd taken to Jane straight away, which helped. It wasn't as if she *didn't* like Beth; she hardly knew the girl. Kate reprimanded herself for being so unfair. And the best thing of all was that Jack was staying in the UK! Bristol wasn't far away at all! He and Beth could even come down for weekends, do some surfing – she could even look after any *babies* they might have! She might even be tempted to swap her sleuthing for knitting baby clothes! She mustn't jump the gun; as usual, her imagination was now running away with her.

Yes, hopefully it would all work out. She and Beth might even become close.

Woody, of course, was a calming influence, as always.

'Jack's not stupid,' he said, 'and if he and Beth are together for a while, then he should be able to suss out if they're OK for each other or not. Particularly if he's as canny as you! Let's face it, it took you a couple of years to realise what a godsend I was!'

Kate laughed. 'Point taken! It's just that... It's just that...'

'You don't like Beth,' Woody supplied.

'I don't *dislike* her,' Kate protested, 'I just hardly know her.'

'Well, make an effort to get to know her then.'

'I seem to remember that you had your reservations about her too,' Kate said.

'I ain't marrying her, you ain't marrying her, so let Jack decide – OK?'

'OK,' Kate replied, resolving there and then to make a bit more effort with Beth.

TWENTY-ONE

Kate, sitting in the kitchen next morning with a mug of coffee, was trying to rationalise her feelings about Jack's plans. She'd been reassured to some extent by Woody, and so decided it was time to put the whole thing to the back of her mind. Instead, she must continue to try to clear her own name, and the only way to do that was to find the killer.

She'd had no further contact with Charlotte, which was a little worrying. She had no idea if she was liable to be hauled back to the police station, or even if she herself was the number one suspect! She wondered briefly if she should inform the detective inspector about Delia's visit to the hairdresser. On the one hand, surely Charlotte would have already checked Delia's movements on the day of Timmy's murder, since Delia was a suspect? And if she, Kate, *didn't* tell Charlotte, would she be impeding the course of justice and all that stuff again? On the other hand, *if* she were to tell Charlotte about Delia's visit to Tinworthy, she would probably have to tell Woody about her most recent visit to Bodmin Moor, leading to more recriminations and more lectures about not getting involved! Either way, it was a no-win situation.

Kate's instinct told her to get on with it herself. It also told her that the only way to pinpoint the killer was to clear all the suspects, one by one.

It was time to get out The List again from the depths of her shoulder-bag, where it now resided. She smoothed out the piece of paper and sat down with it in front of her while she finished her coffee.

Irving was not only top of her list but was also the main suspect. He had reason to hate Sienna because of her affair, and maybe he felt she was making a fool of him, as well as being after his money. He might also have wanted the freedom to marry Sally Brand, his sister-in-law, if indeed they were involved with each other. He'd been with Sienna at the Tinworthy Fair and could well have accompanied her up to Potter's Point. Afterwards, he could have scuttled away down the coastal path, out of sight, or fled back to the fair, hiding behind any gorse bush as necessary. Kate realised she knew very little about Irving Aldridge, and she needed to devise a way to find out more. But where to start?

As regards Timmy's demise, if Irving was in league with Sally Brand, he could have heard from her, via Angie, about the possibility of Timmy being able to identify the killer.

Thanks for passing on that information, Angie – you've given me motives for at least two more suspects! But no bloody solution!

Then there was Sally: Sally's reason for visiting Tinworthy and the fair seemed extremely far-fetched. She'd made no secret of the fact that she hated her sister – but *tailing* her? Just for an article about sisters? She could, of course, have tailed her all the way up to Potter's Point, and then said something like, 'Hiya, darling Sienna!' just as Sienna shouted out in surprise in the split second before she was pushed over the edge. That would make sense. But, more than that, she might have wanted Sienna's *husband*. And because Angie had suggested that Timmy possibly knew who the killer was, that would have given her the motive for paying him a visit with a plastic bag under her arm.

Sally and Irving were definitely the most obvious suspects.

Kate was as certain as she could be that it wasn't Marc Le Grand. Yes, Marc had been furious about Sienna's scathing report on The Atlantic Hotel but – as he admitted himself – it had only affected his business on a temporary basis. Kate couldn't see Marc's fury lasting so long that he'd kill her sometime later. Marc had been at the fair that day and, like Kate herself, had gone to stretch his legs. Had he gone up to the clifftop? Had he seen Sienna standing there? Perhaps the temptation had been too much! Was it the perfect opportunity?

But why would he kill Timmy? How could *he* know that Timmy might have seen the killer? Or perhaps he'd realised that Timmy had seen him as he made his way frantically back down to the fair?

Kate wandered through to the sitting room and gazed out of the window at the sea below. There were some giant waves today and the surfers were out in force, most of them quite unaware that there was a murder inquiry going on. She wished she was one of them.

Her thoughts turned to Delia Moran. Delia had every reason to kill Sienna. There was a definite motive and a great opportunity to kill the woman. Perhaps she'd just *happened* to be making her way along the cliff-top with her dogs on the afternoon of the fair. It might even have been pre-arranged, with Delia making some sort of appointment, using a false name. However, if she was walking with two lively Labradors, surely they would still have been running around somewhere? Or did she walk *without* the dogs?

Delia may have been in Tinworthy at the time of Timmy's murder, but why would *she* want to eliminate Timmy in the first place? Could she have possibly known that *he* knew who the killer was? Bearing in mind how much Delia knew about Timmy, it was surely possible that she could have guessed that Timmy would have been following Sienna around, and so could potentially have seen the killer.

Kate needed to make a plan. She couldn't think how she could justifiably visit Irving Aldridge again if he didn't want any counselling. Even if he changed his mind about that, he'd certainly be looking for a private consultation.

Where did the man go? Did he visit a pub? If he did, it certainly wasn't The Greedy Gull. She and Woody were regulars there and had never seen him. He also spent a lot of time in London on business.

The man was not going to be easy to trace.

Sally Brand, on the other hand, was obliged to stay in The Atlantic Hotel while she remained under suspicion, and Kate felt she had a valid excuse to contact her again by asking when their interview was likely to be published. Then she wondered if Sally could possibly be hand-in-glove with Marc Le Grand. They both hated Sienna, so perhaps they'd planned something between them? Perhaps that was even why Sally was staying there! Why hadn't she thought of *that* before?

Kate was convinced that there was something going on between Sally and Irving. But could the *three* of them have schemed this together – Sally, Irving and Marc? The possibilities were making her head spin!

No nearer any conclusion, Kate decided it was time for another coffee.

At least if she wanted to talk to Delia Moran again, she should have no trouble convincing her to go on an afternoon moorland walk. After all, they were *almost* friends now!

Kate knew that each time you met someone, you got to know a little more about them. They gave little snippets of themselves away without realising it. It was almost an advantage that she, Kate, was a suspect herself so that they were all in the same boat and, hopefully, none of these people would suspect her of studying *them*.

The only thing she was sure about was that whoever had killed Sienna had also killed Timmy. She had a lot of work to do.

But where to start?

TWENTY-TWO

Kate decided there was only one way to know what Irving Aldridge was up to, and that was to tail him – locally, at least. Kate had never tailed anyone in her life, and she could hardly ask Sally Brand for tips on how to go about it.

On Friday, Woody was doing work on his cottage, on the hillside opposite, so it gave her more opportunity to pop in and out without having to explain where she was going. She knew that Woody worried about her and only wanted to protect her, but sometimes it felt a little restrictive.

On previous occasions, when the Hedgefields were still resident at Tremorron, she'd walked Barney on the public land around the Tremorron Estate, which bordered the coastal path. From there, she should be able to see if Irving was at home or not. She'd found an off-road parking spot, bordered by trees, where she could hide her car. Not for the first time, she reckoned she should have bought a green Fiat, or a black one, or a silver one. She should *not* have bought a bright red one but – at the time of purchase – she hadn't been planning any subterfuge.

On the first day of her 'tailing' she didn't see Irving at all, but she did see Sally Brand arrive at around midday in her Renault, and it was still there when Kate decided she could tarry no longer at half past one. Then she had a quick drive round at three o'clock in the afternoon, but Sally's car had gone, and so had Irving's green Jaguar. As she drove back past The Atlantic Hotel, she checked their car park but neither car was there. So where had they gone?

Kate had to admit that her first day's surveillance had been a dismal failure. She realised that she couldn't spend half of her life tramping around Tremorron, so there had to be a better way to do this.

On the second day, she walked Barney early on the beach and up on the cliffs, and then decided to concentrate on The Atlantic Hotel. There was no way to disguise her car there so she hoped that there might be countless red Fiats around and hers wouldn't stand out.

As she strolled along the rows of cars, she saw a dark-green Jaguar and checked the registration against the note she'd made. Yes, it was Irving's. Kate had no idea how long he was likely to be visiting so decided this was a good time to call on Sally, which she'd been planning to do anyway.

When she entered, she found the reception area was very busy, with people checking in and people checking out, and Marc holding court with half a dozen businessmen at the entrance to the restaurant. As usual, he was looking extremely dapper in an immaculate dark suit, white shirt, dark patterned tie and – his trademark apparently – a red rose in his buttonhole.

Kate stood in line for a few minutes before she came face to face with the Danish receptionist again. She still looked cool and immaculate in blonde cashmere which matched her blonde hair and showed off her golden tan.

'I'd like to speak to Mrs Sally Brand please,' Kate said politely.

The receptionist consulted her computer screen. 'Mrs Brand has specifically requested not to be disturbed.' She turned her icy blue stare at Kate.

'Oh.' Conscious of a queue forming behind her, Kate asked, 'Any idea when she might be available?'

'None whatsoever. Sorry.'

Feeling almost chastened, Kate moved away from the desk and caught Marc's eye as she did so. He was now alone and had been heading towards the stairs when he saw her.

'Kate!'

'Oh, hello, Marc. I was hoping to see Sally Brand, but I gather she doesn't wish to be disturbed.'

There followed a good deal of eye-rolling before Marc said, 'Come, have a drink!' He indicated the bar.

'I'm driving, Marc.'

'Well, coffee then?'

Kate followed him into the bar, which was almost empty, apart from Frederick the waiter standing picking his nose behind the counter. He lowered his hand rapidly.

'Espresso, *peut-être*?' asked Marc. 'Or a latte or…'

'An Americano is fine, with some cold milk please,' Kate replied.

Marc fired his orders at Frederick, who promptly headed to the coffee machine. As they sat down by the window, Mark asked, 'Did you have an appointment with Mrs Brand?'

Kate shook her head. 'I only wanted to know when the interview she did with my sister and me was likely to be published. Not important really.'

Marc blew out a long 'eugh', French-style, and then looked round furtively before continuing, 'We are all suspects – *non*?'

'I'm afraid so,' Kate confirmed.

'And do you not think it strange that two suspects should be together so much?'

'I don't know what you mean,' Kate said, knowing perfectly well what he probably did mean.

'I will tell you then.' He sat back while Frederick delivered the coffee. When the waiter was behind the bar again, Marc leaned forward and said, sotto voce, 'Sally Brand and *Irving Aldridge!*' Then he sat back triumphantly to study Kate's reaction.

She decided to be surprised. '*Really?* What do you mean?'

Marc leaned forward again and lowered his voice. 'He is up there right now, in her *room!*'

'I *thought* I saw his car outside,' Kate said, feigning some surprise.

'You did! You did! He is a constant visitor, is Monsieur Aldridge!'

'She is his sister-in-law though,' Kate said.

Marc raised his eyebrows. 'So? Then why do they not sit on one of my beautiful big settees in the reception area, or here, in my bar, to talk about whatever it is they need to talk about? Why must this be in the bedroom, hmm?' He leaned forward again. 'When he is not here, then she is there, at his house.'

Kate wondered how he knew. 'Are you sure about that?'

'Of course. On two occasions I follow her. She is there almost every night, so why does she have a room in my hotel, eh?'

'I don't know,' Kate admitted.

'Well, *I* do! This is because she wants us to think that they are *not* together. And do you know why?'

Kate shook her head.

'Because together they pushed Sienna Stone over that cliff!' He sat back, satisfied.

'That's an interesting theory, Marc,' said Kate.

He tapped his nose. 'It is the truth! *Mon dieu*, it is so obvious! They wanted rid of her so that they can be together!'

'But if you know what they're up to, then surely everyone else does too? Have you told the police?'

'Of course! When they come to interview me – which they do, Kate, they *do* – then I tell them. But no arrests are made yet, so what would *you* do?'

'I don't know.' Kate drained her coffee. 'What about Timmy Thomson though?'

Marc shrugged. '*Je ne sais pas!* He was a stalker, *non*? So, he follows her everywhere, so perhaps he saw them doing it? Perhaps he was blackmailing them, *non*?'

'Possible, I suppose,' Kate said, realising as she spoke that it was indeed *entirely* possible and something which she hadn't even considered. Time to change the subject. 'How is *your* lady friend? I haven't seen her lately.'

'Ah, Jodi is with her son in Brighton because he is having problems with his boyfriend. But she will be back next week.'

Kate recalled a short blonde woman with blue eyeshadow and a forest of false eyelashes. 'Oh, good. Well, I must go now, Marc, but I've enjoyed our chat, and thanks so much for the coffee.'

Marc accompanied her to the door. 'Do not doubt me, Kate. These two are the killers! So, how long must you and I be suspects?'

'I understand you were at The Atlantic today,' Woody said casually as they sat outside on the patio, watching the holiday-makers down on the beach.

'How did you know that?' Kate asked.

'Oh, Charlotte mentioned it.'

Kate could feel her hackles rising. *Charlotte! Always bloody Charlotte!* 'What's it got to do with Charlotte?' *And why did she tell you?*

'Calm down, my love!' Woody patted her hand. 'It's got

everything to do with Charlotte because she and her team have to try to solve this thing. They can't follow each suspect's every move, because they haven't got enough staff. But they do notice when four out of the five remaining suspects are all under one roof. Your car was in The Atlantic car park, as was Irving Aldridge's, Sally Brand's and, of course, Marc Le Grand's.'

Kate sighed. She should have known they'd be keeping tabs on everyone. 'I only went to ask Sally when the interview with Angie and me was likely to be published.' That wasn't *strictly* true, but she could hardly admit to her futile attempt at trying to tail Irving. And she did plan, at some point, to ask Sally about the interview.

'I was told that she was not to be disturbed,' Kate added. She decided not to mention Marc and his theory. 'Irving's green Jaguar was outside, so where was he if he wasn't with Sally? So, as we suspected, something is going on there.'

'Kate, I only want you to be safe,' Woody said, 'and, like it or not, you are still a suspect as far as the police are concerned, so you must be careful about where you go and who you associate with.'

'Does that mean I'm supposed to stay at home and my every move will be monitored?' Kate asked angrily.

'No, but it's probably not advisable to mix with the other suspects. Purely from a police point of view, Sienna's murder *could* have been a joint effort. All of you had reason to hate Sienna, so you could have schemed it together.'

Kate gasped.

'*Purely* from a police point of view,' he reiterated. 'They have to be neutral. You know that.'

Before Kate had time to digest this comment – which echoed more or less what Marc had suggested earlier – Beth's little car pulled up and out she got with Jack.

'Woody, could you have a quick look at Beth's Micra?' Jack asked when the pair of them came over. 'It keeps stalling, and she has to get it back in the next couple of hours because one of the other girls wants to use it later.'

As Woody got to his feet, he squeezed Kate's shoulder, and said, 'While I'm looking at the car, why don't you two ladies have a nice cup of tea and get to know each other better?'

TWENTY-THREE

The 'two ladies' smiled awkwardly at each other as the men made their way across to look at Beth's ailing vehicle.

'Well, we'd better do as we're told then,' Kate said brightly. 'Let's go into the kitchen. Is tea OK for you or would you prefer coffee – or something stronger?'

'Tea's fine,' Beth replied, following her through the door. 'No milk or sugar though.'

Kate studied her slim frame. 'I take it you're not dieting? You certainly don't need to.'

Beth shook her head. 'No, I've never taken milk or sugar in either tea or coffee.'

There was a silence as Kate switched on the kettle and got out the cups. Then, to break the ice, she asked, 'How's the caravan cleaning going?'

Beth sighed loudly. 'I'm really sick of it. You wouldn't believe the state some of these people leave their vans in – absolutely disgusting! Makes you wonder what their homes must be like.'

'How horrible for you!' Kate said.

'And you should see the state of the toilets!'

'Spare me the details,' Kate said, handing Beth a cup of tea. 'I imagine you'll be very glad to get back to hairdressing.'

'I will.' Beth sipped her tea. 'At least I've learned to surf, and Jack has been great.' She glanced at Kate out of the corner of her eye.

'I gather you'll be going back to Bristol and that Jack is looking for work there too?' She studied Beth's pretty little face and lustrous dark hair, and wondered again what it was about this girl that worried her.

'Yes, we want to be together,' Beth said.

'You don't fancy working for a hairdresser down here?' *It's worth a try.*

'No,' said Beth, 'I want to go home.'

'Yes, Bristol's a great city,' Kate agreed, 'although I gather your life there has been pretty mixed?'

'I've had some rough times, but that's hardly Bristol's fault, is it?'

'No, I guess not.' Kate sipped her tea thoughtfully. 'It's just sad that you have no relatives there.'

'I've no relatives *anywhere at all*,' Beth replied sharply. 'Not one.'

'That's such a shame, Beth. Did your mum have no family?'

'No,' Beth replied. 'She was an only child and her parents died before she had me.'

Kate didn't dare ask about her father.

'You must be curious about my father,' Beth said, looking Kate straight in the eye, 'because, if you're not, *I* am!' She gave a little snort. 'I haven't the faintest idea who he was.'

'That's a pity,' Kate said sincerely. 'I take it your mum was single then?'

'Yeah, she was. She had me when she was seventeen, and she was only twenty when she was killed.'

'Oh, I'm *so* sorry. She was just a girl; what a tragedy! A road accident, I believe?'

'Yes. I was strapped in the back.'

'How awful for you!' Kate was beginning to feel increasingly ashamed for ever having doubts about this poor girl.

'I was taken into care of course.'

'What was that like?' Kate asked tentatively.

'Sometimes it was OK, sometimes it wasn't. I don't really want to talk about it...' Beth sniffed and stared out of the window.

'Of course not,' Kate soothed, 'and I didn't mean to pry. I'm just glad that you've found some happiness now.'

Beth's face lit up. 'Jack's wonderful. I can't wait for us to find a flat together.'

'I gather you're going to be able to go back to your old job?'

'Yes, because – believe it or not – an Australian girl has been working there in my place for most of the summer, and now she's moving on. So Australia has done me a favour in more ways than one!'

'Well, Beth, it's done me a great favour too, because I was hoping Jack wouldn't go back to Australia. I know that probably sounds selfish. He had a good life out there, but when you're a mother...' Kate's voice tailed off. She was now becoming quite nervous at uttering the very word 'mother'.

'Yes, I can imagine,' said Beth. 'Of course there's a strong possibility that we'll *both* go there eventually. I mean, he's already a sort of Australian citizen, isn't he? And I'm sure I could get a job there easily. It must be wonderful to be warm all the time, and to have all that Pacific surf on your doorstep! What's not to like?'

Before Kate had time to recover from this, the door opened and Woody and Jack came in, both smiling from ear to ear.

'Woody's fixed your car, Beth!' Jack said triumphantly.

'Couldn't have done it without your help,' Woody added. 'There's no denying we're a good team! How are you two getting on? Any tea going?'

. . .

'I honestly don't dislike her at all,' Kate said to Woody as they drank their after-dinner coffees.

Woody studied her for a moment. 'But you don't like her either,' he said.

'I didn't say that.'

'You didn't need to.'

'Now you're making me feel guilty! And you said much the same thing after that first lunch we had. The poor girl's had a tough life, and has obviously always had to look out for herself. And now she thinks she's found love, so how could I deny her that?' Kate sighed. 'It's just that I can't for the life of me imagine her as my daughter-in-law.'

'Well, don't imagine it then! They're not married yet and – let's face it – they're not all going to be as delightful as Tom's wife.'

'I know you're right,' Kate conceded, 'and I also know that daughters-in-law can be tricky. Just look at Angie and Ingrid; they can't stand each other!'

'Well, that's Angie for you! I'm quite sure that if Jack and Beth do get round to marriage, you'll be a very nice, caring mother-in-law! My advice is to stop worrying about things that might never happen. Anyhow, let's have a nice, quiet rest of the weekend with no mention of marriage or murder!'

TWENTY-FOUR

Kate was back in the surgery on Monday when a familiar-looking woman came into her consulting room mid-morning, sporting a badly concealed black eye. Nevertheless, the woman had plastered blue eyeshadow over her swollen eyelid and set it all off with a generous helping of false eyelashes. She had come for her diabetes check.

'It's Jodi, isn't it?' Kate asked. 'Marc's friend?' She had only met Jodi a couple of times at social events, but she was easily recognisable by the make-up.

'Yeah, and you're Kate. I *asked* for you.'

'Have you brought your urine sample?'

Jodi rummaged in her bag. 'Here it is – looks like a nice drop of champers, don't it!'

Kate refrained from commenting as she stuck a label on the bottle.

'Yeah, I've been up in Brighton,' Jodi went on, 'and only got back Saturday night. Would you believe my son's partner's buggered off and left my poor Roland heartbroken! *Heartbroken*, I can tell you! Terrible business!'

'Yes, I'm sure it was. And I can see you've been in the wars;

how did you manage to get that eye?' Kate asked.

Jodi sniffed loudly. 'Well, I didn't walk into no door, cos that's what everyone says, innit? I'll leave it to your imagination!'

'So, someone hit you? Not your son surely?'

'No, my Roly would never do that. It's just that Marc's got this bloody foul temper.'

'*Marc?*'

'Yeah, it's just the way he is. See, I was a bit late gettin' back Saturday and I suppose we had too much to drink, so we argued a bit. You *know* how it is.'

Kate did not know how it was and thanked her lucky stars for having such a placid relationship with Woody because she was aware that she must drive him crazy sometimes. He was always calm; firm but calm.

'Oh, Jodi, that's awful. I had no idea Marc was like that.'

'No, no, he didn't hit me or nothin'. But when he gets mad, he *throws* things! Can't stop himself. I can't tell you the number of glasses and things he's chucked at the wall. Makes him feel better, he says. Anyway, I just got in the wrong place this time and I got in the way of him chuckin' the TV controller at the wall! I'm only tellin' you this cos you know him well, but don't go tellin' him I told you!'

'I won't, but maybe you should report him for violent behaviour?'

'No *way*! He's just hot-tempered, and I like a man with a bit of oomph, you know? And he gets ever so sorry afterwards. I expect it's his Latin blood, cos the Latins flare up easy, don't they? You know he's half-French?'

Kate was none too sure that being half-French qualified as Latin. 'So I believe,' she said. 'Did you know his mother?'

'Oh no, cos she lived down in France somewhere and she died when he was tiny, so he came back to England to his dad. His dad was in Essex, see, just like me. Anyway, both me and

Marc was married before so we've only been together for about three years. No, wait, I tell a lie – it must be nearly four.'

'You should know him well then,' Kate said, producing a syringe. 'I'm going to take a blood sample now.'

'OK. It's just that he's that stressed, what with all this murder business.' Jodi held out her arm. 'See, I went and asked him if he'd got anything to do with it.'

'Presumably he didn't like that?'

'No, he bloody well didn't – he went ballistic! I mean, I *know* he's a suspect for that Sienna woman, but I never thought for a minute that he done it. But he was out for a couple of hours in the morning before I left, the day that Timmy bloke got himself killed. So that's all I asked him: where had he been?'

'Where *had* he been?' Kate asked, withdrawing the needle from Jodi's arm.

'Well, he wouldn't tell me and that's when he come over a bit angry.'

'Surely if he had a valid reason for being out, he would have told you?' Kate asked.

'Just wot *I* said! Then he says the reason he's mad at me is cos I don't *trust* him. He says it don't matter where he went, because I shouldn't be doubtin' him. But that don't make sense to me...'

'I can understand how you feel. Let me have a look at your face.'

'No, don't worry, it's OK, and God bless Max Factor! See, I've got one of them pan stick things from years back and it's proved bloody useful since me and Marc got together, I can tell you!'

'Does Marc throw stuff around often?' Kate asked as casually as she could.

Jodi shook her head. 'Not often, just now and again. Now, you won't go tellin' anyone wot I just told you, will you?'

'No, of course not,' Kate said. She burrowed in the drawer

of her desk and withdrew a leaflet on domestic abuse. 'Perhaps you'd like to read this? In any case, you know where I live, and I'm there if you ever feel the need to talk, Jodi.'

Jodi nodded. 'Thank you.'

Kate had all but eliminated Marc Le Grand from The List, but now she put him back there, near the top. Could that be why he was so keen to pin the blame on Sally and Irving? To cover up his own movements? Where had he been for the couple of hours on the day Timmy was killed? If he was innocent, why wouldn't he tell Jodi? There were so many unanswered questions.

Kate knew *she* hadn't killed anyone, and presumably neither had Timmy. That left four suspects, and she didn't have the faintest idea which of them might be guilty. She'd always reckoned she was a good judge of character and – up to now – she'd almost always been proved right.

But she couldn't make head nor tail of this lot.

When, on Tuesday, Kate called in at The Old Locker for her after-work drink, she found Fergal on his own and looking most unhappy.

'Where's Angie?' she asked.

Fergal rolled his eyes. 'Don't ask! She won't fecking well come down and I was rushed off my feet at lunchtime!'

'Is she not well?' Kate asked anxiously.

'Nothing wrong with her, just her hair.'

'Her *hair*?'

'She's been colouring it with God-knows-what and it's gone pink.'

'*Pink?*'

'Pink. Why don't you go up and try to talk some sense into

her? Tell her I'm going to be rushed off my feet this evening if she doesn't get her arse down here, *pronto!*'

Kate suppressed a smile, wondering what on earth her sister had done now. There was nothing for it but to venture upstairs.

She was halfway up when she heard a bad-tempered voice shout out, 'Who *is* it?'

'It's only me,' Kate replied as she reached the top landing. 'I'm told you have a problem?' She pushed open the door to their small living room to find Angie sitting at the table with an array of bottles in front of her. Angie's hair was pink. Very, very pink. Magenta, in fact.

'What on earth have you done?' Kate was trying hard not to laugh.

Angie scowled. 'It's all Guy's fault. Last time I was there, I asked for my usual "Bermuda Blonde", but it came out really pale, more silver than blond. I'm damn sure he didn't use "Bermuda Blonde". I've been really unhappy with it for about ten days.'

'So why didn't you go back and ask him to do it again?' Kate asked.

'Time, Kate! My *time* is precious, and my hard-earned *money* is precious, so I thought I'd sort it out myself.'

'And you decided on *pink*?'

'Of course I didn't decide on pink! Don't be so bloody sarcastic! No, I did it last night with one of those home-colouring kits, but it's nothing like the colour on the box, and I'm going to *complain!*' She thrust the box at Kate. 'Look at that!'

Kate studied the picture on the box of the pouting blonde with her ultra-shiny deep golden mane and the caption 'Biarritz Beauty', underneath which was written 'Glorious Blonde with Copper Highlights'.

'Looks like you might have overdone the copper highlights,' Kate said with a grin.

'It's not funny. I'm going to sue them for a false description of the product. That model's hair doesn't look anything like mine, does it?'

Kate had to admit that it didn't. 'Let's see the instructions.'

'Oh, I don't bother with *instructions*. I expect they're around somewhere, probably still in the box.'

Kate fished around in the box and discovered that was exactly where they were. 'It says here to apply Tube A to dry hair, leave on for fifteen minutes, and then use Tube B to wash it off. Did you do that?'

Angie snorted. 'I *told* you. I never bother with instructions, and they never tell you to leave it on for long enough anyway.'

'So how long did you leave the dye on for?'

Angie shrugged. 'I don't know; maybe half an hour, forty minutes.'

'*Honestly*, Angie! You'll wreck your hair!'

'Well, it's too late now. What am I going to *do*? I can't go down to the bar and face everyone looking like this!'

'I think there's stuff you can buy that's supposed to remove hair colour,' Kate said, 'but I don't know what it's called. Why don't you phone Guy and ask his advice, or see if you can get an emergency appointment?'

'He'll think I'm nuts because it's only ten days or so since it was done – the day the stalker was murdered, and I told him it was fine. I shouldn't have said that because it wasn't fine at all.'

'You had your hair done the day Timmy Thomson was murdered?'

'Yes, what's wrong with that?'

'Angie, what time was your appointment?'

Angie thought for a moment. 'Half past eleven, and I didn't come out until gone one. Fergal was going mad.'

'You wouldn't know if there was a lady called Delia Moran in there, do you?'

'Of course I knew! Guy was quite excited because she's the

wife of the director of *SeeVue* – Sienna Stone's programme – the guy Sienna was supposed to be having an affair with. Anyway, Guy told me she's living somewhere up on the moor now and she was having a cut and a colour. She was in there *ages* too, because she was there before me.'

'That's interesting,' Kate said. 'I don't suppose you have an idea what time *she* left?'

'She went out just before me, probably one o'clock. She looked very glamorous. Why do you ask?'

'Oh,' Kate said airily, 'only because I met her when I was walking the dog, and she admired my hair. I recommended Guy.'

'Well, she took your advice then. Now, what am I supposed to do about this hair, Kate?'

'I did read somewhere that you can use washing-up liquid to remove hair dye, but I don't know how true that is, and I don't suppose it's very good for your hair. But if you're desperate—'

'I'm desperate,' Angie confirmed, heading towards the kitchen sink.

Just at that moment, Fergal hollered up the stairs, 'When do you plan to come down, Angela? It's getting fecking busy down here!'

'Time I was off,' Kate said, glad to make her escape. 'Good luck with the hair! And be sure to use plenty of conditioner.'

When Kate got home, she found Woody in the kitchen, in his striped apron, dicing up vegetables for a curry.

'Nice healthy recipe this,' he assured her, planting a kiss on her lips. 'Got it on the internet.'

'Sorry I'm a little late,' Kate said, 'I stopped off at The Locker for a drink but never actually got one.'

'Doesn't she love you anymore?'

'Angie was sulking upstairs and looking like a large pink

chrysanthemum.'

'What's she done now?'

Kate told him. 'I've left her brandishing a bottle of washing-up liquid. How's your day been?'

'Yeah, good. I've been over to see the new tenants, and they seem OK. While I was there, old Mrs Crow next door gave me a load of vegetables: peppers, tomatoes, potatoes, courgettes. Says she can't use them all, so I thought I'd do us a curry. Get yourself a drink, then go sit down and relax. Watch the news or something.'

'Thank you, my love, I will. My feet are aching.' Kate poured herself a large glass of Merlot, settled herself on the sitting-room sofa and kicked off her shoes. She picked up the remote and switched on the television, but her thoughts were very much elsewhere...

Delia Moran had been in the hairdresser's before Angie got there at eleven thirty, and had left just after one o'clock. Kate knew Timmy had been killed sometime before she herself had arrived at Parson's Court around quarter past one. If Delia *had* done the deed, she must have done it before her appointment with Guy. She tried to remember the estimated time of Timmy's death. She didn't want to ask Woody because he'd want to know why *she* wanted to know and – to all intents and purposes – she was no longer involved with this case. Well, as far as Woody was concerned anyway.

She'd double-check with Guy the time of Delia's appointment and try to figure out a way to find out the time of Timmy's death. However, it was extremely unlikely that Delia had gone to Parson's Court, bashed Timmy on the head with something-or-other – probably a saucepan – tied a plastic bag over his head and then sauntered back to Guys 'n' Dolls for her hairdo. No doubt she'd been thoroughly questioned by Charlotte anyway.

Kate took a large gulp of her wine and turned up the volume on the TV. She needed the distraction.

TWENTY-FIVE

This week, Kate was doing an extra shift on Friday morning, and Denise was about to go on holiday. 'Last day, thank God!' she greeted Kate and Sue cheerfully when they arrived for work. 'This time tomorrow I'll be on that plane, gin and tonic in my little paw, heading towards Santorini – yippee! All those lovely Greeks!'

Denise and her friend, Myra, went on a husband-hunt for two weeks every summer, and had apparently exhausted Spain and Italy without success, although they'd gained considerable expertise on Latin lovers in the process.

'And,' she added, waving her arms around, 'this place will go *haywire*! Make you appreciate me when I get back!'

Kate groaned; Denise was right. A temporary replacement was brought in each year and, generally, chaos ensued. Appointments were mixed up, filing didn't get done and angry patients usually took out their wrath on the nurses. Kate was very relieved she wouldn't be working more than two days next week.

The morning was predictable, until just after eleven o'clock when an old man, leaning heavily on a walking stick, hobbled into Kate's treatment room. He looked at her with rheumy eyes.

Kate recognised him instantly. 'It's Sidney, isn't it?' She picked up his notes and saw that they said Ernest S. Bird. 'So it says Ernest on your notes?'

He peered at her again for a moment before plonking himself down on a chair. 'I never liked that name. You be that nurse wot came up when Timmy were killed?'

'That's me,' Kate confirmed. 'How are you, Sidney?'

'I been better, I can tell you. Can't sleep a wink.'

'I'm sorry to hear that. Is that why you're here?'

Sidney directed his gaze to the window. 'I can't get it out of me head, see. I'm just noddin' off to sleep and I see 'im again, like *that*. Horrible it is.' He shuddered.

'Let's try a mild sedative,' Kate said, feeling sorry for the poor man, 'to help you relax.'

Sidney continued staring out of the window. ''E were right next door, you know, just through the bleedin' wall. How could someone do that to Timmy and me not hear it?'

'If they took him by surprise then he wouldn't have had time to yell out or anything,' Kate said. 'Try not to think about it.'

Sidney, however, was now in full flow. 'Everyone thought 'im funny, you know, cos he were mad about that Senna woman – what was 'er name again?'

Kate was tempted to say 'Senna Pod'. 'Sienna Stone,' she supplied.

'But Timmy were OK really. 'E used to come in for a cuppa or a can of cider sometimes. I think 'e got lonely, did Timmy. Funny enough, I saw 'im in the corridor, comin' back from somewhere or another, about twelve o'clock, and an hour later, 'e were dead. *Dead!* Don't bear thinkin' about.'

Kate, who'd been writing the prescription, dropped her pen. 'You saw him *alive* at twelve o'clock – noon?'

'Oh yes, cos 'e said to come in for a cuppa after I'd had me dinner. I always have me dinner at half past twelve, see, every single day.'

Kate handed him the prescription. 'So, presumably, you went in for your cuppa?'

He gave her an odd look. *"Course* I did! That's when I found 'im.'

'So he was alive at twelve and dead an hour later at one?'

'That's wot I keep tellin' everyone! That police lady keep askin' me, over and over.'

'So someone killed him during that hour...'

'While I were 'avin' me dinner! I were in the kitchen, see, cookin' me chop and chips, so maybe that's why I never heard nothin'. It were a lovely chop too, but I lost it all after I seen Timmy...' He clutched his stomach at the memory.

Kate felt sorry for the poor old fellow. 'Take these pills, Sidney,' she said, 'and try not to think about it. The memory will eventually fade, you know. Promise me you'll come back if you still feel bad and can't sleep? Give it a couple of weeks. We can get the doctor to prescribe something stronger if necessary.'

Sidney got up slowly, having stuffed the prescription in his pocket. 'I can't never forget it,' he said, leaning on his stick again, 'and now none of us is safe in our beds, are we? Even in broad bloody daylight! So them police is everywhere now, but what 'appens when they go, eh? Tell me that!'

Kate had some difficulty concentrating for the remainder of her shift and was very relieved to get home at about five o'clock. Woody was out somewhere and she sat down with a large mug of tea, glad to be on her own for a little.

She got out The List. Whoever it was that had killed Timmy Thomson, it was certainly not Delia Moran. Kate drew a line through her name. The police, of course, would be well aware of this.

That left Irving, Sally and Marc; one of them, or two of them together. Or even the trio in league? No, surely that couldn't be possible. Or perhaps it was none of them at all? She had no gut instinct that pointed to any one of them. She'd let her own suspicions be guided by the police list of suspects. But how many people had been walking the coastal path on the day of Sienna's murder, or had been in the area, quite apart from anyone at the fair? Someone from Sienna's dubious past could have been lurking around up there – and had possibly arranged to meet her! The more Kate thought about it, the more likely she thought that to be.

Kate began to have serious doubts that she'd ever be able to solve this one. It was not at all like her other cases and was beginning to give her a real headache, not least because the other suspects were slowly being eliminated and so it was possible that the police might still be considering *her* as suspect. For once, she did *not* envy Charlotte Martin.

TWENTY-SIX

The last place Kate expected to find Sally Brand was on Lower Tinworthy beach.

Saturday morning had dawned warm and sunny. Woody had gone off to look at an allotment that was available in Higher Tinworthy, having recently developed a passion for growing his own vegetables.

'In the States, we'd call this a community garden,' Woody informed her, 'which I think is a nicer name than allotment.'

The Lavender Cottage garden wasn't big enough, and it was on a slope so did not conform to Woody's exacting standards. The house was now full of grow-your-own-vegetables books and seed catalogues – all that was missing was a large level patch of ground. Kate was relieved that he'd found something to do now that he'd finished the repairs at On the Up, and it would be wonderful to have fresh, home-grown vegetables.

She fixed the lead onto Barney's collar, and they set off down to the village and on to the beach. At the far end of the beach were the rocks where she liked to sit and where, over the years, she'd met some interesting people. Not so long ago she'd met Timmy Thomson at this very spot.

Today, as she flung a stick for Barney to retrieve, she could make out, in the distance, a woman, sitting on 'her' rock. As she got closer, she thought it looked like Sally Brand and, when she got closer still, she realised it was indeed her. Sally appeared to be gazing out to sea in some sort of trance.

Kate cleared her throat. 'Good morning, Sally!'

With a visible jump, Sally emerged from her reverie. 'Kate!'

'Sorry if I gave you a fright,' Kate said.

'No, no, that's OK. I just find it comforting to sit here,' Sally said. 'There's something very soothing about the sounds of the sea.'

'There is,' Kate agreed. 'I come here often myself for that very reason. It puts everything into perspective, doesn't it?'

'It does.' Sally continued gazing at the ocean. 'Long before we existed, and long after we've gone, that sea will continue to crash or lap onto the shore, depending on its mood.' She paused and laughed. 'Get me! I'll be writing poetry next!'

'Well, why don't you?' Kate asked as she hurled the stick again for Barney before sitting down on the rock opposite.

'Maybe I will sometime. For now I'll stay with journalism.'

'Talking of which,' Kate said, 'I tried to call on you a few days ago to ask you about the interview and when it might be published, but you were not to be disturbed.'

'Oh, right,' Sally said dismissively. 'I'm not sure of the publication date yet but it looks like it might be November at the earliest. I promise to let you know.'

Kate tried to think of a way to get Sally back to the subject of not being disturbed. She joined her in gazing at the sea for a moment before she decided to take the bull by the horns. 'Sally, what's going on with you and Irving?'

Sally seemed to be taken aback at this. Her eyes widened and she stared hard at Kate. 'I've no idea what you mean.'

'I think you do,' Kate said.

'You've got it wrong,' Sally said, looking down at her shoes and brushing off some grains of sand. 'We've only been making funeral arrangements and things like that.' She looked up and stared at Kate again. 'What business is it of yours anyway? I've already told the police everything they need to know.'

'I seem to remember that you came to my house, Sally, for the express purpose of finding out who might have killed your sister, and you thought I might be able to help. Well, I've been doing my damnedest to find out who *didn't* kill her, and half of the original suspects have been eliminated one way or the other. But when I see you and Irving together, I can't help but be suspicious.' Kate was about to say more when she noticed tears streaming down Sally's face.

Nothing was said for several minutes before Sally, in a strangled voice, said, 'You don't understand! There's absolutely no way I would have killed her!'

'Why not? You said yourself that you hated her.'

'I know,' Sally said, rummaging in her bag for some tissues. She blew her nose lustily. 'I did hate her, but I didn't want her dead, and do you want to know why?'

Kate did indeed want to know why. 'Tell me.'

Sally sighed. 'It's a long story, but it began shortly after Sheila – sorry, I mean, Sienna – married Irving. I was overseas at the time of the wedding so I'd never met Irving and, when I came back, they'd only been married for a few months. They asked me to come to stay with them, which I did, and that's when I met Irving for the first time.' She paused. 'We fell in love with each other instantly, Kate, just like that! It was *unbelievable*! Even at this early stage, Irving realised that he shouldn't have married Sienna, and that she was mostly interested in his money. And *I* realised that I'd met the love of my life!'

Kate was agog. 'My God, what did you do?'

'We didn't do anything then, but we got together each time he went up to London on business. This went on for some years before Irving decided he didn't want to live like that anymore, and he was going to divorce Sienna and marry me. He knew, of course, about her affair with Roger Moran, so he had grounds for divorce anyway.'

'Did Sienna know?'

'No, not at all. She didn't want a divorce because she was enjoying Irving's money, so we were going to give her a *big* surprise!'

'But surely you and Irving had a prime motive for killing her then?'

'Oh, we did. But I told Irving, the last thing I wanted was for her to be dead, because I wanted her to know that I'd got her man! I couldn't wait to see her face! After all the years of her lording it over me, I'd finally got my revenge!'

Kate took a moment or two to digest this. 'I can understand how you might have felt,' she said, 'but what about Irving?'

'No,' Sally said very firmly after blowing her nose again. 'It wasn't Irving who killed her.'

'How do you know that?'

'Because he has an alibi,' Sally replied tersely.

'And the police are aware of that?'

'No, they're not!' Sally snapped.

'Why not, for heaven's sake!'

'I can't tell you, Kate, for sensitive reasons. I'm sorry, but that's *it*.' She set her lips in a firm line, stood up and slung her bag over her shoulder. 'I've already said far too much. Just believe me though – it wasn't Irving or me.' With that, she walked away, leaving Kate in a state of utter confusion.

After a minute, Kate stood up, threw the stick for Barney again and began to wander slowly back along the beach.

When she got home, Kate sat down with a coffee and a buttered scone. She felt guilty about the butter, but it wasn't as bad as the

Cornish clotted cream and jam that normally accompanied it. She had to think about her figure.

Kate got out The List. She was very tempted to draw a line through Sally Brand because she honestly reckoned that Sally had been telling the truth. But what about Irving? What alibi did *he* have? And why was Sally so certain of it? Why had he not produced this alibi for the police? What did Sally mean by 'sensitive reasons'?

Assuming that Sally might be out of the equation, that left Irving, in his tricky situation between the two sisters, and Marc, who was fond of chucking stuff around the room.

Perhaps Woody might have some ideas. She felt she could tell him about meeting Sally because it wasn't at all pre-planned, and it was a very interesting story. And Jodi's visit to the surgery was equally unplanned and interesting.

Life was certainly stranger than fiction at times.

Shortly afterwards, Woody came home, elated. 'We've got 150 square metres of mud, stones and weeds,' he said cheerfully. 'The old boy who had it died recently, but he hadn't been near it for a couple of years. So I've got some work to do, and it's sure going to keep me busy. Anyway, how's your day been?'

'You'll never guess who I met when I took Barney down to the beach this morning?'

Woody raised an eyebrow. 'Daniel Craig?'

'Unfortunately not. Sally Brand.'

'So what was she doing down there?' Woody asked, digging out one of his seed catalogues.

'Enjoying the sound of the sea and being very chatty,' Kate replied.

Woody sat down with his catalogue. 'So what was she chatting about? The weather? The menopause?'

'No, we didn't get round to that. She opened up about Irving; they're in love apparently.'

Woody snorted. 'Well, we guessed something was going on there, but *lust* more like.'

'No, it would appear to be love. She didn't set eyes on Irving until he and Sienna had been married for some months, because she'd been living overseas. She didn't say where. By that time, he'd cottoned on to the fact that Sienna had only married him for his money.'

'For a supposedly successful businessman, he wasn't exactly quick on the uptake, was he?'

Kate ignored the comment. 'So when Sally and Irving met, they fell for each other straight away and had illicit meetings in London when he was up there on business. But lately he'd decided he was going to divorce Sienna and marry Sally.'

'Therefore, bumping her off would cost him a helluva lot less than divorcing her surely?'

'Woody, you can be very cynical at times!'

'It was the nature of the job, my love. So what else did she have to say?'

'She said two very interesting things. Firstly, there was no way *she'd* have killed Sienna because she couldn't wait to see Sienna's face when she realised that Sally had stolen her man! Don't forget Sienna had been stealing her thunder for years.'

Woody laid down his catalogue. 'And you believed her?'

'I like to give people the benefit of the doubt, *and* it made sense. Then I suggested that Irving might be the killer and she said absolutely *not*, and that he had an alibi to prove it.'

'So what's the alibi? The police will be checking it out anyway.'

'That's just the thing,' Kate said triumphantly. 'They haven't told the police about the alibi because it's a "sensitive issue" – her words, not mine.'

'Kate, just sometimes I cannot believe how gullible you are!

A sensitive issue!' He held out his leg. 'Pull the other one! Now, what do you say to carrots and parsnips for a start? We could be eating them *all* winter.'

'Yes, fine,' Kate replied absently, her mind elsewhere. What on earth was a sensitive issue? What could possibly be so sensitive that you couldn't produce it as an alibi?

TWENTY-SEVEN

At Woody's insistence Kate had taken the day off work on Monday, 16 August, to celebrate her birthday. It hardly seemed like a year ago since she'd celebrated her sixtieth, and now here she was, sixty-one!

Woody drove her to Boscastle where they had a walk up the beautiful Valency valley, followed by a pub lunch. In the evening, they dined at their favourite restaurant, The Edge of the Moor. Unlike last year, when he'd laid on a surprise party, this time it was just the two of them.

'I'd like you to buy yourself a nice dress or something,' Woody said, holding her hand across the table, 'because I haven't a clue what you might like. Perhaps something special, in case we get invited to something-or-other?'

'How lovely!' Kate said, knowing full well they rarely got invited to anything special. She'd probably spend the money on some decent jeans but decided not to say so. Nobody did much dressing-up in Tinworthy and, if they did, her green dress was perfectly fine. But it was the thought that counted, and for now she was happy to enjoy spending the evening with her lovely husband.

. . .

When Kate arrived at work the following day, she was waylaid in the corridor by Andrew Ross. 'Can I have a word, Kate?'

'Yes, of course,' Kate replied, following him into his office and wondering what she might have done or not done.

He sat down behind his desk and indicated the chair opposite. 'Have a seat, Kate, while I try to find what I'm looking for.'

Andrew was an excellent doctor but notoriously untidy. His desk, as usual, resembled a disaster area. While he shuffled about amid layers of documents, Kate studied the framed photographs of his wife and sons, all lined up and wearing kilts. Andrew never forgot his Scottish roots and took the family back up home to Perthshire every September for three weeks.

'Ah, here we are!' He'd unearthed a pamphlet which he was studying over the top of his spectacles, before passing it across the desk to Kate.

The heading was 'HHH' which underneath was explained as 'Help, Health and Harmony' but before Kate could begin to read what it was all about, Andrew said, 'They do bereavement counselling courses, you see. Now, I know that you've done some psychiatric and counselling courses in the past, which I'm sure has been useful since you came down here.'

'Occasionally,' Kate said. Some of what she'd learned had, in fact, helped her through some of her sleuthing, rather than being of benefit to the community. She glanced down at the brochure. 'Looks interesting, Andrew.'

'Now, they're offering four-day bereavement counselling courses, and I wondered if you'd be interested? I know you already have some knowledge, but apparently these courses are really state of the art and full of new treatments and ideas.'

'Hmm,' said Kate.

'We could spare you for the first week in September. The courses for the South-West take place in Bristol. All expenses paid. Now, they've notified me that they have a cancellation for the course beginning Tuesday, 31 August, right after the Bank Holiday weekend, and I realise that's rather short notice, but I think it might be a very beneficial extra qualification for you to have.'

'I'll certainly think about it,' Kate said.

'Good. So why don't you go home tonight and talk it through with your husband and family and let me know if *they* can spare you for a few days. It's less than a couple of weeks away, so let me know as soon as possible.'

Kate stood up. 'Thanks, Andrew. I'll talk it out with them and come back to you on it. But I would rather like to do it.'

Andrew was shuffling papers around again. 'I'll be glad when Denise gets back from holiday,' he said, 'because that agency girl's no damn good at filing!'

Kate could never recall seeing him with a tidy desk with everything filed away, even with the ministrations of the much-missed Denise, but decided not to mention it.

It would be an interesting course, she thought, as she made her way back to her treatment room. She fancied Bristol. Perhaps Jack might even have found a job up there by September! If she had enough time, she might even check out the hairdresser where Beth had worked before she came to Cornwall and where, apparently, she would be working again.

Then a thought occurred to her. Where did Beth live in Bristol? She'd never asked. Did she share a flat with other girls? Did she have a place of her own? Maybe she would have registered here at the medical centre when she first arrived in Cornwall? When she had a spare moment, Kate decided she would check to see if she could find out Beth's home address.

In the meantime, she would discuss this with Woody, although she didn't think he could possibly object. After all, it was only for four days; she could drive up there on the Monday night or Tuesday morning, and drive home on the Friday evening.

Jack was at home that evening, because Beth had gone to the gym with one of the other girls, and he insisted on treating Kate and Woody to takeaway pizzas.

Takeaway pizzas were new to Lower Tinworthy. At the end of June, an enterprising couple had taken over the old shoe-repair shop and converted it into Hot Stuff, where they prided themselves on their Cornish pasties, sausage rolls, pies and all manner of hot takeaway items. They'd now installed a pizza oven and were hoping to do a roaring trade.

Kate made a green salad while Woody rummaged in the cupboard to see if he could find some Italian red and unearthed two bottles of Chianti.

Kate settled for the Neapolitan pizza because she liked the crisp base, and this one was liberally embellished with anchovies and capers, both of which she adored but which were scorned by Woody.

'The cheese, tomatoes and basil should be sufficient,' he informed her, 'but then, of course, this is *not* Napoli!'

Kate was pretty sure she had sampled something similar to this in Naples but refrained from commenting.

Both Woody and Jack opted for margheritas, which Woody agreed were 'not bad for Tinworthy' and said he might even consider having a wood-fired oven in the garden so he could make his own.

'This is nice,' said Jack, on his third glass of wine. 'We should do this more often!'

Kate wondered when to bring up the subject of Bristol. She topped up her glass and looked at her husband and son. They both seemed happy and contented so perhaps this was as good a time as any.

She cleared her throat. 'I had a chat with Andrew Ross today at work. He's keen for me to do a counselling course.'

'That's good,' Woody said, 'although I thought Penelope Bowen was our local so-called counselling expert.'

'This,' said Kate, 'is *bereavement* counselling, which is a little more specialised.'

'Go for it, Mum!' Jack said, picking up his glass. 'Mind if I go through to watch TV?'

Kate shook her head, and Jack got up and left the room.

'As you know, people get bereaved every day, Woody, particularly with the murders we've had round here.' For a moment, Kate thought about Timmy and wondered if anyone might mourn the poor man. Only Sidney probably.

'So when and where's the course?' Woody asked.

'Quite soon, the thirty-first of August to the third of September,' Kate replied. 'They've had a cancellation – hence the short notice – and it lasts for four days. In Bristol.'

'Bristol?' Woody said. 'Can't you do a course closer to home?'

'No, it's quite specialised, and they only do it in big local centres. It's also where the company's headquarters are. I'll obviously have to stay up there for three or four nights, but I'd be home for the weekend. You wouldn't mind, would you?' She touched his arm.

'Well, if it's to do with work, then of course you must go.'

'While I'm up there I thought I might check on where Beth worked and lived.'

There was silence for a minute, the only sound coming from Jack, in the next room, flicking through the TV channels.

'You want to check up on *Beth*?'

'Well, sort of. Just to see where she lived and everything...'

'But why, Kate? It's not even as if they're engaged.'

'I know, but—'

'I *get* it now. You're so keen to go to Bristol, just to be able to check on Beth?'

'I'm going to Bristol for *work*! It wasn't my idea – it was Andrew Ross who wanted me to go.'

'Kate, this is *ridiculous*! You're going to Bristol to do yet more so-called sleuthing on a young girl who may, or may not, marry your son! Surely that's down to Jack, not you?'

'Yes, but I just want to feel better about her, and I'm sure I will when I see her background,' Kate said. She only wanted to know more about the person that her son was in love with. Because there was something about Beth that she couldn't quite put her finger on...

'I'm sorry, Kate, but I think this whole idea is bloody ridiculous! Will you have to pay for accommodation as well?'

'Dr Ross said all expenses were paid.'

'Why do you have to be so inquisitive? I think you should forget about checking on Beth.'

'I'd like to see how *you'd* react if one of your daughters was planning to get tied up with someone they knew nothing about, and who *you* weren't too happy with!'

'I would not interfere, Kate.' Woody pushed back his chair and stood up. 'I've heard enough. This is crazy. I'm out of here!' With that, he headed out of the back door, slamming it behind him.

Kate sat still for a moment, badly shaken. She'd really thought he would understand.

'Mum?' Jack had come quietly into the kitchen and sat down on the chair vacated by Woody. 'I heard all that.'

'Jack, I'm sorry. Am I being silly?'

'No, Mum, you're not,' Jack said. 'To be honest, I myself would like to find out a little more about Beth, but she doesn't seem interested in showing me where she lives and works in Bristol, and I'd like to know why. I mean, we could go up there on her day off, but there always seems to be some excuse. I love her and, if there's a problem, I'd really like to be able to help her.'

'So you think I should see what I can find out?'

'Listen, Mum, you want to go on this course anyway, right?'

Kate nodded.

'So, as you're going to be there anyway, anything you could find out about Beth would be really, really helpful.' He smiled at her reassuringly.

She leaned across and squeezed his hand. 'Thank you, Jack.'

Woody came back just over an hour later, noticeably inebriated. Kate could guess where he'd been.

'Des and I have sorted out the world,' he said, 'and all the women in it. We have decided' – here he hiccupped – 'that we aren't even going to *try to understand* the fairer sex anymore! Am I allowed to say "sex" these days? Do we come from Mars, and you come from Venus, or is it the other way round? Planets apart, I still love you!' He yawned. 'Guess I'm going to hit the sack. You coming?'

Kate rolled her eyes. Men! At least they weren't going to bed on an argument.

TWENTY-EIGHT

The chaos continued at the medical centre. One agency girl had replaced the other, but neither was anywhere near as efficient as Denise. Then again, Denise had worked there for around twenty-five years so naturally she was on top of the job – if not on top of Andrew Ross's filing. Thus, it was with some relief that Kate drove home on Tuesday evening knowing that Denise would be back, with or without a Greek in tow, next week.

One advantage of Denise's absence, however, meant that Kate could check the records without interference, and this she did. Beth's surname was Hart, Jack had told her, and she kept everything crossed that she had registered at the surgery. She was very relieved to find the file, which had little on it apart from Beth's name and her home address: 28 Barrymore Road in Bristol. She made a careful note.

As she drove up to Lavender Cottage, she saw an unfamiliar white Vauxhall Astra parked in Woody's spot. As Kate emerged from her car, so Jodi emerged from her own.

'Coo-ee!' she yelled.

Kate could not begin to imagine what Jodi might want.

'Hope you don't mind me callin', but I thought you got

home about this time. I wanted to set the record straight but didn't think it was a good idea to come into the surgery when there was nothin' wrong with me, like.'

'Oh, quite,' Kate agreed, her dream of a quiet cup of tea rapidly dissipating. She had little choice but to invite the woman in.

Jodi followed her into the kitchen, pulled out a chair from under the table and sat down heavily. 'I got somethin' to tell *you*,' she said with a coy smile and a flutter of blue eyelids.

Kate was filling the kettle when Jodi added, 'We're *engaged*!'

'Engaged?'

'Yeah, to be married, like. Marc and me!'

'Well, congratulations!' Kate said sincerely. 'That's wonderful!'

Jodi stretched out a chubby finger sporting a large diamond. 'Ain't that lovely? But wot I came to tell you is that I now know where he was that day – the day wot I told you about? When that bloke was murdered?'

'Where was he?' Kate asked, almost dropping the two mugs she'd just got out of the cupboard. 'Milk and sugar?'

'Oh, ta! I could murder a cuppa! Milk and two sugars please.'

'So where...?'

'Well,' said Jodi, placing her hands round the mug Kate had just set in front of her, 'he didn't want to tell me cos it was supposed to be a surprise, see. Wot he'd arranged was a meeting with *SeeVue*, that Sienna Stone programme, you know? They was doin' this programme about oldies like us gettin' wed again so they wanted to film Marc proposin' to me, like, and then they was goin' to film the weddin'. So Marc had gone to Plymouth to meet the film people, like. They got a different producer and director now since Sienna. Anyway, on Saturday, Marc says to me to dress up a bit, look nice and all that. Well, I didn't know wot was goin' on, did I? So next thing I know, this TV crew comes into the sittin' room, and Marc gets down on one knee and asks me to marry him!'

'Wow! How exciting, Jodi! I presume you said yes?'

'Well, I did! And then he put the ring on me finger! He'd bought the ring while he was in Plymouth too! This programme, see, is all about love second time around. Ain't that nice? I didn't go tellin' them it was my *third* time around in case they stopped filmin' us.'

'And they're going to film the wedding too?'

'Yeah, and we're havin' the weddin' at the hotel on Saturday, the twenty-eighth! In about ten days' time – unbelievable! It's almost like they want to make up for the Sienna Stone programme, innit? Anyway, that's where Marc was for them few hours I was tellin' you about. He was in Plymouth, and he wanted it to be a surprise.'

'Well, this is *certainly* a surprise,' Kate said with considerable feeling.

'Yeah, and you and Woody's goin' to be invited,' Jodi said, draining her tea.

'That's something to look forward to,' said Kate.

Was it? Ten days' time, and to be *televised*! What on the face of the earth was she going to wear? Then, with some relief, she thought of Woody's birthday present. Perhaps she should treat herself to something new after all.

Woody got back, muddy and happy, about an hour after Jodi departed.

'I've moved most of the big stones,' he said, 'but there's still loads of digging to do. The soil is lovely though, very rich and loose.'

'Oh, good,' Kate said absently, still mulling over what Jodi had said.

'I've ordered some bags of horse manure from that farm up near Tremorron,' Woody continued happily, 'and I'll get that well dug in once I've got everything cleared. I've been thinking, would you like me to plant some flowers for you up there? What do you think?'

'Yes, lovely...' Kate said distractedly. 'I had a visitor when I got home from work this afternoon.'

Woody was examining his black fingernails. 'Yeah? Who was that?'

'Jodi whatever-her-name-is, Marc's friend.'

'I gotta have a shower and scrub these nails,' Woody said. 'So what did *she* want?'

'She wanted me to know that Marc had an alibi for the few hours when he'd gone out on the morning of Timmy's murder.'

'Really? What excuse did *he* come up with?'

'This one is genuine.' Kate went on to tell him about the engagement and the TV programme. 'Furthermore, *we* are going to be invited to the wedding!'

Woody blew out a long breath. 'Do we *have* to go? And what the hell do we give people like them for a wedding present?'

At that point Jack came in and asked, 'Who are you buying wedding presents for? Us, ha ha? A bottle of wine will do for now, so is it OK if I help myself, Mum? Me and Beth thought we would like a drink while we make our own wedding plans! It's all right, Mum, only joking!' He helped himself to a bottle of good Burgundy and two of Kate's best glasses, then carried them down the steps into the sitting room and snuggled up on the sofa with Beth.

'No idea what to give them, Woody,' Kate said. 'But I *do* think we have to go, and I *do* know that Marc couldn't have killed Timmy.' She waited for Woody's comment, but none was forthcoming, so she said, 'That just leaves Irving and Sally.'

'Now you're going to tell me you've removed Marc from The List?'

'Well, sort of,' Kate admitted. 'He could have killed Sienna, I suppose, but he couldn't have killed Timmy, assuming only one killer is involved.'

Woody sighed. 'Do you want to know what I think?'

'What do you think?'

'I think you could probably tear up that list of yours. I very much doubt that any of the original so-called suspects did it. I think it was someone she met up there, someone perhaps who'd arranged to meet her up on the coastal path. Could be anyone at all, coming from any direction.'

'So where would you *begin* to look for all the people who might have been up there at the time?'

'Good question. If it wasn't for Timmy's death, I think the police might well have been tempted to write Sienna's off as a suicide. But Timmy's death sure as hell was no suicide, and the two have got to be connected. Like I've said a thousand times before, leave it to the police, Kate. They will find the necessary clues – they always do.'

I wouldn't put money on that, Kate thought. *But probably best not to say so.*

The wedding invitation arrived the very next day. The gold-edged card invited Mr and Mrs W. Forrest (they didn't know that he was Abraham Lincoln Forrest officially) to the marriage of Jodi Ann Cottle to Marc Alexandre Le Grand, at The Atlantic Hotel, Higher Tinworthy at 3 p.m. on Saturday, 28 August. Underneath was printed, 'This event will be televised as part of the *SeeVue* Second Time Around programmes.'

'That's at the end of next week!' Woody exclaimed. 'Isn't there any way we can get out of going to this thing?'

'No, there isn't,' Kate said firmly, 'and it might just be fun! It should certainly be interesting. I wonder who else will be invited?'

Woody gave out a loud groan.

Kate decided she definitely could not wear the green dress again because she'd worn it so many other times, including for her own wedding. No, she couldn't possibly appear on the TV screen wearing that. It was time to go shopping. Good old Woody!

'I'm taking Barney for a walk on the beach,' she called out to Woody, who was preparing to set off for the allotment again, 'and I'll probably pop in for a cake with Angie afterwards.'

'Behave yourself then!' he called out cheerily.

Kate was delighted with the allotment, not because she was much bothered by what Woody planned to grow up there, but because he looked so happy and purposeful. Not only that, if he was so engrossed with his new hobby, he wouldn't forever be asking her where she was going and why. He seemed to have accepted the fact that she'd taken his advice to 'not get involved' and had agreed that it was hardly her fault that Jodi had appeared on the doorstep and that Sally had been on the beach.

Sally was not on the beach today, but plenty of others were. Lying prone on surfboards on the sand were around twenty children, listening to the instructor telling them how to stand up. As Kate well knew, it was one thing to hoist yourself upright on a nice, flat patch of sand, and quite something else to get yourself upright on the wild Atlantic surf. She herself had left it a bit late to learn properly, but no doubt these kids would do fine.

She wandered the length of the beach, throwing sticks for Barney, before strolling back to The Old Locker. There she found Angie in the tiny kitchen making sandwich fillings.

Angie's hair was now – almost – back to blond, although there was still a trace of pink here and there in her tresses, which she said were '*strawberry* highlights' that she'd come to like.

'You'll never guess what,' Angie said as she mashed some tinned tuna with a fork. '*We've* been invited to a wedding!'

'At The Atlantic Hotel? In ten days' time?'

Angie stopped mashing and chucked in a dollop of mayonnaise. 'How did *you* know that?'

'Because we've been invited too.'

'Fancy that,' said Angie as she resumed mashing. 'Did you know we're going to be on telly?'

'Yes, I heard about that first-hand from Jodi,' Kate said. 'She'd been very concerned about Marc's whereabouts on the morning of Timmy Thomson's murder, but apparently, he'd been in Plymouth fixing up all this with the TV people – and buying her a whacking great diamond to boot.'

'Hmm,' Angie said, 'but I don't see how Sienna Stone can slate him on one of her programmes and then the same people want to film the wedding; doesn't make sense, does it?'

'There are different people doing the programme now apparently. Perhaps they wanted to make amends?'

Angie shrugged. 'Who knows? You could be right.'

'So I take it that you and Fergal are going?'

'Hopefully. We're training a young lass to help out here in the bar, and we think she'll be OK on her own for a few hours, but they haven't given us much notice, have they?'

'Million-dollar question, Angie – what are you going to wear?'

'No idea! What about you? Don't tell me you're dragging out the green number again?'

Kate sighed. 'Well, we haven't exactly got much time, have we? Could Fergal and your girl hold the fort on Saturday while we go shopping in Exeter? Or do you prefer to buy online?'

'Online is great, and very convenient, if you have the time to send it back and get something else if necessary. But we don't have time for all that, do we?'

'So we're going shopping?'

'Yes, let's go shopping.'

'I'll be glad to get away from here for a day,' Kate remarked, 'to take my mind off this damn case.' Although she'd said nothing to anyone, she was still worried about being a suspect and was already looking forward to doing something normal.

TWENTY-NINE

Exeter was extremely busy. Kate finally found a parking spot at the very top of one of the multi-storey car parks just as a huge black cloud, which had been hovering over them ominously for the past half hour, decided to burst. By the time she and Angie had reached cover, they were both drenched and bad-tempered.

'How the hell are we going to try on dresses when we're soaked like this?' Angie wailed.

Angie had wailed most of the way from Tinworthy because the girl who was to be their relief had arrived very late, and Fergal had had a hissy-fit about being on his own all day. 'You've got a whole fecking rail of dresses up there – why would you need another one?' he'd said, or words to that effect.

'He has no idea how easy it is to put on weight,' Angie groaned, 'particularly as he never puts on a bloody ounce!'

They had a coffee to give them time to dry off, and then headed to the first store where Angie picked up a selection of size sixteen dresses and couldn't fit into any of them. 'The sizes are all wrong in here,' she complained bitterly to the bored-looking assistant, who merely shrugged.

Kate eventually found a couple of size sixteen dresses that

fitted her well enough, but she didn't like any of them. She made a mental note to get dieting again as she pulled up a protesting zip.

'For goodness' sake, Angie, try on an eighteen!'

Angie looked daggers at her. 'I am *not* an eighteen!'

'You obviously are! If you like one of these dresses, look for an eighteen. Come on, we haven't got all day, and you can always cut out the label before you get home if it bothers you that much.'

'I am *not* an eighteen!' Angie repeated as she picked up her bag and headed towards the exit.

Having found nothing either, Kate sighed and followed her out onto the street.

'They make them far too tight round the middle these days,' Angie ranted on as they dashed through the heavy rain to the next shop. 'And why doesn't Exeter have a decent covered shopping precinct, eh?'

The next shop proved to be even more disastrous than the first, as they didn't appear to have anything larger than a fourteen.

'It's a shop for trendy young girls,' Kate explained patiently to a seething Angie. 'We probably set off the wrinkly alarms!'

'But I'm young at heart!'

But not round the middle, Kate thought.

Store number three was quite successful. Kate found a dark blue silk midi-dress with a flattering V-neckline which suited her well and slimmed her outline.

'I'd have liked that,' Angie said enviously as she surveyed Kate in the changing cubicle.

'It's a sixteen, Angie, and I'm going to have it. This is my birthday present from Woody.'

Angie was now in full panic mode as Kate paid for the dress with Woody's bank card.

'It's no good, I can't find anything, so *I* won't be able to go!'

Angie's remark brought back memories to Kate of her fifteen-year-old sister shouting, 'I'm not going to the school disco in *that!*' as their long-suffering, exasperated mother lifted dress after dress off the rail in their local department store, whilst trying to convince Angie that tiny mini-skirts would not be approved of at Appleford High School for Girls.

Now, as she stared at Kate's large carrier bag, Angie said, 'You are so lucky!' Then she espied a well-known logo. 'Ah, I forgot about *here!*' She dashed across the street to yet another store.

As they scanned the rails, Kate picked up a very attractive loose deep-pink dress in a size eighteen. 'How about this, Angie?'

For the first time all day Angie brightened up. 'That's nice – is it a sixteen?'

'Yes,' Kate lied. 'Want to try it on?'

'Maybe I will,' Angie muttered.

Kate accompanied her into the changing rooms, still holding the dress. Fortunately, Angie did not examine any of the labels before she stepped into the dress and studied herself in the mirror. 'What do you think?'

'I think it's lovely, and it suits you,' Kate said truthfully.

'Should I buy it then? I mean, we're going to be on television, so it's got to look *sensational!*'

'It'll look great.'

Angie, with her pretty face and strawberry-blonde halo, did look very good. However, she was not about to be easily satisfied. After trying on a couple of sixteens which did not fit, Angie finally decided on the pink dress. Then, as they sat munching sandwiches in the Marks & Spencer café, they discussed the problems of shoes and bags.

'You should wear red with that dress of yours,' Angie declared, getting out her screw-topped bottle of tonic water. Kate had seen this bottle on many occasions and knew perfectly well that it contained fifty per cent gin. Angie poured it into an empty glass and took an enormous gulp.

'Ooh, I needed that!' she said with relish. 'I do like this dress.' She lifted the top part out of her carrier bag to admire it. 'Lovely colour...' She stopped for a moment, then: 'Bloody hell, it's an eighteen!'

'Is it?'

'You *knew* that!' Angie glared angrily at Kate. 'I've a good mind to take it back!'

'For heaven's sake, Angie, it looks terrific on you, so what does it matter what the label says?'

'I shall never forgive you for this, and now I shan't enjoy wearing it one little bit!' She took another hefty swig from her tonic bottle.

'Don't be ridiculous!' Kate said. 'Look, I've got some nail scissors in my bag so why don't we just cut the label out if it bothers you so much?'

Angie sniffed, took another gulp and then cut the label out, placing it carefully in her scrunched-up serviette alongside her coffee cup. 'Don't know about you, but I've had enough of these damn shops for today. Shall we go home?'

It was on the Wednesday before the wedding that Kate had a phone call from Sally Brand.

'Just wondered if you'd like to join me for a coffee,' she said, 'because I have something to tell you.'

'Well...' Kate hesitated. She had just decided to cook some meals for the freezer and had laid out all the ingredients on the kitchen work surface.

'I know it's short notice, but I'd really like it if you could come.'

'OK, Sally, give me half an hour.' Kate then hurriedly did some chopping and slicing and decided the rest could wait until

she got back. What on earth could Sally want to tell her? Whatever it was, it could be important, and she couldn't afford to
ignore it.

A little later, Kate walked into the reception area of The
Atlantic Hotel and found Sally waiting for her on one of the
large settees. She stood up, smiled and indicated that Kate
follow her into the bar area where Frederick was again in
charge of the coffee machine. Sally made a sign to him and he
nodded.

'Let's sit by the window,' she said to Kate.

'How's things?' Kate asked after Frederick appeared with a
tray of coffee and biscuits.

When he'd gone back to the bar, Sally said, 'Things are just
fine.' She beamed. 'I know it's not long since Sheila – sorry,
Sienna – died, but Irving and I are so tired of hiding away and
we've decided to "come out", so to speak.' She poured the drinks
and offered Kate a biscuit.

'I can understand how you feel,' Kate said, 'but don't you
think that going public would have everyone pointing at you
both as the likely killers?'

'That's a risk we're willing to take,' Sally said, munching a
piece of shortbread. 'We are *so* fed up with not being seen
together.'

'Well, of course, it's up to you,' Kate said.

'I wanted to know what you might think,' Sally continued.
'You see, I don't know many people down here, and we've
become sort of friends, haven't we? So I thought I'd ask your
opinion.'

'Just don't let the press get hold of it,' Kate said. 'You *know*
how they'll react.'

'The thing is, we've been invited to Marc and Jodi's
wedding on Saturday, so we're going to be seen together then

for sure. We thought we might have dinner, in the hotel here, on Friday night, to kind of break the ice. What do you think?'

Kate felt rather flattered that her opinion might matter to Sally. What could she say? Of course, word would get around and people would point the finger but, if they really did have an alibi, then no amount of finger-pointing should be relevant.

'I think you should do it if it's what you both want,' Kate said diplomatically. 'Just be prepared for the media to find out though, because they'll have a field day.'

'I know that,' Sally said, 'but thank you for listening and not saying that the whole idea is ridiculous.'

'I wish you all the luck in the world,' Kate said.

'Thank you so much.' She offered the plate of biscuits to Kate again. 'Have you tried the chocolate gingernuts? God, they're wonderful!'

Kate got home to find Woody, Jack and Beth all sitting in the sun. She knew she should continue cooking but decided to join them for a few minutes.

'I've just been up to The Atlantic,' she told Woody, 'at Sally Brand's request. Apparently, she and Irving have decided to make their relationship public, and she wanted my opinion.'

'Who's Sally Brand?' Jack asked.

'She's the sister of Sienna Stone, who got pushed off the cliff. She's been having an illicit relationship with Irving Aldridge, Sienna's husband, for some years.'

Jack snorted. 'You couldn't make it up, could you!'

Kate looked at Woody. 'What was I supposed to say to the woman?'

'What *did* you say?' Woody asked.

'I said that I could understand that they wanted to, but that the press would go bananas if they found out.'

'That about sums it up,' Woody said.

'Anyway, they're going to Marc and Jodi's wedding, as a couple, and they're going to dine together at The Atlantic restaurant on Friday night – to test the water, so to speak.'

Jack laughed. 'I thought Tinworthy was just a quiet, quaint little village, but there's a lot goes on round here, isn't there?'

'Your mother and I both thought the same,' Woody said drily.

'Surely if the woman's sister and husband were having an affair,' Beth piped up, 'they should be the main suspects for the murder?'

'Apparently, they have some sort of alibi,' Kate said, 'but they won't tell anyone what it is.' She stood up. 'Now I must continue with what I was doing in the kitchen before I was summoned to The Atlantic.'

As she worked, she heard Jack on his phone booking something.

'Guess what, Mum?' he said a couple of minutes later, coming into the kitchen. 'I've just booked a table for Beth and myself at The Atlantic for Friday night. Beth says she wants to see how the other half live!'

The other half live as prime suspects, Kate thought, as she returned to her chopping. All she could think about was, if they did have an alibi, why on earth had they not presented it to the police?

THIRTY

Kate was trying to sort out what to pack for going to Bristol, while getting herself glammed up for the wedding.

'I cannot imagine what this wedding is going to be like,' Woody sighed as he pulled up the zipper on his new cream trousers, 'and I'm going to look real poncy in this!'

Kate had finally persuaded him to buy a lightweight summer suit – and to leave the dark grey one hanging in the wardrobe. 'You look very nice,' she said admiringly. Which was true, particularly as Woody had acquired a deep Mediterranean tan from working outside for much of the summer.

'And you look lovely,' Woody said, grabbing Kate by the waist as she pirouetted around the bedroom in her new dark-blue dress. She'd added a white pearl choker necklace and navy-and-white shoes. 'You look like you've lost weight too.'

He couldn't have said anything nicer; surely music to the ears of any woman. The dress was cleverly cut and skimmed her body in all the right places, but she hadn't expected Woody to notice.

'Thank you,' she said sincerely. 'And cheer up! I'm sure

we'll enjoy ourselves, although I've no idea who'll be there. At least we'll know Angie and Fergal.'

'Hallelujah,' Woody said without enthusiasm.

'Come on, they're not so bad!'

'Kate, I have nothing against your sister other than she's likely to get smashed as a rat when she hits the gin, and Fergal will probably end up doing his Irish dancing all over the place!'

'Never a dull moment,' Kate agreed as she straightened his blue tie. 'Is that the taxi I'm hearing?'

They were sharing a taxi with Angie and Fergal because both men had said they had absolutely no intention whatsoever of remaining sober on such a remarkable occasion.

Barney had been given a long walk in the morning and was now roaming the garden, which was dog-proof. Woody had built him a large kennel so that, in good weather, the dog could be in the garden when they were out. Barney did not like being shut up indoors on his own.

They got into the taxi which then headed down to The Old Locker to pick up the other two. Angie – a vision in pink – came tottering out on some very high-heeled silver sandals, which Kate could see being abandoned as the afternoon wore on, because Angie was not one to keep footwear on for any length of time. Fergal was looking quite suave, having had his hair and beard neatly trimmed, and he too was clad in a lightweight suit.

'I do love a wedding,' Angie said as she got carefully into the taxi. When she sat down, she said, 'I wonder who else is going to be there? At least we'll know Marc and Jodi – and Guy. As far as I know, he's still single at the moment.'

On this occasion, Guy had styled an elaborate creation on Angie's head, which Kate hoped was securely lacquered into place. Kate had not had her own hair specially done for this event, so she didn't know that their hairdresser had been invited. She was pleased, because she was very fond of Guy.

Then Kate wondered if Charlotte might be there, although

it was highly unlikely that any member of the police force would be included on the guest list, even if Marc was now, presumably, in the clear.

The taxi lumbered its way up to Higher Tinworthy.

The Atlantic Hotel car park was full, and there was a huge television-broadcast vehicle at the side door where two jeans-clad young men were standing amidst a sea of cables.

The notice outside the main entrance declared: 'We regret that the restaurant is closed to the public today'. The Danish receptionist, sporting a pink rose on her plain grey dress, had been commandeered into directing everyone across the hallway to the function room, now rechristened The Ocean Room, at the rear of the building, and didn't look as if she was particularly thrilled to be doing so.

The reception area was decorated with garlands of pink roses and greenery, with a great deal of gold ribbon everywhere, and on the gold-framed notice at the entrance to the function room was written 'Jodi and Marc' in elaborate gold lettering. Inside the room were rows upon rows of dainty gold chairs, each sporting a large gold bow attached to the back, and most of them already filled. At the far end was a platform with an enormous arrangement of yet more pink roses adorned with gold leaves and gold ribbons. Privately, Kate thought it would look marginally more tasteful with less gold and more greenery. Alongside was a TV camera, which was now directed towards all the guests.

'Holy moly,' said Woody.

Several people looked round and waved; some were patients of Kate's whose names she couldn't recall. As she cast her eye around, she noticed Sally Brand and Irving Aldridge sitting close together near the front.

'Stay near the back,' Woody muttered, taking Kate's arm

and guiding her along one of the rear rows of spindly seats, which teetered alarmingly as the four of them sat down.

'Jaysus,' said Fergal with a frown, 'there won't be room on these things for your big arse, Angela.' He shuffled about and managed to knock his gold bow off the back of the chair. 'There's hardly enough space for mine.'

'I wouldn't recommend the charm school Fergal Connolly went to,' Angie remarked drily before kicking him on the ankle. Hitching up the skirt of the pink dress, she sat down carefully then turned to Kate. 'I *knew* I should have left that Irish buffoon behind the bar!'

More people were filing in, and shortly all the chairs were filled, and, as more bottoms wriggled, so more bows came adrift. Soon there were more bows on the floor than on the chairs.

'I can't believe Sally and Irving are here,' Kate murmured.

'Well, you did say they were going public,' Woody reminded her.

'It's a bit blatant though, isn't it?' Angie asked. 'I mean, Sienna's hardly cold.'

'They plainly want to be acknowledged as a couple now, rather than hiding away,' Kate said. 'Ah, I've just seen Guy!'

The lovely Guy was a few rows in front, chatting with the elderly couple next to him. In front of him was the vicar's daughter, Jane, alongside her partner, Joanne.

There – in front of them – was the party-giver herself, clad in royal-blue satin: Penelope Bowen. Penelope was one of those women who ran everything, was president of this and chair-woman of that, not to mention having a husband detained at Her Majesty's pleasure. Penelope was not the type to hide away over a mere detail like that, and was accompanied by the portly self-important local magistrate, Peter Edwards, with whom she'd been having an affair for years.

The registrar, Mrs Pettigrew – a large, chubby lady with a big smile – had now arrived at the front, along with the groom.

Marc was looking very dapper in tight dark trousers, a white shirt with voluminous sleeves gathered into frilly cuffs, an embroidered waistcoat in greens and purples, and a bow tie to match. He caused such a sensation that there was a round of applause, and much laughing, which caused him to bow gracefully, just as Mrs Pettigrew requested everyone to rise in anticipation of the bride's arrival. The cameras were rolling as, on cue, the door behind opened to admit Jodi – a vision in what looked like pale pink satin, her hair precariously arranged on top of her head with a confection of roses and ribbons, and she was carrying a bouquet of what else but pink roses. With gold ribbons.

Angie nudged Kate. 'She looks like a fairy elephant! Look at that fat tummy!'

Jodi was accompanied by a good-looking dark-haired man, balding on top, who Kate assumed was her son. Was he the one from Brighton? she wondered. He, too, was dressed in a white shirt beneath a gold-and-silver patterned waistcoat, but as they wandered ahead down the aisle towards a beaming Marc and Mrs Pettigrew, Kate was unable to see if he was wearing a matching bow tie or not.

'I'm beginning to feel distinctly underdressed,' Woody whispered with a grin.

For some inexplicable reason, a recording of Abba singing 'Take a Chance on Me' was then played at full volume for a few minutes, while Jodi and Marc stood admiring each other. Then, abruptly, the music was switched off and, in the sudden silence, Mrs Pettigrew cleared her throat and began, 'Ladies and gentlemen, we are here today...'

Kate found herself thinking of their own simple ceremony in St Piran's some three months before. Woody, who must have been thinking along similar lines, squeezed her hand.

The ceremony went ahead and, within minutes, the new Mrs Le Grand and her husband were making their way slowly

up the aisle, beaming at everyone like royalty, while 'Knowing
Me, Knowing You' bellowed in the background. The TV
cameraman was walking backward, ahead of them, filming.

Kate was relieved to stand up as her bottom had become
quite numb. Judging by the number of people rubbing their
behinds, she wasn't the only one.

'I had my right cheek hanging out in space,' Angie admitted
in a whisper as they followed the happy couple, along with
everyone else, back across the hallway and into the bar. Frederick and a gang of waiters stood filling and handing out glasses
of champagne as everyone formed a line to meet up with and
congratulate the bride and groom.

'Lovely ceremony!'

'You look gorgeous, Jodi!'

'What a handsome couple!'

'Hope you have many happy years together!'

Kate tried to think of something different to say as she
approached the pair. There was a lot of kissing going on, but
Kate managed to offer her congratulations by shaking hands and
wishing them every happiness. Woody, in her wake, was saying
something similar before they emerged at the end of the line.

True to form, Angie's glass was already almost empty. 'Did
you see the bottles on display when you got your champagne?'
she asked. 'Bollinger! They must be doing all right if they can
have the Bolly flowing!'

Woody took a sip and looked doubtfully at his glass. 'I'm not
so sure about that.'

''Tis a well-known ploy,' said Fergal, draining his glass, 'that
you have the fancy bottles on display, and so everyone thinks
that's what they're drinking when, in fact, underneath the table
is gallons of supermarket stuff. Who's to know when they refill
your glass with a fancy napkin round the bottle?'

Woody laughed. 'Not that you'd dream of doing anything so
underhand in The Old Locker?'

'Never!' replied Fergal with a wink as he held out his glass for a refill from a large white-napkin-swathed bottle.

'I suppose we should circulate,' Kate said.

'*Must* we?' asked Woody.

She turned to her right to find herself face to face with Jane and Joanne. Jane was draped in a voluminous floor-length dress patterned with what looked like orange marigolds, while Joanne sported a badly creased green linen trouser suit.

'How are you both?' Kate asked.

'Very well,' said Joanne.

'Absolutely tickety-boo,' confirmed Jane.

'Jane has taken up dressmaking,' Joanne said proudly. 'Don't you love her gorgeous gown?'

Jane did a little twirl in acknowledgement of her prowess. 'Next thing I'll be making my wedding dress,' she said, 'because Jo-Jo and I are having a civil ceremony, *right here*, just before Christmas!'

'Congratulations! I'm so pleased for you,' Kate said.

'Of course Mummy and Daddy won't be coming,' Jane said, looking suddenly gloomy. 'No change there.'

Joanne snorted at this, and Kate had vivid memories of her giving the vicar a black eye at Penelope Bowen's party.

'We're keeping it very small of course,' Joanne went on.

Kate hoped that meant there was little danger of herself and Woody being invited to the event and said sincerely, 'That's probably best, but I hope you have a lovely day.'

She looked round to see Woody talking to a tall horsey-looking woman who she'd never seen before, just as someone nudged her right elbow.

'Hi, Kate!' said Sally Brand. 'We *did* it! We're openly together, and no one's said a thing so far.'

'It's no one's business but your own,' Kate said, 'but I'm very pleased for you both.' She'd just said something similar to Jane and Joanne, and to Jodi and Marc, so it was beginning to feel as if the whole world was pairing off.

'Well, *you* knew, *Marc* knew, and we'd already told the police, so what was the point in hiding away?'

'Oh, absolutely,' Kate said.

Sally waved an arm at the crowd around them. 'This is all very nice of course, but I think we'll have something rather more low-key in the circumstances, and then have a church blessing like you and Woody did. We certainly won't want to attract publicity.'

Kate couldn't help but think that they were very unlikely to avoid publicity when Irving's wife had recently been murdered and he was now about to marry her sister. The press would have a field day.

'Come here, darling,' Sally ordered Irving, who was standing just behind. 'I know you've met Kate of course.'

Irving's handshake was disappointingly limp. 'Well, I'm sure Sally's told you our story so, obviously, I certainly won't have need of your counselling.'

The Danish receptionist had now appeared on the scene and – with a surprisingly strong, authoritative voice – was ordering everyone to please proceed to the dining room.

'Talk later,' Sally said chummily, before taking Irving's arm and joining the throng.

As Kate watched them saunter off, her mind was once again wandering back to the case. There was no escape from it.

THIRTY-ONE

The guests trooped obediently into the large dining room. More roses, more gold ribbon. At least the chairs looked substantial, but they too were adorned with gold ribbons. The room was set up in the traditional manner with a top table, at which Jodi and Marc already presided in the centre, with two young men seated next to Jodi, including the one who'd walked her up the aisle, so presumably her sons. Next to Marc was a cross-looking miniature female version of himself, who could only be his daughter. And next to her was a scowling, spotty teenage boy, gazing at his phone and looking like he'd rather be anywhere else on earth than here.

The other seven round tables were each set for six people – a pyramid of pink roses and trailing gold ribbons in the centres – with little gold cards indicating who was to be sitting where. Angie and Fergal were seated at the far end of the room, and Kate and Woody found themselves opposite each other at a table with Guy, an ancient lady and a middle-aged couple: a very thin woman and a vastly overweight man.

'So glad you're here, Kate,' Guy said, giving her a hug. 'I'm now sandwiched between two delightful ladies – yourself and

Edith here!' He indicated the ancient lady. 'Edith is the bride's aunt, believe it or not.'

Kate leaned across and shook Edith's bony, freckled hand. 'Hi, I'm Kate, and my husband over there is Woody.'

Edith looked from one to the other and said, in a very cultured, high-pitched voice, 'I did *not* want to be here, you know!'

'Oh,' Kate said, taking her seat, 'why is that?'

'My late brother married beneath himself,' Edith said, fingering some ruffles at the neck of her cream blouse and looking with distaste at the top table, 'resulting in a *very* flighty daughter. Let me tell you, this is the *third* wedding of Jodi's I've had to endure, and I daresay this marriage won't last long either. I wouldn't have come, but they sent a car to my *door*.' She sniffed and picked up the gold card with her name on it. 'I'm the token aged relative, you see. Everyone else is dead.'

'Oh dear,' said Kate, exchanging an amused glance with Guy, 'but perhaps you'll enjoy it more than you think.'

'I shall escape just as soon as I can,' said Edith, 'but *not* on an empty stomach.'

'I daren't tell her she's sitting in the wrong seat,' Guy muttered to Kate, just before Edith announced, 'I am aware that I should be sitting one seat along, but this one's nearer the door so I can escape more easily.'

There were murmurs of approval all round as the other couple moved together and Woody moved next to Kate. 'Do you suppose they'll come round to check and frogmarch us back to where we should be sitting?' he asked with a grin.

'Who cares?' Kate said.

The couple, now seated next to Woody, were studying the gold-printed menu.

'Smoked salmon,' the thin woman said sadly. 'I'm not a lover of fish, am I, Bob?'

Bob agreed she wasn't but said, 'Never mind, love, there's lamb to follow and you like that, don't you?'

She looked doubtful then sniffed. 'I'm Hazel, by the way, and my husband here is Bob. We live next door to Jodi, see, so that's why we're here.'

Kate and Woody gave a brief account of themselves, as did Guy. Then the old lady said, 'I'm Edith, I'm Jodi's aunt and I live in Surbiton.' She looked round the table. 'That's where they set *The Good Life*, you know, years ago.' She paused for breath then added, 'That dress Jodi is wearing is far too tight. I could see her *belly button* straining through the fabric!'

There was a deafening silence before Hazel leaned forward and said, '*I* made that dress! That was when she was supposed to be getting married last time though.' She looked at her husband. 'When was that, Bob? Four or five years ago, would it be? Anyway, the bloke did a runner at the last minute, and I said to her, "Jodi," I said, "you hang on to that dress because you'll meet somebody else!"' She looked triumphantly round the table before continuing, 'The only trouble is she's put on at *least* a stone since then!' She snorted.

'Let's just hope it holds together for the rest of her big day,' Guy said.

'It'll be a lot more fun if it doesn't,' Woody commented.

The smoked-salmon starter had arrived, with all sorts of decorative garnishes, including a minute amount of caviar. Wine was served and everyone got stuck in, the chatter subsiding round the dining room and being replaced by the clicking of knives and forks.

'I can't eat *that*,' Hazel said, pushing her plate towards her husband. Bob happily scraped the contents onto his own plate and ate the lot. Kate was beginning to see where his weight problem might be coming from.

'So,' Kate asked politely, 'are you a dressmaker, Hazel?'

'Yeah, and I could've made her something better than that if I'd had the time, but this has all happened so sudden, like.'

'None of us had much time to prepare,' Guy said. 'I've had to cancel all my appointments at the salon today so I could do Jodi's hair and come to the wedding. And let me tell you, all that gold rubbish on top of her hairdo was *her* idea, not mine!' He turned to Kate and said, in an undertone, 'Never mind, she's got a dishy son!'

'Was he the one who gave her away?' Kate asked.

'That's the one. Roly, he's called. Isn't he *de-lish*? I had a collie once called Roly – lovely dog he was. I'm taking that as a good sign.'

Plates were cleared, glasses refilled, and the roast lamb was served and pronounced delicious.

'It's full of garlic!' wailed Hazel.

'That,' said Woody, loudly and slowly, 'is one of the reasons why it's so delicious.'

'I don't like garlic,' said Hazel.

'Is there anything you *do* like?' Woody asked politely.

Kate kicked her husband under the table. 'Go easy!'

Edith, in the meantime, had almost cleared her plate. She dabbed her mouth with a napkin, leaned forward, looked Hazel in the eye, and said, 'When it comes to taste in general, my dear, perhaps you are a little deficient? I mean, who chose that awful satin for Jodi's dress?'

'Well, we both did,' said Hazel, 'and why are you all getting at me?'

'Calm down, dear,' said Bob, helping himself to Hazel's lamb. 'Pudding will be here shortly.'

'Any chance you might like *that*?' Woody asked.

Guy nudged Kate. 'I *do* like your husband!'

'Thank the Lord I moved seats,' said Edith, laying down her knife and fork, and frowning at Hazel, 'otherwise I'd have been between you two, with all that food slopping about from plate to plate.'

Before there was time for Hazel to reply, the dessert was served: a creamy concoction with apricots and a sprinkling of chocolate. Kate reckoned that Marc – or, in this instance, his head chef – had excelled himself. Even Hazel gobbled it all down.

'I'm going now,' said Edith, dabbing her mouth again. 'I can sense a speech coming on, and I can't *abide* speeches.' With that, she got out of her chair and was through the door with amazing agility.

'She told me she was ninety-three,' Guy said admiringly. 'Can you believe it?'

It all became easier as the wine flowed, and Bob turned out to be a good joke-teller, as did Guy. Even Woody was persuaded to talk about some of the Tinworthy murders by the time they got to coffee. The buzz of conversation continued all round, interspersed with much raucous laughter.

Then *ping, ping, ping* – the sound of spoon on glass. 'Your attention please!' somebody bellowed.

There was a hush as everyone obediently, and expectantly, turned their attention towards the top table.

Champagne glasses were being filled up all round as Marc stood up, waving his arms around in a Messiah-like gesture to make sure he had everyone's undivided attention.

'*Mesdames et messieurs*! You'll be relieved to know that there will be no best man's speech because there is no best man!'

There was much cheering at this.

'So *I'm* going to keep it short!'

Clapping and foot-stamping followed.

Ten minutes later, he was still talking, the French accent having completely disappeared. He stopped only to gulp down more champagne at regular intervals. He praised his parents, particularly his wonderful late *mère*, he praised the day he'd bought The Atlantic Hotel and made it into *such* a success. He praised his *wonderful* chef – who he himself had personally trained of course – and his *terrific* team who had produced and served this *wonderful* banquet, and then he remembered to praise his beautiful, *beautiful* bride, who was knocking back the champagne at an alarming rate and was peering up at him with slightly unfocused eyes. Then, as a further afterthought, he praised the wonderful people of Tinworthy who'd stood by him when he was – *unbelievably* – a suspect in the recent tragedies, and who were here to share this magical day with him.

He might have been cleared of killing Timmy, Kate thought, but what about Sienna?

There was more cheering and whistling before Marc concluded, 'Now please make your way back to The Ocean Room, where you will find the floor has been cleared for dancing to our lively local band. And don't forget, the bar is still open, folks!'

There was the sound of chairs scraping on the floor again as people began to stand up.

'Just one more thing,' Marc bellowed, having been elbowed in the ribs by Jodi's son. 'A *toast* to my beautiful bride!'

The beautiful bride had been toasting herself continuously for some time, and now appeared a little bewildered and not a little tipsy. The son, who had given her away and done the elbowing, now stood up and added, 'And a toast to the happy couple!'

Marc hauled his bride to her feet, and she stood swaying happily while everyone left in the dining room raised and clinked their glasses. Then followed a noisy stampede out towards the bar and The Ocean Room.

'Do you think we can escape now?' Woody asked Kate.

'No,' replied Kate firmly, 'I think we should have a dance first.'

As she stood up, Kate was astounded to find Jodi's son who, only moments earlier, had been at the top table, was now sitting down next to Guy in the seat Edith had vacated, and both were deep in animated conversation.

'*He* didn't waste any time,' Woody remarked admiringly.

'Less inhibited than us,' Kate said, steering him towards The Ocean Room. She looked round for Angie, who she could see nursing what looked like a large gin and tonic at the far end of the room, along with Fergal, who'd removed his jacket and was holding court to a group of people who were in hysterics, no doubt at one of his dubious jokes.

The Tinpots formed Tinworthy's six-piece pop group who played at most local events. They were enthusiastic, if not brilliant, and were currently belting out Stevie Wonder's 'I Just Called to Say I Love You'. This, apparently, was the happy couple's favourite song, and so everyone waited for them to take to the floor first.

Jodi was walking a little unsteadily, but Marc had his hand firmly round her waist, and then round most of the rest of her as they gyrated slowly to the music. After some applause and cheering, a few other couples began to shuffle around as well, including Kate and Woody.

'This is nice,' Woody murmured into her hair. 'We haven't danced together for ages.'

'*You're* the one who wanted to go home,' Kate reminded him.

'OK, so maybe we'll stay for another jig or two. I have to say you're looking very desirable, Mrs Forrest!'

'You're not looking too bad yourself,' Kate said.

Then, just as The Tinpots got to the last line of one of the choruses – 'And I mean it from the *bottom* of my heart' – there was a thump as Jodi landed in an undignified heap on the floor, bottom in the air. One of the exhausted seams of the pink dress had torn asunder, exposing two very large pink cheeks to the unsuspecting, gawping crowd.

The new Mrs Le Grand was wearing no knickers.

Jodi had been shepherded away by a pink-faced Marc, but the dancing and jollity continued. Kate and Woody, highly amused, stood watching during the next dance, as everyone's inhibitions appeared to have taken flight. There was Jane and Joanne dancing together, Penelope Bowen and Peter Edwards practically devouring each other, Irving and Sally, and then, out of the blue, came Guy and Roly, gazing into each other's eyes as they took to the floor in a lively attempt at what looked like a foxtrot.

Fergal appeared, minus Angie. 'She's having a little rest,' he informed them, pointing towards the bar. 'She's kicked off her shoes and found a comfy chair. You know Angie!'

Kate did indeed know Angie, who had obviously overdone the gin again.

'But this looks like turning into a great party,' he added, 'and wasn't that business with the bride better than any fecking cabaret?'

'Wasn't it just!' Woody agreed. 'It was worth coming, if only for that.'

The band then turned to some Cornish sea-shanties and, after a chat with Fergal, some Irish music. Fergal – as he'd no doubt planned – came into his own and, ignoring the now-asleep Angie, began his speciality – his own form of Irish dancing. There were cheers all round, howls of laughter, much foot-tapping. Even Marc and Jodi had reappeared – she in a loose flowery number – and had joined in the frivolity.

Nobody saw the blue lights flashing outside, or heard the line-up of police making their way in across the reception area. Not until they burst in through the door, led by Charlotte.

As they crashed into The Ocean Room, the music stopped, everyone turned round and watched as Charlotte made her way towards Irving Aldridge and Sally Brand, who were still entwined together on the dance floor. Then, in a voice loud and clear, she announced, 'Irving Aldridge and Sally Brand, I have come to arrest you both for the wilful murder of Sienna Stone. You do not have to say anything, but it may harm your defence if you do not mention when questioned something which you later rely on in court. Anything you do say may be given in evidence.'

Their 'togetherness' was short-lived, Kate thought sadly, although she wasn't altogether surprised. Now, would they produce this mysterious alibi?

THIRTY-TWO

Even Angie woke up with the commotion that ensued. 'What's going on?' she asked grumpily. 'Why are people leaving?'

Woody had already summoned the taxi. 'We're getting out of here, pronto,' he said.

Angie continued bleating. 'But I want to dance!'

'You've left it a little bit late, Angela,' Fergal said as he hauled her to her feet. 'We're going home now.'

'But we've only just *come* in here!'

'No, we haven't. You've been asleep for an hour,' Kate said. 'Come on – Woody's organising the taxi.'

There was much shuffling around while Angie located her shoes. Then, unwillingly, she followed them out through the reception area while Kate explained patiently what had happened. They weren't the only guests leaving – around half of them were already making their way out.

Marc had taken up position at the front door and was apologising profusely for the interruption to his wedding reception. 'The band will play on, you know,' he said somewhat desperately, 'so you can all stay!'

Everyone made sympathetic noises and said what a lovely wedding it had been but...

As Kate thanked him, Marc said, 'I *told* you those two were up to something, didn't I?' He sniffed loudly. 'But they didn't have to wreck my bloody wedding!'

The taxi was already waiting outside. 'I thought you'd be a couple of hours yet,' the driver said as they got in.

'Yes, we did too,' said Kate.

'Come back to The Locker for coffees,' Fergal said. 'The night is young!'

'I just do *not* believe this!' Angie was still moaning.

'Well, it certainly killed the party spirit,' Kate remarked. 'And I do feel so sorry for Marc and Jodi on their wedding day.'

'What a shambles!' Kate exclaimed as they drew up outside The Old Locker. Woody paid off the taxi, having assured the driver that he and Kate would walk home later.

The bar was half full, and the new 'hired help', whose name was Emma, seemed to be coping perfectly well. She told Fergal she had a system going and she'd like to stay on until eleven o'clock, as planned, and suggested they sat at a table, and she'd call for help if she needed it.

'She's put me firmly in my place,' Fergal said as they headed for a table in the corner, 'but I'm going to make us some of my special coffees.'

They all knew what Fergal's coffees were like: more alcohol than coffee. Nevertheless, they all felt the need for some sort of pick-me-up to round off the evening.

'Why on earth did they have to arrest Irving and Sally right in the middle of a wedding reception?' Kate asked as she sat down.

'I had a brief word with Charlotte,' Woody said, 'and, apparently, an eyewitness has now come forward, but she didn't tell me who that was.'

'An *eyewitness*? At this late date?' Kate was astounded.

'How can we find out who it was?' Angie asked eagerly. 'Surely you can wangle it out of her, Woody?'

Woody shrugged. 'I keep telling everyone that I'm no longer a police officer, which means that she doesn't have to tell me a damn thing. And she probably won't. It'll come out eventually of course.'

Fergal had returned with a tray of Irish coffees. 'You get yourselves on the outside of that,' he instructed them, 'and you'll be ready to party all over again!' He sat down next to Angie.

Kate turned to Woody. 'So who do *you* think the eyewitness was?'

Woody sipped his coffee. 'Wow, that's good, Fergal!' He set down his glass cup. 'To be honest, I have no idea who it could have been.' He thought for a moment. 'It could, I suppose, be your friend, Delia Moran, Kate.'

'Even if it was, why would she wait until now to tell the police?' Kate asked. 'It just doesn't make sense.'

'It could be anybody,' Angie said. 'It could be anyone at all who was walking on the cliffs that day.'

'For sure,' Fergal agreed. 'It could even have been a holiday-maker who's gone home.'

'But surely,' Kate protested, 'if you saw someone being pushed off the top of a cliff, you'd go straight to the police there and then?'

'That is what normal people would do,' Woody agreed.

'So are you suggesting that this person might not be normal?' Kate asked.

'I'm not suggesting anything,' Woody said, 'but I shall try to find out. Now, can we change the subject?'

'Are we ready for another of these?' Fergal asked, indicating the rapidly emptying glass cups.

'I'd rather avoid a hangover,' Kate said, 'as I've had a fair bit to drink already and I have to drive up to Bristol on Monday.'

'So you've plenty time to recover, so you have,' said Fergal, picking up his own empty cup and heading back to the bar.

'They didn't give you much notice of this course, did they?' Angie asked Kate.

'Seemingly, it was a last-minute cancellation,' Kate said, 'and Andrew Ross managed to get me on to it. It's all about bereavement counselling, so I'm not expecting it to be a bellyful of laughs.'

Woody had got up to join Fergal at the bar and help him to carry back the refilled glasses.

Kate lowered her voice. 'I'm going to check on Beth while I'm up there, Angie – see where she lives and try to find out something about her.'

'Will that not upset Jack if you go interfering?' Angie asked.

'I'm not the only one who wants to know more about her – Jack does too. Woody doesn't altogether approve though; thinks I should leave well alone.'

'He may well be right,' Angie replied, just as Woody returned with a couple of drinks.

'Who may well be right?' he asked as he sat down.

'Oh, just the Queen of Sheba,' Angie replied.

All the way to Bristol on Monday evening, Kate could think of nothing else but the arrest.

She and Woody had lain in bed discussing the event for about an hour after they'd woken up.

'I guess we shouldn't be surprised,' Woody said, 'because – by a process of elimination – everyone else was pretty much in the clear.'

'Why would an eyewitness suddenly appear now, after so long?' Kate asked, still unable to believe it.

'That's hard to say. Maybe they saw something on the press or on TV. Or perhaps they'd been sitting on the information and had a sudden attack of conscience, but I shall do my damnedest to find out,' Woody said.

Kate sighed. 'I'm beginning to wish I wasn't going to Bristol now as I'd so like to know what's happened.'

'What's happened is that these two have been arrested,' Woody said, 'and I shall keep you informed of any events in your absence.'

'I keep thinking about how Sally said they had an alibi,' Kate went on, 'but that it was *personal*. I wonder what that means?'

'I've no idea,' said Woody. 'But if they do have an alibi, this is the time to come out with it, no matter how personal it is.'

Now, en route to Bristol, as she drove past Taunton Dene, Kate was hopeful that Woody might indeed be able to find out something in her absence.

She'd eaten before she left home at 6 p.m., and Woody, being Woody, had popped two screw-top bottles of her favourite Shiraz into her bag, along with a 'proper wine glass' because, he said, 'you cannot drink wine out of those horrible little plastic bathroom glasses'.

Kate just hoped that the glass would survive the journey.

'I'm going to miss you,' he'd said as he kissed her goodbye. 'But we'll FaceTime every evening.'

'I'll tell you about my counselling course if you tell me what's going on with Sally and Irving,' Kate said.

'At least *this* time, you aren't dangerously involved, thank God,' he said.

In truth, Kate was rather sorry that she hadn't become more involved. By the process of elimination she had, of course, come to the same conclusion as the police. However, she really *had* believed Sally Brand when she'd said that she wanted to see Sienna's face when she, Sienna, discovered that her sister had stolen her husband. That made perfect sense to Kate. So had Irving done the deed himself? Or was Sally as good an actress as her sister had been?

Bristol was manically busy when she got there, which came as something of a shock. Kate had forgotten that the world didn't go to sleep in the evenings because – apart from visiting the pubs – not a lot happened in Tinworthy after 6 p.m.

She then got hopelessly lost trying to find the Holiday Inn where she'd been booked for four nights and found herself driving round in circles, and usually in the wrong lane, before she finally saw a sign for where she was supposed to be going.

The hotel's underground car park resembled a dark dungeon, and it took Kate some time to find a space. Then, feeling quite nervous, she made her way up to the reception area, which was completely deserted but with machines everywhere: machines for snacks, machines for coffee and hot drinks, machines for checking in, machines for checking out. Kate fumbled with her phone, beginning to feel more and more like a country bumpkin. Had she *really* spent most of her life in Greater London?

Finally in her room, Kate unpacked her bag and withdrew the bottle of wine and the still intact wine glass. This she filled to the top before propping herself up on the bed, taking a large gulp and calling Woody. He didn't have any updates for her yet, but, of course, she hadn't been gone too long...

THIRTY-THREE

The course, which was held in the function room of the hotel, began each morning at ten and finished at three, which made Kate wonder why they didn't make the day longer and the week shorter.

However, it was going to give her the opportunity to wander around a city she'd always liked, and to revisit some of the well-known spots, such as Brunel's iconic SS *Great Britain*, the Harbourside and, not least, to drive *across* the Clifton Suspension Bridge instead of under it, as she always did when coming from Cornwall.

There were seventeen would-be counsellors on the course, almost all from the local area, the only exception being a tiny, very plump lady called Ella. She hailed from Dorset, appeared to be around fifty or so, walked with a stick, wore a permanent scowl and questioned everything. Ella was the only other attendee staying in the hotel and Kate decided, after one day, they were unlikely to be compatible.

The lectures were much more interesting than she'd anticipated, but it meant that Kate was forced to imagine the unimaginable: the death of a loved one. She could hardly bear to think of a life without Woody, without her two sons and even without Angie. She could feel tears prickling at the back of her eyes at the mere thought of it, so how on earth could you bear the reality? And particularly if it came out of the blue – an accident; a suicide; a murder even? What could anyone possibly say to you that would begin to alleviate the pain and the grief?

Several of the other course members had experienced just that, and so they were able to contribute from first-hand experience what – if anything – had brought them any degree of comfort. Strangely enough, it appeared that, often, it turned out that it was easier to pour your grief out to someone you didn't know but who just listened. But listening wasn't as easy as it sounded, because it was necessary to really concentrate on what the person was saying. At their lowest point, the grief-stricken do not really believe that time will heal... or believe in any of the other platitudes normally offered.

The course gave them the opportunity to do some role play, with each of them taking a turn at being the bereaved and then the counsellor. It was intense, and Kate found that they were all drained emotionally by three o'clock every afternoon, which was probably why they finished at that time. Each day she felt a desperate need to escape back into the world of people chatting; laughing; living.

Sitting next to Kate was an extremely tall, thin, dark-haired young man by the name of Eric, who had very nice blue eyes and a luxuriant black beard. He also had a sense of humour and, on a couple of occasions when things had become very intense, he'd come out with a remark which made everyone relax and even smile a little.

On the Tuesday afternoon, as they were all gathering their bits and pieces together and preparing to leave, Eric said to Kate, 'Fancy a drink?'

Kate fancied a drink very much.

'I know a nice little pub about five minutes' walk from here,' he said.

Kate felt dwarfed as they walked along. 'How tall are you?' she asked.

'Six feet, six inches, or two metres if you want to go metric,' he replied, 'and please don't start asking me what the weather's like up here!'

Kate laughed. 'I wouldn't dream of it!'

The Belvedere was a modern pub with gleaming white walls, wooden floors and comfortable leather chairs.

'Let me get you a drink,' he said and, as Kate began to protest, added, 'But you can buy the next one!'

Kate had a lemonade shandy and immediately began to feel better. 'I really needed to unwind,' she told him.

'What better way?' he asked with a grin, taking a huge sip of his pint of ale.

'So, do you live locally?' Kate asked.

'About thirty miles out,' he said, 'but there's a good train service, so I don't need to do any driving. What about you? Cornwall, eh? I bet it's heaving with visitors right now.'

Eric was easy to talk to and she found herself chatting about Woody, and Jack, and the current crime investigation. During the course of their conversation, Kate discovered that Eric was forty-two years old, he'd once backpacked round the world, was now a social worker, his girlfriend had just walked out on him and he could speak fluent Russian, due to his mother having come from Estonia. 'Not that it's a lot of good around here,' he said sadly, 'but if you ever come across anyone that speaks Russian, send them to me!'

He liked to get the 4.30 train home so, when they left the pub, he bade her a cheery farewell and asked, 'Can we do this again tomorrow?'

Kate agreed that they could, because it still gave her time to do her sightseeing and shopping. She enjoyed his company, and it was also someone she could talk to about the course.

On Wednesday he asked, 'Shall we have a final beer together tomorrow before you head back to your Titworthy on Friday?'

'*Tinworthy*,' Kate corrected. 'But no, I'm afraid not, Eric, because I have an address I want to try to find while I'm here.'

Eric grinned. 'You know how to break a guy's heart! Anything I can help with?'

'I'm looking for a Barrymore Road.'

He shook his head. 'Sorry, no idea where that is.'

There was a moment's silence and Kate reckoned she knew him well enough now to tell him of her concerns. 'It's someone I want to check on, someone I met in Cornwall,' she said. 'A girl. A girl my son is besotted with.'

'And you're not?'

'Not what?'

'Besotted with her.'

Kate smiled. 'Not very, no, although I don't know why.'

'You can't love everyone, Kate!'

'I know that, but there's just *something* about her...'

'So she gave you this address?'

Kate shook her head. 'No, she didn't, but I got it anyway.'

'I won't ask you how you managed that, although I can probably guess.'

'OK, so I got it from the medical centre where I work. For some reason I thought that if I could see where she normally lived, I'd get a better understanding of her, perhaps. Does that make sense?'

Eric grinned. 'Depending on whether it's a palace or a slum?'

'Something like that, I suppose. She has no relatives, you see, because her mother died when she was tiny, and there was no one else. So it's most likely a flat share or something.'

'What is it about her that worries you?'

Kate thought for a moment. 'It's just that Jack, my son, has recently come back after working in Australia for a few years, and where he lived with a lovely girl. Unfortunately, she's left the relationship and he's probably very vulnerable at the moment because he was only with us for a matter of hours when he met this new girl. I just fear it may be on the rebound. It's all moved on so quickly, and now he's even talking about getting married.'

'I can understand why you're worried.' Eric drained his beer. 'Another? Go on!'

'OK then, just a small white wine please.'

Kate watched him as he sauntered up to the bar and hoped he wasn't thoroughly bored with all this family talk.

When he came back with the drinks, he sat down, took a swig of his beer, wiped his mouth and asked, 'What is it you dislike about her?'

Kate thought again. 'That's just it, Eric, I honestly don't *know*! There's just something, something in her manner...' She paused for a moment. 'Woody, my husband, thinks I should just let them get on with it, and I suppose he's right, really. But shortly before I left, even Jack suggested I look up where she lived, so he must have his doubts too.'

'Then you must go, if only for your own peace of mind. Frankly, Kate, I always go on my gut instinct and, from what you've told me, I think that's what you're doing too. If there's something dodgy about the girl, surely it's better to find out now? And will you let me know?'

'Of course I will!' They'd already exchanged addresses. 'And you promise to visit us next time you're in Cornwall?'

'You bet!' said Eric.

· · ·

Every evening, she and Woody had FaceTimed. And every evening he asked if she was behaving herself, and she told him she'd met another man and so he'd better watch out. 'I've always fancied a bit of cradle snatching,' she said.

'I hope you've investigated him thoroughly,' Woody said. 'There's still an axe murderer roaming around somewhere that hasn't been found.'

Then, every evening, she asked if he'd discovered anything interesting about Irving and Sally's arrest and, every evening, he said he hadn't. He had to go to Launceston on the day she was due back and, knowing how desperate she was to know the details, he promised he'd pop into the police station and have a chat with Charlotte. 'So I just might have something to tell you when you get back,' he said. 'But,' he added, 'don't hold your breath because I honestly don't know how much she's likely to tell me. And, of course, they can't be kept in custody indefinitely without proof.'

On the penultimate day of the course, she dug out Beth's address from her notes: 28 Barrymore Road. That gave nothing away; it could be a flat, a house, or even a room in a shared house.

There was only one way to find out.

THIRTY-FOUR

Kate studied the map of Bristol, at the same time wondering if she shouldn't be leaving this investigation to Jack. After all, what business was it of hers really? If she even found where Beth lived then the chances were that there'd be no one there anyway, as they'd all be at work. She knew she was dithering, and she wasn't normally a ditherer.

There was nothing *wrong* with the girl after all. Kate was sure that, if only she could find some common ground with Beth – apart from Jack – they could probably get on really well. However, Kate knew nothing about hairdressing and very little about surfing. She was also sure Beth was unlikely to know much about nursing, or sleuthing, or wayward sisters for that matter.

She'd almost talked herself out of going to find Barrymore Road then reminded herself that, for Jack's sake, she really *should* make this pilgrimage. He had, after all, *wanted* her to go. And even Woody had finally agreed there was no harm in having a look.

.   .   .

The only Barrymore Road Kate could find on her map was on the outskirts of the city, in the direction of Bath. She got into the Fiat, switched on 'SatNav Lady' and prepared to listen to instructions from the disembodied female voice, although she'd already mapped out a route for herself.

Twenty minutes later, Kate was well on her way to somewhere in the outskirts of Bristol, having been held up by roadworks, with a resulting diversion, but SatNav Lady sorted that one out. She was now deep in suburbia and was directed by SatNav Lady to 'take the next right turn into Barrymore Road'. Then she added, 'You have now reached your destination.' Kate found herself in a leafy road of 1930s-type bungalows, mostly detached.

She drove on to the end of the road in search of a sign to confirm that this really was Barrymore Road. She found one, and it was. She parked the car and looked around; this was not at all the type of area she had imagined Beth living in but more likely one for retirees.

Kate got out of the car and began to look for numbers. As with many roads populated by older folk, most houses had given themselves a name and not a number, but finally she found number 36 and calculated that number 28 was either a few houses back the way she'd come, or a few houses in the direction she was going. Which way did the numbers run?

She walked for about a hundred yards before she found number 42 so knew she was heading in the wrong direction. Having established that the even numbers did all appear to be on this side, she made her way back to 36 and calculated that 28 must be four houses back from there. In fact, the 28 had at one time been painted on the glass panel above the door but was now barely decipherable. The little bungalow didn't have a name. It was bog standard with a bay window each side and a door in the middle, all needing painting.

Kate pushed open the gate and walked up the path, and

there, on his knees, weeding a flowerbed beside the front door, was an elderly, bald-headed man. She *must* have the wrong address.

He heard her approaching, turned round and grinned at her.

'Do you happen to know if a Beth Hart lives here?' Kate asked hesitantly.

He shrugged. 'I'm not sure, my dear. I live three houses up.' He pointed vaguely over his shoulder. 'I only do a bit of gardenin' for all the old ladies round here, including Mrs Hart, but she's in, so you should ask her.'

Mrs *Hart*! An old lady! For a moment, Kate considered turning on her heel and walking straight back to her car. Then she thought that, having come this far, she might as well find out for sure. Nervously, she pressed the doorbell and waited. She could hear no sound and wondered if she should press it again.

'She takes a bit of time to get to the door,' the old man shouted cheerfully.

Kate pressed the bell again and this time she could hear a faint rumbling sound coming from within. After what seemed like minutes, the door finally swung open and Kate found herself face to face with an elderly woman in a wheelchair.

'I'm so sorry to bother you,' Kate said, 'but I wondered if a Beth Hart lived here?'

The woman looked her up and down for a moment before asking, 'And who are you?'

'My name is Kate Palmer. I'm a nurse and I met Beth in Cornwall and I have this address for her.'

'What's wrong with her? What's happened?' the woman asked.

'No,' Kate replied hurriedly, 'she's fine. Nothing bad has happened.'

'*Why* do you want to know about her then?'

Kate had practised some replies. 'Well, she's become

involved with my son and, as I'm here on a course this week, I just thought I'd check out where she lived.' Kate wondered if she was being too honest.

'She gave you this address?' The woman kept staring at her.

'Not exactly, but – as I said – I'm a nurse and her address was on the records at my practice.'

The woman hesitated for a moment then asked, 'And you want to know something about her?'

'Yes,' Kate replied, 'I do.'

The woman propelled herself back a few feet, opened the door wide and said, 'Well, you'd better come in.'

'Are you related then?' Kate asked.

'I'm her grandmother,' said the woman.

For a moment Kate stood stock-still. Then she found her voice. 'But she hasn't *got* a grandmother!'

'Oh yes she has!' said the woman. 'Are you coming in or not?'

Kate tried to regain her composure. 'Yes please.'

She stepped into a tiny hallway and stared at the woman in front of her, who said, 'What did you say your name was?'

'Kate. Kate Palmer.'

'Well, I'm Laura Hart. Please come this way.' She trundled herself slowly into what was obviously a sitting room. It was carpeted in frenetic orange-and-black swirls, competing with the armchair covers and curtains, which came in various floral patterns, all faded badly. The patio door looked out onto a little lawn, where an empty clothes dryer whirled in the wind.

'Please sit down.'

Kate studied her new acquaintance as she settled herself into a feather-cushioned armchair, wondering how she'd ever be able to hoist herself out. Laura Hart was silver haired, fresh complexioned and smartly dressed in a dark-green patterned blouse and black trousers. Kate reckoned she must be at least eighty.

Kate cleared her throat. 'I know you'll find this hard to believe, Mrs Hart, but Beth assured us she had no living relatives.'

Laura Hart snorted. 'Well, there's enough of me still alive to assure you that she has.' She hesitated for a moment. 'Alas, only myself though.'

Kate shook her head. 'Why would she tell us that? I really don't understand.'

'Beth is not an easy girl to understand, Mrs er...'

'Please, I'm Kate.'

'She's not exactly an easy person to understand, Kate.'

There were framed photographs on the mantelpiece which Kate was straining to see.

'Please do have a look at the photographs,' said Laura Hart. She was obviously a woman who didn't miss much. 'You'll see three generations of women who look very much alike.'

Kate heaved herself out of the armchair and crossed the room to look at the photographs. Centrally positioned – in pride of place – was one of Beth, which looked as if it had been taken a few years previously. But Beth it was, without a doubt.

On the right was a photograph of a woman who looked very much like Beth, cradling a baby, and on the left was an old wedding photo. The bride gazing adoringly at her tall husband was almost certainly Laura. The resemblance between the three women was quite remarkable.

Kate was aware that Laura was studying her for her reaction.

'I can certainly see the likenesses,' she said, continuing to stare at the photographs.

'The picture of Beth was taken when she'd be around sixteen or seventeen. The one on the right is the last picture I have of her mother before she died, with Beth as a baby, and the other one is of me and my late husband, Bill, on our wedding day.'

'Three very attractive ladies,' Kate said truthfully, 'and *so* alike.'

Laura nodded. 'Yes, the physical resemblance is all on the female side of the family but' – she paused for a second – 'that is the *only* way my granddaughter is like either her mother or myself.'

Kate wasn't quite sure what to say next. But she hoped that Laura Hart would offer more information.

'Would you like a cup of coffee?' Laura asked. 'Or tea?'

Kate, deep in thought, came back to earth. 'Well, thank you. Shall I...?'

'I am perfectly capable of making hot drinks,' the woman said briskly. 'What shall it be?'

'Coffee would be lovely. Just milk.'

Laura propelled herself into what was obviously the kitchen, and Kate could hear the sounds of a kettle being filled and cups rattling. Hopefully, over coffee, she'd be able to find out what had happened to this strange little family and why Beth had denied having any living relatives at all.

After a few minutes, Laura reappeared, a tray with two mugs of coffee balanced on her knees. 'Help yourself,' she said. 'Yours is the one with the William Morris design; I do love William Morris patterns.'

'Yes, I do too,' Kate said, picking up her mug and placing it on the table next to where she was sitting. She took a sip then said, 'What I don't understand, Laura, is why she said she had no relatives?'

'Well,' Laura replied, 'there is only me and she's never forgiven me...' Here her voice tailed off for a moment, then she continued briskly, 'She needs an address for her mail and everything, and I expect I'm cheaper than a box number or whatever it is that rootless people do. I also forward her mail to her, wherever she happens to be. So, right now, I do know that she's in some caravan park or other in Cornwall.'

'Which is where she's met my son,' Kate said.

'I do hope he's not besotted with her?'

Kate sighed. 'I rather fear he is.'

'He shouldn't be. She flits from man to man.'

In spite of her reservations about Beth, Kate was shocked. 'But they're talking of moving in together here, in the Bristol area, and eventually getting married. Jack, my son, is even looking for a job round here.'

'It won't happen – the marriage I mean.' Laura spoke firmly. 'She'll move on; she always does. There's a list as long as my arm of all the addresses she's had in the past couple of years alone.'

'But why?' Kate asked. 'What makes her so restless?'

'Well, that's a very short question with a very long answer.'

'Can you try to explain it to me?'

'It all stems back to the accident I suppose. That's the reason she dislikes me so much; it goes back to when she was only three years old.'

'Yes, she told us that all of her family had been killed in a road accident.'

'Not *all* her family. She and *I* survived. She was strapped into the child seat in the back, next to my daughter. My husband was driving and I was in the front passenger seat.' She paused to drain her coffee. 'It was a very cold day and the roads were icy, but the accident was not Bill's fault. The driver of the other car, who was speeding, had lost control and came straight at us, hitting us head on. Bill and my daughter, Jenny, who was sitting directly behind him, both died instantly. I was left like this.'

'I'm so sorry,' Kate said.

'It was snowing heavily and both cars had zigzagged across the road so, by the time the police arrived, it was difficult to tell who had been where, particularly as the other driver only sustained minor injuries and insisted that we were at fault. But we weren't, I can assure you of that. The legal battle continued for months, but the other party had more money and better lawyers.'

'That is *awful*!'

'It was. I had massive injuries, including a shattered spine, and spent the best part of a year in hospital, flat on my back. There was no way I could look after Beth, so she was taken into care. She's never forgiven me.'

'But that doesn't make sense!' Kate was appalled.

'Seemingly it makes sense to Beth. When I was eventually released from hospital and moved into this bungalow, which is adapted for me, I had carers coming in and out, and there was absolutely no way I could look after a child. So Beth was farmed out with various foster parents, some better than others. The social worker would bring her to see me once a month. She was a sullen child and hardly spoke to me.'

'Surely when she got older she realised that the situation was from necessity and not from choice?'

Laura sighed deeply. 'For some reason she never did understand. I've no idea how she thought I could look after her when I could barely look after myself.' She looked away. 'I don't know who her father was, but I do know she is nothing like my lovely daughter. It's a very sad business.'

Kate was blinking back tears. She did feel sympathetic towards Beth but she now knew for certain that she did not want her son to become any more involved with her. 'Oh, Laura, I really don't know what to say. How incredibly sad!'

'Yes, it is sad.'

'It must be absolutely awful to know your granddaughter feels that way about you when I know all you wanted was the best for her.'

'Yes,' Laura replied, 'it is awful because I know she hates me. But if she hates anyone more than me, it has to be the driver of the car who decimated our family and got away scot free.'

'Perhaps that's understandable,' Kate said, 'when you think how many lives he wrecked one way or the other.'

'That's something else,' said Laura. 'It wasn't a man – it was a woman. And I'm quite sure she'd been drinking but I don't recall that she was ever breathalysed.'

'A woman?'

'Yes, I'll never forget her. Her name was Sheila Potts.'

THIRTY-FIVE

On the Friday morning, as Eric took his seat next to hers, he asked, 'How was Barrymore Road?'

'Unbelievable!' Kate replied and gave him a brief résumé of what had transpired.

He shook his head sadly. 'Your gut instinct was right, as I thought it would be. What will you do now?'

'I'll go home, talk it through with Woody and hopefully he'll know how to deal with it.'

'And you'll tell your son?'

'Without a doubt. I couldn't sleep last night thinking that she could potentially be a killer and my son could be in danger.'

'Then you should call him immediately and tell him to keep his distance,' Eric said.

'That's just what I'm going to do.'

Later, Kate could barely remember the last day of the course other than that she was awarded a certificate at the end of it. She remembered even less of the journey home, the piece of news from the previous day having obliterated all thoughts of anything or anyone else from her mind.

Could it all be purely coincidence? Surely Beth had come to Cornwall to learn to surf while cleaning caravans and not for any sinister purpose? Was it even the same Sheila Potts? But why had Beth lied about having no living relatives? Why did she not acknowledge the existence of her grandmother, a grief-stricken paraplegic old lady who'd lost all her family that fateful day?

She'd phoned Jack, who'd said he probably wasn't seeing her that day anyway, but what was all the fuss about? Beth was hardly likely to be a killer, was she! All quite ridiculous! Then again, given the fact that an eyewitness had now come forward, so Irving and Sally would not be in custody without good reason surely? How should she handle this? Obviously, she would tell Woody everything she knew, but the most important thing was to ensure that Jack had no further contact with Beth until everything was sorted out. Jack *must* have had some worries about Beth by the time he'd asked Kate to check on where she lived, and he had to be told the full story about the grandmother. Should they talk to Beth on her own to establish whether or not she had set out to kill Sienna? Or should she go straight to Charlotte and tell her of her suspicions?

Kate's head was in a spin as she finally, gratefully, pulled up outside Lavender Cottage two and a half hours after leaving Bristol.

'I've missed you,' Woody said, holding her tight. 'I don't like being alone anymore.'

'I've missed you too,' Kate said, following him into the kitchen and a rapturous greeting from Barney. There was a mouth-watering aroma of something cooking.

'Dinner's all organised,' Woody said, producing a bottle of Moët & Chandon from the fridge.

'Wow, champers!' Kate said. 'Are we celebrating something?'

'Yes, we're celebrating that you're home, and that the killers are safely in custody. I've got something interesting to tell you about that, *very* interesting!'

'I've got something very interesting to tell you too,' Kate said. *Understatement of the year.*

'Let's have a drink first,' Woody said, handing her a glass of champagne.

Kate sank gratefully into the sofa, kicked off her shoes and took a large sip of her drink. 'Bliss!'

Woody sat down next to her. 'How was the last day of the course then?'

'It was good. I mean, the whole thing was an eye-opener. Not very cheerful and quite intense, but I must say I enjoyed it, and I think I'll find it a very useful qualification.' She looked round. 'Where's Jack?'

'Surfing with Beth. Said he'd be back for supper.'

Kate's heart sank. He obviously hadn't taken her seriously. 'Is Beth coming too?'

'No, I don't think so,' Woody replied.

'Perhaps that's as well,' Kate said.

'Meaning what?'

'Meaning I'll tell you in a minute.' Kate took another sip. 'So, are Sally and Irving still in custody?'

'Yes,' Woody replied, 'they are.'

Kate snorted. 'So much for the famous, mysterious alibi then!'

Woody leaned forward with a mischievous grin. 'You're going to *love* this!'

'Love what?'

'You'll never guess what the alibi was?'

'Don't keep me in suspense, Woody!'

'They had taken a video of themselves, on her phone,

naked, entwined and *on the job*, timed and dated for more or less the exact moment that Sienna met her fate!'

Kate gasped. 'Tell me you're kidding!'

Woody was plainly enjoying himself. 'Oh no, I'm not!'

'Then why haven't they been released?' she asked.

'Charlotte's not altogether convinced by it,' Woody replied. 'She reckons that the video could have been doctored. I hadn't considered that when she showed it to me, and I think she over-estimated my technical ability. I told her I had no idea if it had been doctored or not.'

'What happens now?'

'Irving and Sally remain in custody until Charlotte can find someone who can authenticate the time and date. Don't ask me how she's going to do that. She says that, at the moment, she's more inclined to believe the eyewitness.'

'Who is...?'

'No idea. She won't tell me because she says she needs to keep it a secret for now, for the eyewitness's own safety.'

'This,' said Kate, 'is becoming weirder and weirder.'

'It certainly is,' Woody agreed. 'But as far as I can see, it boils down to one of two alternatives. Either Irving and Sally *have* had their porn video doctored to cover the fact that one or both of them were with Sienna on the cliff that day, or else the eyewitness is lying.'

'Why on earth would the eyewitness lie?'

'Million-dollar question, Kate. Why indeed?'

'And why has the eyewitness only just come forward?'

Woody shrugged. 'You tell me.' He topped up their glasses.

'Well,' said Kate, 'I, too, have some interesting information which may, or may not, be relevant.'

'Let's hear it,' Woody said.

'I found 28 Barrymore Road,' Kate said, 'which was a little bungalow, in a road full of little bungalows.'

'Not exactly where you'd expect to find a young, single girl then?' Woody said.

'Not at all. Anyway, an old lady in a wheelchair answered the door and, after a few relevant questions, she invited me in. Her name is Laura Hart, and she's Beth's grandmother.'

'What? Beth hasn't *got* a grandmother!'

'Oh yes she has,' Kate confirmed.

'So why would she tell us she had no living relatives?'

Kate shook her head. 'The grandmother, Laura, provides an address for Beth, forwards on her mail to wherever she happens to be, that sort of thing. She was concerned when I said that my son was besotted with Beth and that they planned to marry. She said that Beth flits from man to man, address to address.'

'Well you've always had reservations about her, and it's beginning to look like you were absolutely right.'

'There's more,' Kate said. 'The road accident that occurred when Beth was tiny killed both her mother and her grandfather. Beth survived of course, and Laura survived with horrific injuries which meant months in hospital and left her paraplegic. There was no way whatsoever that she could have looked after a young child.'

'Which is why Beth was put into care?'

Kate nodded. 'And she's never forgiven her grandmother for handing her over to the authorities.'

'But that doesn't make sense! What else was the poor woman to do?'

'Exactly. Although Beth didn't have an easy upbringing, so part of me does feel for her. Now we come to the interesting bit. I discovered the name of the person who was driving the car that smashed into them.'

'Don't keep me in suspense!'

'Sheila Potts.'

Woody rubbed his brow. 'I've heard that name somewhere before.'

'She became Sienna Stone.'

He let out a long, lingering breath. 'You're saying that Sienna Stone wiped out most of Beth's family?'

Kate nodded. 'Apparently, the roads were icy, but Sienna was – again – on the wrong side of the road, but that couldn't be verified for certain because of the snow and ice. Laura also reckoned – even in her injured state – that Sheila Potts had been drinking, but she was never breathalysed for some reason and got away with it because she could afford the best lawyers.'

Woody was silent for a minute. Then he said, 'We can check up on all that on police records, once we have the date of the accident, which I'm sure the old lady can tell you.' He paused. 'So is it possible that Beth came down here not to learn to surf but to avenge the death of her family?'

'It's certainly a possibility, but what proof is there?' Kate asked. 'If someone witnessed Irving and Sally doing the deed, then that would certainly let Beth off the hook.'

'Nevertheless, we need to take this information to Charlotte, because it may just be important.'

Kate nodded. 'I think, too, that we need to invite Beth for supper at some point, perhaps tomorrow?'

Woody let out a long, slow whistle. 'That could be interesting.'

Kate thought for a moment. 'I've just remembered something.'

'Mmm?'

'Do you recall when I told you, in the kitchen, that Timmy said he knew who had killed Sienna?'

'Yes...'

'Jack and Beth were next door, in the sitting room. She could easily have overheard our conversation.'

Woody shook his head. 'You're sure?'

'Yes, I am.'

He thought for a moment. 'You know something else? Beth

was with Jack next door too when you explained where Marc had been at the time of Timmy's murder, and that he couldn't be a suspect.'

'And I probably said that left Sally and Irving as the likely killers.'

'Yes, you did say that.'

'There are an awful lot of coincidences, aren't there?'

'There are a helluva lot of coincidences, Kate.'

Jack came back in the morning to shower and to change his clothes.

'Hi, Mum, good to have you home! How was Bristol?'

'Bristol was fine – very interesting in fact. I'll tell you all about it later. I wondered if you and Beth would like to join us for dinner this evening?'

'That would be great, and I'm sure Beth will agree. She's working all day anyway, so I won't see her until later. Funnily enough, she's been a bit withdrawn this past week for some reason; a bit closed up, but that's Beth. She acted a bit strangely when I said you were in Bristol, but no idea why. What exactly did you find out?'

Kate felt relief that at least he wasn't spending the day with Beth. 'Like I said, I'll tell you later. Go have your shower now.'

When Jack, showered and changed, had taken Barney for a walk, Woody decided he should phone Charlotte.

Kate, listening in, heard him say, 'Sorry to bother you on a weekend, Charlotte, but Kate has some interesting information which might be of importance in the Sienna case.'

There was a moment's silence before Charlotte, on speaker-phone, said, 'Woody, I'm in St Ives with my friend today. Can it wait until tomorrow morning?'

Woody sighed. 'Well, I suppose so.'

'Can you tell me, briefly, what it's about?'

'It's about Beth Hart, Kate's son's girlfriend.'

'Beth Hart?'

'That's right. Kate found out some interesting stuff about her while she was up on a course in Bristol.'

There was a further pause before Charlotte asked, 'You consider it important?'

'I'd say so,' Woody replied.

'In that case would you mind if I called in this evening when I get back to Tinworthy?'

'No, we don't mind at all. Beth may be here, but we can talk privately.'

The line went so quiet that Kate wondered if she was still there.

Then Charlotte said slowly, 'You see, Beth Hart's our eyewitness.'

THIRTY-SIX

'How are we going to handle this, Woody?' Kate had set about preparing the meal and was becoming increasingly nervous.

'We are going to have dinner and act normally,' Woody replied. 'If we're going to have any sort of dramatics, then let's have them on a full stomach.'

Dramatics? Was he expecting dramatics? Kate wondered. Would Beth even agree to come for that matter? She had asked Jack to confirm that she *was* coming with him, but it was now 3 p.m. and she still hadn't called him. There was no reason, of course, for Beth to be in any way suspicious, because why would she think that Kate had visited her grandmother anyway? Kate decided she would tell them all about the course, about Eric, about visiting the SS *Great Britain* – which she'd meant to do for ages – while they were eating dinner.

'I shall certainly ask her about being an eyewitness though,' Woody remarked.

'What? While we're eating?'

'For goodness' sake, Kate, why not? We need to know, if she *did* see Irving and Sally push Sienna off the cliff, why she didn't come forward with the information sooner. It's a perfectly reasonable question.'

'I suppose it is,' Kate said doubtfully. 'But Charlotte was supposed to keep the name of the eyewitness secret, was she not?'

Woody shrugged. 'Well, we can say I'm still seconded to the police or something.'

Kate thought for a moment. 'I wonder if Jack knows she's the eyewitness? Would she have told him, I wonder?'

'Who knows? We'll see how he reacts.'

'If we'd known about this before he went out, we could have asked him.'

'Well, we didn't,' Woody said, putting an arm round her. 'And probably best to say nothing to him for the moment. Now stop worrying about it and stuff that damn chicken.'

Jack confirmed that Beth would be happy to come to dinner and asked if half past six would be all right. Kate replied that that would be fine and they'd be eating around seven. She then resumed worrying as she prepared the vegetables.

Sometimes she almost convinced herself that there was a perfectly good reason for it all – there had to be. Then she'd wonder, even if Beth had nothing whatsoever to do with the killings, why she had lied about her grandmother.

Only one thing was certain: whatever the outcome, she did *not* want Beth marrying her son.

Beth arrived on time and the four of them sat drinking wine in the kitchen while Kate put the finishing touches to the meal. The conversation was mainly about surfing, how Beth was improving and how sorry she'd be to leave the sea. Perhaps she might relocate, she said, and not go back to Bristol after all.

Maybe, Jack said, they should be looking at the Newquay area or similar, Tinworthy even? Perhaps Guys 'n' Dolls had a vacancy for a hair stylist, perhaps Jack could find work locally, perhaps they could find a little flat to rent? And so it went on.

When they sat down to eat, Kate spoke of the bereavement counselling course, she spoke of Eric and she spoke of her visit to the *Great Britain*, exactly as she had planned to do.

They were just finishing the main course when Woody said casually, 'I understand that you were the eyewitness who saw Sienna Stone being pushed off the cliff, Beth?'

Beth looked startled for a moment. Jack dropped his fork and stared at her in amazement.

So he didn't know!

The girl quickly regained her composure. 'That,' she said, looking directly at Woody, 'was supposed to be confidential information.'

'Oh, it is,' Woody agreed, 'but I'm still seconded to the police on cases like this, and so the information was available to me.'

'I thought you'd severed all ties with the police,' Jack put in.

'Not *all*,' Woody lied. 'But what surprises me – what I don't understand – is why it took you so long to come forward with the information?'

Beth laid down her knife and fork, leaned forward and looked him straight in the eye. 'I'd seen them with her but had no idea who they were until Jack took me to dinner at The Atlantic last Friday.'

'Yes,' Jack said hurriedly, 'everyone was staring at this couple because, seemingly, they were so *blatantly* together. Neither of us knew who they were until we asked the waiter.'

'And then I realised, of course, that this was the couple I'd seen,' Beth added.

Jack touched her arm. 'You didn't *tell* me you'd gone to the police.'

'Well, I felt it was my duty,' said Beth piously. 'They told me I mustn't tell anyone, so that's why I couldn't tell you. I'm sorry.' She picked up her knife and fork again and continued calmly eating for a moment. 'It's obvious,' she said, looking at them all in turn, 'the *husband* and the *sister*.'

'I wish you'd told me though,' Jack said, 'because we agreed to have no secrets from each other, remember?'

Kate exchanged glances with Woody. *Oh, Jack, you know nothing yet!* He'd asked her several times during the day what had transpired in Bristol, and she was beginning to wonder if she should have told him all of this earlier.

'Like I told you, this was a police matter,' Beth said as she scraped her plate clean.

Kate had been inwardly rehearsing all day exactly how to bring up the subject of Barrymore Road. Now her mind was a complete blank, but she knew she had to say something. She took a large swig of her wine.

'I met your grandmother, Beth,' she said.

'Mum, what the hell are you talking about?' Jack was pushing back his chair. 'You know Beth hasn't got—'

'Oh yes she has,' Kate said, surprised at her own calmness. 'A very nice lady by the name of Laura Hart.' She noticed, with some satisfaction, that Beth was now openly fighting to regain her composure.

She gave Kate a look of pure hatred. 'I've no idea what you're talking about,' she snapped.

'Oh, I think you do,' Kate said as she laid down her cutlery. She was beginning to wonder if the pudding she'd made was going to be necessary.

The three of them were now staring at Beth.

'Number 28, Barrymore Road,' Kate continued, 'a bungalow adapted for a handicapped old lady.'

Beth leaned forward. 'Where did you get that address from?'

'Not important,' said Kate. 'What is important is that I went there.'

'You don't understand,' Beth said, looking at them all in turn.

'That's true, I don't,' Kate agreed as she took another gulp of wine.

'She always hated me.' Beth spoke slowly. 'She never wanted to have me around, *never*. Just dumped me with the authorities. So I disowned her.'

'You fail to mention that she was hospitalised for a very long time as a result of the crash that killed your mother and grandfather,' Kate said. 'There was no way she could look after a child when she could hardly take care of herself.'

'Beth, is this true?' Jack asked.

'Your mother has been interfering in things that do not concern her,' Beth said, standing up. 'And you know what? I'm getting *out* of here!'

Jack stood up and went towards her. 'Beth...'

'*Don't!*' She pushed him away with an outstretched palm.

'Before you go,' Woody said quietly, 'perhaps you can tell us why you're *really* here, Beth. Just to learn to surf?'

Beth was looking towards the door. 'Why else would I want to come to a bloody one-horse town like this?'

'To find Sienna Stone perhaps? To get your revenge for her decimating most of your family? Back in the day, when she was Sheila Potts?'

Beth was now looking around, desperation in her eyes. Then Kate watched in horror as, suddenly, Beth picked up the carving knife from the counter behind and held it out in front of her.

'None of you come *near* me!' She waved it around. 'I'll kill you all before I'll be punished any more for what that woman did!'

With that, she was out of the kitchen door like a bullet.

THIRTY-SEVEN

For a split second, the three of them were transfixed before Woody leaped up and raced out of the door, Jack hot on his heels, along with Barney, who obviously considered this to be some new and exciting game. Kate hesitated for only a moment before she too bolted after them.

It was a rugged path that zigzagged its way up to the cliffs from this side of the valley, and Beth was way ahead, sprinting like a gazelle, the setting sun glinting on the blade of the carving knife which she was still brandishing.

Halfway up, Kate had to slow down as she was becoming breathless, but both Woody and Jack were still ahead, moving at speed, about fifty yards behind Beth. Kate continued running more slowly, terrified that either of her men might be tempted to tackle the girl, and wishing fervently that Woody still had his taser, but those days were gone. In any case, he would hardly have been likely to have it at the ready when eating dinner.

They were nearing the top now with Beth still sprinting ahead, and ignoring both Woody's and Jack's pleas to stop. Where the hell was she going?

Then Kate realised, with horror, that Beth had arrived at

the exact spot, Potter's Point, where Sienna Stone had been when she was pushed. She was standing with her back to the edge, defiantly waving the knife in front of her.

'Don't you bloody well come near me!' she yelled at the two men as they slowly approached her.

Kate felt physically sick as she watched Woody and Jack advance towards the girl.

'Lay down that knife, Beth,' Woody said calmly as he inched towards her.

'Yes, come on, Beth,' Jack echoed from just behind him. 'No one need know about this! We need to talk!'

As she neared, Kate could plainly see Beth's eyes full of hatred as she took a step backward. Kate held her breath, convinced that, at any minute, Beth was going to topple over the sheer drop, now only inches behind her – and which was clearly her intention.

'Don't. Come. Near. Me.' Beth spoke hoarsely. 'I'll die happy, knowing that I finally found the woman who annihilated my family. It's taken years, because she changed her damn name, but I *got her!*' She laughed manically.

'Beth, we *understand!*' Jack shouted, a desperate note in his voice. 'Just please get away from the edge – *please!*'

Beth was now waving the knife menacingly towards Jack.

Jack tried again. 'Please, Beth, can't we at least *talk?*'

'*Talk?*' She glared at him with ill-concealed disdain. 'Talk? Talk about *what?* There's nothing to talk about!'

'What about poor Timmy Thomson?' Jack asked. 'Did you kill him too?'

'He *saw* me, sneaky little rat. No great loss there!'

While she'd been looking at Jack, Woody had taken the opportunity to edge even closer on her other side. She spun round, now aware of this, and swung the knife from side to side, eyes wide, glaring from one to the other.

'Do not come one bloody *inch* closer to me!'

Kate watched, hardly daring to breathe, and offered up a silent prayer.

It was at that moment that Beth turned towards Woody, pointing the knife within inches of his chest. In that split second, Jack leaped forward, in what could only be described as a rugby tackle, and grabbed her left ankle. Beth began to keel over backward, but Woody, in a flash, grabbed the other ankle. The knife sailed off into space, almost followed by Beth, who was dragged back by her ankles onto terra firma. She lay stunned for a moment while Woody removed the belt from his trousers and strapped her hands together before she had time to recover. Then he and Jack manhandled her into an upright position and, between them, began to guide her back down the path.

Kate was trying hard not to cry at the thought of what might have happened, what so nearly *did* happen. She shuddered as she looked down the cliff-face at the sand beneath where Sienna had so recently met her death, and where Beth had very nearly followed suit.

Nobody spoke as they retraced their steps and the poor girl, half-dazed, let them guide her down towards Lavender Cottage.

As they approached the garden, a voice could be heard coming from their doorway.

'Where have you been?' Charlotte shouted, running towards them. 'And what the hell are you doing with my eyewitness?' She looked from one to the other in disbelief. Finally, her eyes rested on Beth. 'What's going on here, Beth?'

Beth, her face twisted with fury, said nothing – only spat.

'We have a lot to tell you,' Kate said.

'Understatement,' Woody added.

Beth was recovering fast. 'I don't give a damn,' she snapped. 'I'd do it all again; I just wish I'd been able to make her suffer first.'

Charlotte, visibly shaken, was phoning for police back-up.

'Later,' she said, looking from Kate to Woody, 'I'll be back to get a full statement.'

True to her word, Charlotte came back after an hour and a half.

'I know it's late,' she said, glancing at her watch, 'but I really need to hear this tonight.'

Kate related the story of her visit to Beth's grandmother and Beth's reaction when faced with the information. The more she spoke, the more she began to feel incredibly sorry for Beth. 'You know, the girl never stood a chance,' she said to Charlotte. 'From the age of three, she's been on her own, farmed out to various foster parents and harbouring this justifiable hatred for Sienna Stone. I know you shouldn't go around killing people, but surely some allowance will be made for the life she's had?'

Charlotte shook her head. 'The judge and jury will have to sort that one out, Kate,' she said, 'but I'm sure they'll take all the facts into account. Don't forget that this woman killed *two* people. She told us at the station that Timmy Thomson's life wasn't worth much anyway. Just like that.' She looked across at Jack, who was slumped on the sofa. 'Did you honestly never suspect that Beth could be involved in this?'

Jack sighed loudly. 'No,' he replied. 'I mean, when Mum said she was going up to Bristol, she did act a bit weirdly. Kept asking about the course, and where it was to be held and would she have much free time. I didn't think much of it at the time, but in retrospect...'

'In retrospect we're all a great deal wiser,' Charlotte said, switching off her recorder. 'But full marks to you, Kate. If it wasn't for your doubts about the girl, we might never have solved this case.' She grinned. 'I had Sally and Irving's naughty video checked, and the timing *was* correct, so we were about to release them anyway.'

As she accompanied Charlotte to the door, Kate's thoughts

were in turmoil. She felt relief that the case was solved and that all of the original suspects were now blameless, including – not least – herself. But more than anything, she felt a deep hatred for Sienna, who had ruined that little family's life, and a great sorrow for the resulting bitterness which had blighted Beth's life.

'Well, I suppose I have to hand it to you,' Angie said as she poured out two coffees. 'You really are becoming very good at this detective business. Your nosing around really paid off. You never liked the girl, did you?'

'It wasn't that I didn't like her, Angie, but there was just something about her that worried me. Call it intuition, call it what you like. It was only because of her relationship with Jack of course, otherwise I'd never have set eyes on her.'

'How are you feeling now, Kate? I mean you *were* a suspect.'

'I feel very relieved, and so glad the whole thing is finally over.'

'You must be. What about Sally Brand and Irving Aldridge?'

'They've obviously been released and, last I heard, had put Tremorron on the market and have moved to London for the moment,' Kate replied.

'That house only brings sorrow and grief to its owners,' Angie remarked sadly. 'I wonder if they'll be able to sell it.'

Kate shrugged. 'They've already decided, apparently, to move up to the Bath area at some point.'

'And how's Jack?'

'He was gutted of course, but he's recovering. I think we're all in need of a holiday after everything that's happened.'

THIRTY-EIGHT

The sun was shining as they approached the Scottish border.

Kate and Woody were on their way to Edinburgh, where they planned to spend a week with Tom and family before returning, via Yorkshire, to spend time with Carol, Woody's older daughter, and her brood. Kate gazed out of the window as they approached the rolling Cheviot Hills and marvelled at how many variations of scenery there were in this one small island.

In the rear seats were Jack and Barney. According to Tom, they were looking for personnel in the building trade in the Edinburgh area, so Jack thought he might accompany them, stay up there for a bit and have a look around. He'd been withdrawn and morose for a short while but was rapidly recovering. 'I knew there was *something* about her,' he'd said, 'but could never fathom what it was. I suppose I felt protective of her because of her tragic childhood. She seemed so alone in the world – and so vulnerable.'

Kate felt a mixture of emotions. She knew it had been her visit to Barrymore Road that had led to Beth's eventual arrest, but she was very worried about how it might have affected Laura Hart. Beth was hardly the model granddaughter, but nevertheless, she was Laura's only remaining flesh and blood, and perhaps Laura had harboured a secret hope that one day there might have been some sort of reconciliation. Kate vowed to visit the old lady. Perhaps Laura visiting her granddaughter in custody might help to build a newer, more loving relationship, which they both needed. She still felt a deep sadness for Beth, for the little girl who'd lost her mother when she was so young. Who knows how Beth might have turned out in normal circumstances. Kate vowed she would visit Beth in jail too.

In the meantime, she was very much looking forward to seeing her older son again. And Jack was showing no inclination to go back to Australia, so she felt indeed blessed to have both her sons on British soil.

Kate was aware that her so-called sleuthing had endangered her own life on several occasions, and vowed to keep herself out of trouble from now on. If only she wasn't so fascinated by crime-solving!

And as for Woody? What could she say about Woody? Her rock, her lover, her *raison d'être*! It had certainly been her lucky day when she first met Abraham Lincoln Forrest.

A LETTER FROM DEE

Dear Reader,

Thank you so much for choosing to read *A Body on the Beach* and I very much hoped you enjoyed it. If you did, and want to keep up with all of my books, just sign up with the link below. Your email address will never be shared and you can unsubscribe at any time.

www.bookouture.com/dee-macdonald

And if you enjoyed the book, I would be so grateful if you could write a review. I'd love to know what you think, and it also helps new readers to discover my books for the first time.

You can get in touch with me at any time via my Facebook page or through Twitter.

Thanks,

Dee x

facebook.com/AuthorDeeMacDonald
twitter.com/DMacDonaldAuth

ACKNOWLEDGEMENTS

Firstly, as always, my thanks to Natasha Harding, my lovely editor at Bookouture, for being so patient with me and so supportive and enthusiastic about my work.

Thanks too to my agent, Amanda Preston, and everyone at LBA who looks after my interests.

I'm particularly grateful to my dear friend and mentor, Rosemary Brown. She must have the patience of a saint for listening to me reading aloud my week's output and for her invaluable comments. Sadly, her husband, Mike, passed away suddenly just before Christmas, and he is very much missed. I'd like to dedicate this book to his memory.

Thanks to Stan, my husband, for putting up with my long writing sessions, for taking the phone calls and making the cups of tea! And to my son, Dan, for checking my reviews, etc., and for frequently getting me out of trouble with technology.

Thanks to all the Bookouture team who have contributed to the production of this book, including: Ruth Tross, Aimee Walsh, Natalie Butlin, Alex Holmes and the brilliant marketing team. And to Kim and Noelle for all the promotion they do afterwards. Apologies to anyone I may have inadvertently omitted to mention.

Finally, thank you to all of my readers and to book groups, particularly those who've taken the trouble to contact me. I do try to reply to each and every one but, being the old technophobe I am, I apologise profusely if I ever leave anyone out.

I am very grateful to you all.

Made in the USA
Middletown, DE
25 September 2023